Undertow

Also by Jazzy Mitchell

Leveling Up

You Matter

Musings of a Madwoman

Lost Treasures

Undertow

Jazzy Mitchell

Undertow

By Jazzy Mitchell

©2020 Jazzy Mitchell

ISBN (trade) 9781633040526
ISBN (eBook) 9781633040519

Launch Point Press
4804 NW Bethany Blvd, Suite I-2 #148
Portland, OR 97229

Editor: Nat Burns
Cover Design: Michelle Brodeur

Blurb

Maggie Ambrose is a fifty-six-year-old career politician who plans to run for president. To kick off her presidential bid and introduce herself to the masses, she's writing a revealing memoir. Her publisher insists she divulge more than her political pedigree to gain the nation's attention, but Maggie's not eager to confess the details of her challenging childhood, complex familial relationships, or her failed first marriage. Will the nation embrace a female lesbian candidate after she opens the door to a painful past?

Chapter One

MAGGIE AMBROSE, EYES CLOSED, floated on top of the rolling waves. She listened to the Atlantic Ocean roaring around her, the seagulls screaming, and the distant cadence of people talking. Cars whizzed by at a constant pace, traveling along the boulevard hugging the coast, just as regular as the waves smacking the wall behind her. Her thoughts drifted as she felt her body lifted by the waves, the slight breeze kissing her face, her knees, and her toes.

The late afternoon sun felt good on her now, no longer the same strength as the brutal heat she'd sought to counteract by immersing herself in the cool ocean water. The noise around her floated on the wind, fading away as she daydreamed about the future. A future where she could eat what she wanted every day. One where she felt safe enough to sleep through the night. One where she could read in her room without unwanted interruptions.

A wave took Maggie by surprise, crashing over her head and sucking her under the surface. She popped up moments later, sputtering and coughing while kicking her feet to keep afloat. Looking around, she realized she'd drifted away from the shore, past Red Rock Park, past the curve of the cove. Heads and torsos bobbed far away, close to the seawall, so small she couldn't identify anyone. Not her brother or the neighborhood boys.

A person waved at her, using one arm, and when Maggie didn't wave back he started waving both arms from side to side. Maggie pushed upward as a wave surged beneath her, waiting until it passed to begin her trek toward the shore. The riptide pushed her toward the right, and Maggie dog-paddled to fight the current.

It's okay. I can swim back. I'm okay, she thought.

Focusing on the seawall and the three specks she guessed were her brother and their neighbors, Maggie took a deep breath and began to swim. She allowed her head to be submerged as she stroked for several seconds. Lifting her head, she took a deep breath and repeated her actions, kicking hard. Her stomach hurt, but she kept going. After ten breaths she paused, bobbing as she took stock of where she was. She'd swum half the distance. Tears gathered at the back of her eyes as she kept kicking in place.

You can do this. It's not a big deal. Let's go, Maggie. Be strong.

Feeling the ocean pulling at her back, Maggie turned in time to see a large wave about to break. Taking a deep breath, she dove under it to avoid being pummeled. Once it passed, she broke through the water's surface, focusing once more on her task. She oriented herself toward the seawall and pushed her body through the water, one stroke at a time. The waves pushed and pulled at her like unwanted hands, and she fought off each uninvited attempt, slicing through the water. She'd learned long ago how to compartmentalize, how to beat back fear in favor of a goal. Although only ten, she'd taken care of herself for as long as she could remember. So for now, in this moment, she ignored her fatigued muscles and her sick stomach and the voice she heard in her head telling her she was going to drown.

I can do this. I'm nearly there. No one will know I was afraid. No one will know I was in danger. It's nothing. This is nothing. It will all be over soon, she told herself.

Stopping, Maggie was relieved to find herself back in the cove's shelter. She was still far away from the wall, but no farther than usual. She could hear conversations—laughter and trash-talking—floating on the breeze. A wave lifted Maggie up before it passed her, rushing toward the shore and cresting twenty yards later before kissing a wave that bounced off the wall. She watched her brother, Mike, get pushed to the apex of the two waves, laughing as he dropped toward the ocean floor once the waves passed in opposite directions.

With a surge of energy, Maggie swam toward him, her stomach settling as she got closer. Once she reached him, she shot him a smile. An incoming wave lifted them and they rode it toward the wall, arms extended and legs behind them. Once they slowed down, he pointed toward the right, and Maggie nodded. They allowed the tide to push them in that direction, correcting course every so often to reach the shore. Once they could see sand ahead of them, they rode a wave toward shallow ground. Maggie steadied herself on the murky, stone-strewn ocean floor and dragged herself out of the water. Although exhausted, she did her best to hide it.

"I couldn't see you for a minute," Mike said, grinning. "You went really far out."

"Yeah. It was great." She thought about telling him what happened but dismissed it. Telling him would make him feel as helpless as she'd felt. She was okay now.

She wondered what made her inattentive enough to float out of the cove's protection. She couldn't remember thinking about anything in particular. It had felt good to let herself go, not caring about who she was with or where she was or what she needed to do when she got home. For a few minutes, she'd existed without a care in the world. Until she realized how far she was from the shore. Until she realized she was in danger. Until she realized she could disappear, and no one would notice. Not at first. Not for a while. But Mike had noticed.

Tony and Chris joined them, and they clambered up the concrete stairs to the boardwalk, dripping on the pavement and the yards they cut across to get to their street. Twilight approached, but the day remained hot and humid. Maggie was careful with her footsteps, not wanting to cut her bare feet on broken glass or other debris. By the time they arrived home, her shorts and shirt were no longer dripping. They said their goodbyes, and then Mike picked up a rock at the side of the apartment building, tucked close to a bush, and found the key hidden underneath. They climbed the three worn wooden porch steps and after jiggling the key in the lock, they were able to enter. Mike jogged back to the bush to replace the key while Maggie trudged up the steep wooden stairs. As she reached the top step, she heard Mike bounding up them.

"I'm hot again already." Mike said as he passed her to get to the kitchen.

"I know, right." Maggie wasn't hot, though. She felt ice-cold, the events at the beach catching up to her. At the beach she'd felt like a kite spinning out of control, the string unspooling too fast as the wind lifted it up, only to dive toward the ground when the wind shifted. Although she'd tamped down her fear when she'd realized she was far from shore, she'd felt it. She recognized the danger she'd allowed herself to get into, and she resented it.

I need to take better care of myself. No one else will, she reminded herself.

Their mom wasn't even home, and it was nearly nine at night. Mike was a kid, only a year older than her. What would he have done if he'd realized she was in danger? What could he have done? A shiver worked its way through Maggie, and she wondered whether she'd ever feel warm again.

Chapter Two

"YOU HAVE FIVE MINUTES before you need to leave to meet with your publisher, Senator Ambrose. Do you need anything?"

"No, no. I'm as ready as I'll ever be." Maggie looked around the office before slipping on her winter coat and striding toward the door. Alice Lane, her assistant of three years, fell in step beside her as they navigated the third floor walkway arcade. Once they rounded the atrium toward the elevator banks, Maggie changed course. "Let's take the stairs."

She nodded her thanks when Alice held the door open, and soon they were in the car. Maggie swept away the few freezing raindrops on her coat and sighed. "What do I have this afternoon?"

"After you meet with Stephanie Fabulier, you're due back at the office for a meeting with the team."

As they made their way off I-395 and headed toward Mount Vernon Square, rain tapped on the car windows, the staccato beat soothing her.

"Is my schedule still clear for the long weekend?" She angled her head enough to indicate she was listening even as her eyes followed the paths of the raindrops sliding down the cool glass.

"All set. Did you need me to arrange anything?"

"No. I took care of it." Maggie grinned. "Helen's going to flip when she finds out what we're doing."

She gathered her purse and messenger bag as the car pulled over. The door opened a moment later, the driver and an umbrella shielding her from the rain. After stepping out, she looked back at Alice, holding up a hand when she moved toward the open door. "Stay here. I won't be long."

Entering the high-rise building, Maggie took deep breaths and jutted her chin. She was ready for this meeting. It would launch her on a national trajectory, a path that she needed in her run for president. Although she was well known in Massachusetts and on Capitol Hill, Maggie's campaign wouldn't get off the ground unless she became a readily recognized name. At present, she was just one among many jockeying to be chosen for the next democratic ticket. Squaring her shoulders, she swept into the outer office and nodded toward the young man who looked up from his desk.

"Senator Ambrose, I'll let Stephanie know you're here. Can I get you something to drink?"

"No, thank you." Maggie sat down on a leather chair against the wall and took out her cell phone. She opened the text she had received from Helen and smiled as she sent a quick message to let her know where she was.

At the publisher's office. Wish me luck.

She received a response a few seconds later.

You create your own luck, babe. You've got this!

Helen always knew how to calm Maggie's nerves.

Before she could respond, she heard her name called. Looking up, she saw a tall, blonde woman in her mid-forties standing at the doorway to her office. Rising, Maggie shook the publisher's hand, producing a polite smile as she studied the woman. Light gray eyes, porcelain skin, and a ready smile.

"Please come in, Senator Ambrose. It's a pleasure to meet you." Stephanie led the way to the right side of the room, waving toward two cream-colored sofas. "Have a seat. Can I get you anything? Coffee? Water?"

Spying the glass pitcher filled with water, Maggie nodded. "Water's perfect." She accepted the filled glass with a smile and leaned into a corner of the sofa, crossing her ankles.

Stephanie sat on the other end of the sofa, donned a pair of reading glasses, and opened a laminated green folder. "I read the proposal for your memoir," she said as she tapped the paper. "And I have some comments."

Glancing across, Maggie saw a typed paragraph with handwritten notes in the margins. Words, her words, were circled, underlined, and crossed out throughout the page. All for a five hundred word pitch. "So it seems. I'm here to answer them."

"And I do appreciate that. I know you're a busy woman." Stephanie leaned forward. "Here's the thing. Memoirs are a tough sell. You need to have a hook, a compelling plot, and a point—just like in fiction. It helps that you've been a working politician for twenty-five years, but you're not as well-known on the other side of the Mississippi. What doesn't help is the number of politicians writing them. But the difference is they write memoirs as glorified curricula vitae. Readers become acquainted with their political platforms, but they know little about the politician's personal life. And that's how we can make yours stand out."

"You want me to write about my personal life instead of my professional one." Maggie's voice was flat. She pressed her lips together while shaking her head. "I'm not that interesting."

"I beg to differ. You're interesting. You're a champion for marginalized groups. You've done incredible work in Massachusetts and on the Hill, pushed into place legislation to protect domestic abuse victims, increase LGBTQ rights, and rehabilitate non-violent criminals. All of that's important and should be in your book, but so should your motivations. What formed you? How did your belief system develop? What challenges have you overcome to be who you are today? This is what will sway the nation. Your humanity."

Pinching the bridge of her nose between her thumb and forefinger, Maggie sighed. She wasn't good at being vulnerable, and she loathed the thought of delving into her past. It was a bandaged cut and ripping off the binding was bound to make it bleed again. No, it was worse. It was a wound with stitches that Stephanie seemed to want to pull out. It would be painful and ugly.

"So, if I write about how I got into politics?"

"More than that. Write about your formative childhood experiences. Friendships, schools, family members. Write about how they influenced you. Your romantic relationships. People want to find connections. Show them your path. Better yet, place them on it by revealing how you're like them. Reveal the challenges you overcame. And the ones you couldn't. That's the memoir we want to publish. We'll place the full weight of the publishing house behind it to maximize its impact when you announce you're running for president."

"I didn't say I was going to…" Maggie stopped when she saw the look on Stephanie's face. Her lips were twisted into a smirk, one eyebrow hiked up on her forehead and her eyes twinkling.

Maggie knew it was no use denying her motivation for having the memoir published at this point in her life. "Will we be able to publish by February?"

"Yes. I'll draw up a timeline within the book contract and get it to you by Monday." Stephanie handed her the folder. "My card's in here. Contact me if you have any questions. I'm glad to help."

"Thank you. I'll be in touch." Maggie made her way out of the building, her mind racing. She was good at ignoring her childhood. She'd worked hard to distance herself from her roots while never quite disavowing her hometown.

Am I ready to shine a light on my past? she wondered. If she were serious about running for president, she realized she would have to be. People would find out soon enough. Her past didn't embarrass her—she'd done nothing wrong.

She would write the memoir, and then decide whether to allow the world to read it. She smirked. She knew Helen would give her an honest opinion. It was a double-edged sword, Helen's brutal truthfulness, but she preferred her unvarnished honesty above what the sycophants would say—those disingenuous frenemies who said what they thought she wanted to hear. She was surrounded by them because she was in politics, most attempting to play nice so she would endorse their pet projects. Most had no knowledge of her background other than that she began her political career in Massachusetts. She wasn't sure she was ready for them to know more. Shaking her head, she decided to write the damn thing before panicking. After this weekend, though. She smiled. This weekend she intended to relax with her wife.

Chapter Three

MAGGIE SAT ON A neighbor's front lawn, pulling at the burnt blades of grass while she watched her brother and the neighborhood boys ride a bike down their street. It was a steep hill with a large bump in the middle of the sidewalk, courtesy of a maple tree's roots splitting through the concrete like bony fingers.

"Maggie, try this. It's fun. Come on!"

She didn't like the bike they were using. It had no seat, no chain, and no brakes. She found it too hard to navigate while standing, and it was worse having to crouch over the handlebars to pedal, the jerkiness threatening to throw her over. Joey let out a whoop as he sped by, rolling into a wide driveway and letting the momentum push him onto the overgrown lawn. He circled around until the bike slowed enough for him to plant his feet on the ground.

"It's my turn," Greg shouted, running toward Joey.

"No. Let Maggie try," Mike insisted. He smiled at Maggie, waving her forward as Joey walked the bike up the hill.

It was the day before school was to begin and Maggie was excited. She liked reading books and rhyming words and counting numbers. She liked gaining the approval of her teacher. Although she enjoyed playing with Mike and his friends, she wanted to meet new people. She wanted to go to other people's houses and see what their lives were like.

Maggie climbed up the hill with Mike, dread and excitement making her stomach churn. She was afraid to ride the bike down the hill. It did look like fun. Mike, Joey, and Greg hadn't had any problems. If they could do it, she could do it. She swung her scrawny leg over the crossbar and stood with her hands on the handlebars while Mike coached her.

"When you get to the bump, don't pedal. Just hold on tight and bend your knees. It will feel like you're flying for a minute. And keep the tires straight so you land the right way. You're gonna love it." Mike patted her on the back and stepped back a few paces.

"Go on," Joey said. "It's fun."

Nodding, Maggie stepped on the upper pedal, rising above the bike frame and with a small wobble, and she felt gravity take over. For a moment, she felt free. The breeze caressed her cheeks and kissed her teeth when her face cracked into a wide smile. She was encouraged by the boys' shouts, the warm summer day, and the feeling of invincibility. As she gained momentum, she sped along the uneven sidewalk. Maggie looked for the tree root, the hurdle to overcome, the test of whether she was as cool as the boys. She tensed a second before hitting it, hands gripping the handlebars hard enough for her fingers to turn white. The pedals jolted under her feet, pushing her across the handlebars as the bike stopped for a moment, bumping against the tree roots before veering to the side, the back tire swinging out to the left.

Time slowed down as Maggie realized she was falling across the front of the bike. She saw the broken sidewalk, the reaching tree fingers. She heard a roaring in her ears, and although she knew she was falling, knew it would hurt, she was unable to stop. In the next moment, time sped up again, the sounds of shouting overlapping with the impact of the hard ground. Stunned, Maggie felt pain bloom in her legs, her shoulder, and her face.

"Are you okay?" Mike pulled her away from the mangled bike, helping her sit on the sidewalk. "Your face!"

The pain was overpowering, and her mouth and chin felt like they were on fire. Tears streamed down her face and Maggie screamed, eyes widening as blood filled her mouth and dripped off her teeth. The taste of copper and salt made her gag. Mike ran down the street while Joey and Greg hovered close to pat her shoulders, her back, her hair.

She sat on the ground, screaming and bleeding and shaking. Greg moved the bike to the side as Joey reassured her. "It's okay. You're okay."

Hearing a shout, Maggie looked up and saw her mom running toward her, Mike behind her. "Oh, my God. What did you do?"

Maggie felt fear race down her back. She hadn't realized she might be punished for getting hurt. She trembled, head down, wanting to replay the past few minutes. She wished she'd said no. Wished she'd sat on the burnt grass and watched the boys play. Wished one of them fell instead of her. Wished she were stronger and more coordinated and less likely to fail. But wishing never got her anywhere. She watched blood drip on the concrete between her legs, and her eyes burned.

Arms looped around her torso and lifted her. She swayed on her feet, and Mike reached out to grab her. Joey and Greg stayed near the bike, talking too softly for Maggie to understand their words.

"I'll be right back," Mike said to the boys before wrapping an arm around Maggie's waist. "I'll help you home. Did you hurt your leg?"

Looking down, Maggie saw one knee was scraped and bloody. It stung. She shook her head, grimacing as blood splattered the ground. She looked at her mom, who held her arm in a tight grip, one she maintained all the way to the open apartment door. She released Maggie to lead the way up the stairs, and Maggie watched the white marks on her forearm fade away before following.

She couldn't fall asleep that night. The pain was too great. After her mother pressed a towel in her hands and directed her to hold it against her mouth, Maggie heard her on the phone. Mike sat with her for a few minutes, restless. His leg bounced, eyes jumping around the living room.

Maggie lowered the towel from her mouth. "Go outside. You can't help me." She saw his look of relief and waved toward the door. "Mom won't care."

He nodded and was gone before Maggie returned the bloody towel to her face. She heard the buzz of silence, signifying her mom was off the phone. Her mom came in the room with a plastic bag full of ice and another towel.

"Let me see." She motioned for Maggie to remove the towel and stared. "It's swelling up. This will help." She wrapped a bag of ice in a towel and handed it to Maggie. "Hold it against your lips." She nodded once as Maggie did as she was told. "Good. You can watch some TV."

Mom moved across the room and put on an afternoon talk show. Now Maggie knew she was really hurt. She never got to watch TV. She went through three bags of ice that night, and her arms hurt from holding each one against her lips until the ice turned to water. She was given a children's pain reliever before being sent to bed, where she lay awake gingerly touching her mouth. She could feel where the lower lip was split, feel the uneven skin beneath it, feel how puffy and sensitive the area was.

The next morning, Maggie looked at herself in the mirror and whimpered. She looked like a monster. The right side of her face was swollen and bruised, her lower lip three times its normal size, and her chin scraped raw. She swiveled as her mother opened the bathroom door. "I can't go to school like this. Don't make me go."

She noticed her mom was dressed in black slacks and a pale, yellow blouse.

"You have to go to school. It's the first day. Don't worry, I'll talk to your teacher. I laid your clothes on your bed, so get dressed."

Maggie followed her out of the bathroom, her steps slow. She knew arguing would not help. Her mom was going to work, and that meant she was going to school. She got dressed in jeans and a pink T-shirt before joining Mike in the kitchen. She didn't eat, afraid chewing would hurt too much. Her gaze skittered away from her brother's wide eyes. She knew she looked horrible. All the kids would call her names. She sat at the table, drawing nonsensical patterns with her fingers on the scratched walnut laminate table. She didn't bother moving until it was time to leave.

Walking into the school, Maggie felt eyes studying her, heard the whispers. She kept her head down, allowing the curtain of her straight black hair to obscure her face. She stopped in the coatroom, loitering near the cubbyholes as she heard the teacher and her mom talking in low voices. A hand on her shoulder made her look up. "I have to go to work. You have a good day and walk home with Mike."

Maggie trudged to the far corner of the coatroom, not daring to leave school but not wanting to enter the classroom. Her classmates would see her face and ask questions. Call her names. Laugh and point. She heard the chatter stop as the teacher welcomed everyone to their first day of second grade. Tears ran down Maggie's face, faster and faster.

Miss Goodall talked about her summer, and Maggie wondered why her voice was getting louder even though the students remained quiet. She squawked in surprise when she felt a hand on her arm, pulling her into the classroom. She looked up at her teacher, surprised to see a smile on her face. She continued talking while directing Maggie to a seat in the second row.

Maggie slouched in the seat, swiping at her tears and sniffing. A tissue appeared, and Maggie looked to her right, seeing a pretty redhead with freckles sprinkled across her nose. Maggie accepted the tissue and whispered her gratitude. It gave her hope. Maybe school wouldn't be so bad.

Chapter Four

LISTENING TO THE SURF'S susurration soothed Maggie, who exhaled a long breath as she leaned against the back of the claw-foot tub. It was at the perfect angle to watch the waves hitting the pier, as the sun's rays reflected off the whitecaps. It felt decadent to take a bath in the middle of the day. She lifted a hand, letting water drip on Helen's neck before licking it off.

Humming, Helen squeezed Maggie's thigh, dropping her head to give better access. Maggie took a deep breath, the lavender scent filling her senses as she nosed the juncture of neck and shoulder. An open window allowed the unseasonably warm spring day's breeze to ruffle Maggie's hair. She smelled the salt coating the humid air, and she smiled at how it reminded her of countless days swimming in the ocean while growing up. Although many childhood memories were painful, the ocean continued to soothe her, ironing out the multitudinous worries which plagued her. She delivered several small kisses before leaning back and lacing her fingers around Helen's belly. Lulled by the combination of the bath, the breeze, and the repetition of Helen's fingers running down her forearms while she acted as Helen's body pillow, she closed her eyes.

"Did you want to go out for an early dinner or order in?"

Maggie jolted, realizing she had fallen into a light sleep. Helen turned her head to kiss her shoulder and whispered a soft apology. Maggie squeezed her around the middle. "Let's go out. We can walk the boardwalk and eat some seafood."

"That sounds perfect to me." Helen rose, water sluicing off her body as she stood. She had a solid build with a rounded belly and long legs. She'd put on weight during the years, often complaining that no matter what she did, she couldn't lose that extra ten pounds she'd gained. Maggie was sure the number was closer to twenty, not that she cared. She loved every inch of the woman.

Helen leaned to grab an oversized towel before stepping out of the tub to the heated floor. After wrapping it around her body, she turned toward Maggie. "Thank you for bringing us here. It's been too long."

Maggie had to agree. Rehoboth Beach was far enough away from DC to be counted as a getaway, yet not too far if they needed to cut the weekend short. Although it was the off-season, the warm weather had enticed people to meander on the boardwalk, sit at the beach, and check out the local shops and eateries. It was an unpretentious, small-town beach city, one where they could relax.

She got out of the tub, a small smile blooming when she felt Helen wrap a fluffy towel around her shoulders. "Thanks, love." She leaned back a bit, her smile broadening when Helen embraced her and rested her chin on Maggie's shoulder. She relished these moments of stillness. It seemed she was always on the go. Spending time with Helen without the threat of another meeting or phone conference or deadline was rejuvenating.

Maggie twirled in Helen's arms and gazed at the well-loved face. Tracing the features with her eyes, Maggie marveled at how they'd changed during the years. Helen's brown eyes had become lighter, as if she'd shucked off the stress which used to shadow them in the early days of their relationship. More laugh lines, softer features, and graying eyebrows all indicated the inescapable passage of time, but they also proved Helen was happy. Her pixie-shaped face was like a refolded map, the lines forged by time bracketing her pale lips. Crow's feet served as exclamation points to her gold-rimmed eyes, which sparkled with laughter the longer Maggie stared.

"Planning on moving any time soon, Maggie? Even though you believe love can feed the soul, my grumbling stomach still needs sustenance. Especially after the work out we got earlier." Helen wiggled her eyebrows.

Laughing, Maggie delivered a short kiss before moving to the armoire to pick out some clothes. "So sorry, babe. You know I love to look at you. I have to admit I'm hungry, too."

Maggie donned a black T-shirt with the Massachusetts state seal and some comfortable pale blue culottes. Moving back to the bathroom, she used some hair paste to wrangle her short, spiky hair into something more manageable. She liked how the white streaks in her dark hair made her look respectable. It was probably the most respectable part about her. Grinning at herself in the mirror, Maggie added some mascara before brushing her teeth. Her face reflected the kiss of the sun, and she slathered face cream on her cheeks, forehead, nose, and chin, clucking at the puffiness under her eyes. No matter what she tried, she looked like she hadn't slept in a week. Shaking her head, she reentered the bedroom and slid her feet into open-toed sandals.

Picking up her phone, she saw a text Alice had sent letting her know her weekend remained clear and to check her email for a list of messages, all of which could be addressed on Monday.

"She really is the best assistant." Maggie pocketed the cell phone.

"I agree one thousand percent." Helen grabbed a windbreaker. "Ready?"

Nodding, Maggie grabbed her purse, looking inside to confirm she had money, her license, and the hotel keycard before joining her at the door. "Lead the way."

They strolled down the boardwalk, hand in hand. "You know, once you launch your campaign, we won't be able to do this without someone recognizing you." Helen's voice held a note of melancholy, a wisp of missing something that wasn't yet lost.

"I don't have to run. I can run for the Senate again. Wait to run in the next election."

"Don't be ridiculous. We've talked about this how many times? You've made a name for yourself in politics, and no one lining up to run has your pedigree or desire to help others. People are disillusioned by our current administration. You can help them believe in themselves and in America."

Maggie chuckled. "Maybe I should make you my campaign speechwriter. You make me sound wonderful."

"Easy to do." Helen squeezed her hand. "Want to go in here?" She jerked her head toward a seafood restaurant with outdoor seating.

"Sure."

They were greeted by the hostess and shown to their seats.

"Two mojitos, please," Maggie said. She accepted the menu and scanned it before putting it down on the table.

"So, you haven't said much about your memoir," Helen said.

"Yeah, I know. They want me to write about my childhood, my relationships, our relationship. If it were centered around my political career, I'd jump at the chance." Maggie shook her head. "I don't know whether I want to dredge up all that shit."

"You know people will research it anyway, right? Once you're in the national eye, all your secrets will come out. Isn't it better to beat everyone to the punch? This way you'll be able to control the narrative."

"As logical as that sounds, I still feel like I'm going to vomit every time I think about reliving my childhood. Or my first marriage." Maggie blanched. "And how are you okay with my writing about our relationship? You're one of the most private people I've ever met."

"I've made my peace with it. You've been in politics for what, twenty-five years? You were running for Congress when we met. I'm aware people will be interested in your life, and by extension, mine. I may not like it, but that's why these little getaways are special."

"Do you know what you want?" the server asked as she placed the mojitos and some cheese and crackers on the table.

The server looked to be in her mid-twenties with smooth skin and expertly waxed eyebrows. She wore a T-shirt bearing the restaurant's name and tight denim shorts. The name tag on her chest identified her as Jenny.

"We'll share a shrimp cocktail. I'll have the baked scallops and a baked potato." Maggie handed the menu to Jenny.

"Do you want a salad?"

Glancing at Helen, Maggie sighed. "Yes. House dressing's fine."

"And for you?"

"I'll have the salmon and a side Caesar salad, no anchovies and dressing on the side."

"Great. Let me know if you need anything else."

After the server walked away, Maggie stared at the boardwalk. The dunes obstructed her sight enough so that she couldn't see the waves. She inhaled the briny air, her lips turning upward, and raised her glass. "Salut."

"Salut." Helen allowed their glasses to touch before taking a sip. "Why do you always use a French toast? Why not cheers?"

"I don't know. Maybe because I took French for years and it stuck." Maggie took another sip while extending her free hand.

Helen took it, the ritual complete. They held hands all the time—at restaurants, walking, even sitting on the couch watching television shows. One of them always reached out, needing the connection. Maggie often did it without thinking. Even in the middle of the night—though since menopause hit, she was a furnace at night—neither of them could drift off to sleep without some form of physical connection. During the summer when Maggie was too hot, they settled for positioning their feet together. On cold nights, Maggie acted as a hot water bottle for Helen. And some nights they cuddled for a while before Maggie had to roll to the edge of the bed, seeking the coolness of the unused sheet.

Their dinner progressed the same way countless ones had before. They voiced whatever came into their minds, whether it was politics or the weather or books they were reading. All while they ate with one hand and held hands with the other. All with small smiles shared. When the conversation slowed to a stop, they didn't search for more subjects to discuss. It had taken Maggie many years to become comfortable with the silences. She hadn't imagined they would run out of things to say, and when it happened the first time, she worried Helen was no longer interested in making the effort to connect. She knew now they didn't need to engage with one another during every moment they spent together. In fact, she felt comforted by Helen's presence, a balm to her frazzled nerves, a safe place where she could breathe.

A squeeze to her hand captured her attention. "Coffee?" Helen raised her eyebrows.

Realizing the server was waiting for her answer, Maggie nodded. "Thanks." She watched the server clear their plates, not remembering eating her food. She looked up to see Helen's forehead crinkled, her focus centered on Maggie.

"You okay?"

"Yeah. I guess I'm a bit scattered. This is helping, though." She shot a smile at Helen. "You help."

"Oh stop, you sweet talker."

Maggie loved the fact that Helen still blushed for her.

After paying the bill, they wandered the boardwalk, the late afternoon sun weakening as the sea breeze kicked up. Helen donned her jacket and linked their arms. They ignored the small storefronts, content to find a bench and watch the waves.

"If you write the memoir the way your publisher wants, do you anticipate blowback from your family or anyone else?"

"Well, it would only be my brother, but I think he'd get over it. Mom, I don't really care what she thinks. No other relatives really play a part. As for anyone else...well, you can image how the ex will feel about exposing that part of my sordid past." Maggie grimaced.

Helen rubbed her back with slow motions.

"What if this back-fires? What if people read it and think I was an opportunistic asshole willing to do anything to get ahead? What if people think I had some devious plan of fooling everyone so I could get away from my family?"

"Those are all good questions, and your fears are valid. Some people will judge you. They'll take the information you give them and twist them into ugly lies to hurt you." Helen leaned forward, catching Maggie's eyes. "That's not what happened, though. Tell them the truth and stand tall knowing what you did and why you did it. That's all you can do. We all make mistakes. The people I admire are those who own up to those mistakes and even better, learn from them. You can do this."

Fear buzzed through Maggie as she took in Helen's words. She knew she'd blocked out much of her childhood, not wanting to remember. Some of the most traumatic events had stayed with her, though. At least writing them out might prove to be healing. She could process everything, lay them out, and put them away for good. "Thanks, babe."

"You bet. I'm with you every step of the way." And Helen proved it, as she had for so many years, by walking in concert with Maggie all the way back to the hotel.

Chapter Five

1971

EVERY MORNING MAGGIE GOT dressed, brushed her hair, and watched cartoons before going to school. It was just around the corner, and she made sure to walk the same route so she wouldn't get lost. Her brother went to a different school, but he walked with her to kindergarten before making his way to his elementary school. He was in the first grade, and her mom said next year she'd attend the same school.

With a yawn, Maggie watched Wile E. Coyote chase the road runner. She laughed when he got smushed by the anvil he'd rigged to hit the fast bird. It served him right. After this cartoon, *Tom and Jerry* would come on. They would leave for school once that show ended.

Maggie's favorite commercial came on, and she listened to the familiar words. "Call the Technical College Institute today. Six one seven…"

Maggie jumped off the couch and grabbed a thick phone book, placing it under the phone that hung on the wall. Stepping on it, Maggie confirmed it wasn't high enough to reach the phone, same as all the other days. Stepping down, she took the other phone book and placed it on top of the first one. Now she could reach. She took the receiver and dialed the number as directed on the television. She was glad the commercial kept repeating the number since the rotary phone took more time when dialing a larger number like seven. Once she finished dialing the numbers, she listened to the ringing.

"Technical College Institute. This is Elaine. How can I help you?"

Maggie listened to the nice lady, wondering what to say. Each day she called, like the commercial told her to, and each day she got a different person asking how she could help. Maggie had no idea. Could she help her get to school? Could she help her find something to eat for breakfast? Could she help her get the mud stains off her checkered pants? Maggie didn't know what to ask for or if she would get in trouble for talking to a stranger. All she knew was the commercial told her to call, so she did. Every day.

"Hello? Are you there?"

Maggie kept listening, holding on to the phone with a tight grip. She glanced at Mike, who was sitting on the couch, tossing a tennis ball in the air. She watched the ball hit the ceiling before he caught it. Again, the ball hit the ceiling, and Mike caught it. The repetition was soothing.

"I can hear you breathing. Are you okay?"

That got Maggie's attention. No one ever asked if she was okay. "Yes." Maggie's eyes widened when she realized she'd spoken out loud.

"I'm so glad. What's your name? I'm Elaine. Where's your mommy?"

"She's at work."

"And your dad?"

"I don't know." Maggie glanced at Mike, glad he wasn't paying attention. "I shouldn't be talking to a stranger."

"Oh, that's okay. I'm a friend and I have your phone number right here. Is there another adult with you? Can I talk to an adult?"

"No. Bye." Maggie hung up the phone and stepped down. As always, she lifted the thick yellow pages and placed it back in the kitchen drawer, repeating the action with the remaining phone book. She went to the bathroom, washed her hands, and then sat next to Mike. Bugs Bunny was on. He was so funny. Elmer Fudd was stupid.

"Catch."

Turning, Maggie bobbled the ball before closing her fingers around it. She grinned.

"Throw it back."

"What if I want to play with it?"

"You are. We're just sharing." Mike clapped his hands and looked at her.

She lobbed it toward the ceiling, and he caught it. He repeated her action, and she caught it. They began an easy exchange of throwing the ball up for the other to catch. Maggie glanced at the television and saw Bugs Bunny eating a carrot stick. Her stomach grumbled. She ignored it, knowing she'd be able to eat breakfast at school in a little while.

"Throw it."

Maggie realized she was still holding the ball while watching the show, and her eyes snapped back to Mike. "Sorry." She threw it toward the ceiling a bit too hard, and it bounded toward the TV. She jumped forward to grab it before it could hit anything. "Oops."

She restarted their game, concentrating. She didn't want Mike to get mad at her. Every so often she looked at the TV, but only between tosses. When *Tom and Jerry* started, she caught the ball and placed it next to her hip. "I want to watch this."

They sat in silence, the cartoon's music filling the corners of the room. Just as it was ending, Maggie heard a commotion at the door and turned. She watched her mother push the door open, her keys hanging from the deadbolt and purse spilling onto the floor. She was talking fast, and Maggie leaned forward to see who was with her. She reared back when two police officers entered.

"I swear my mom was supposed to be here. I had to leave five minutes earlier today for a company meeting. I guess she missed the bus, but she's on her way here now. I swear this has never happened before. You know how hard it is to be a single mother. I'm doing the best I can."

As the police looked around, so did Maggie. The apartment door opened into the living room. It had a dirty brown rug, a tan overstuffed chair they weren't allowed to sit in, the orange couch, and an overhead light. The television was across from the couch, its antenna wide like welcoming arms. A black table next to the couch had a large black bust of Buddha. Maggie liked to run her fingers on the bumpy parts of the head, collecting dirt on her fingers.

"Right. Well, make sure we don't get another call. If we do, we'll have to file a report." He turned to Maggie and Mike. "Everything all right here?"

"Yup. We're fine." Mike took Maggie's hand and squeezed it before shooting a smile at the policeman. "We knew Nana would be here soon."

"Okay then." He returned to his partner near the door. "I'm assuming you're staying here until your mom arrives."

"Of course. Thank you, officers. This won't happen again." Mom opened the door for them, giving them the fake smile Maggie remembered from when her mom talked to anyone she didn't like but knew she had to be nice to. Once she closed the door, she leaned her head against it and took some deep breaths.

Maggie felt her chest tighten. When her mom straightened up and glared at her, Maggie knew she was in trouble.

"How many times have I told you not to use the phone? Not to talk to strangers?" Mom stepped into the living room, her face and hands animated. "If Nana hadn't been listening to the police scanner, I wouldn't have gotten here in time. I nearly didn't. And do you know what would have happened?" She raced across the room and grabbed Maggie's arm. "Do you?"

Maggie screeched, trying to pull her arm away. "I was doing what I was told."

"What do you mean? Did Mike tell you to call?" She swung toward Mike, still holding Maggie's arm, and poked her finger in his chest. "Did you think it would be funny?"

"Mike didn't tell me to. The man on the TV did. The Technical College Institute. When the commercial comes on, I call like the man says to." Maggie pulled at her arm and was surprised when her mom let go. The motion made her fall into the side of the couch. She watched the anger fall away as understanding lit her mom's brown eyes.

"Well, don't call again. Now go wash your face. I'll take both of you to school."

Maggie edged around her mom and ran to the bathroom. She was sure her mom was going to demand she get the gold metal ruler. It might still happen later, once her mom thought some more. Fear raced through her. The ruler hurt. She hated being spanked. She tried to be a good girl and do what she was told.

"Maggie, come on." Mike's knock on the door startled her.

"Coming." Maggie washed her face and dried her hands. She opened the door and ran to the front door, where her mom and Mike waited. She followed Mike out the door and down the stairs, their footfalls heavy, surprised when her mom took her hand as they walked down the street. The relief was so great, Maggie let out a huge breath and grinned. She was okay. Everything was okay.

Chapter Six

SITTING AT ONE OF the front tables, prime real estate for those who wanted to be seen, Maggie sipped from her water glass and did her best to seem interested in the conversation about extending the MBTA commuter rail to the North Shore. This was one of Congressman Knaff's favorite topics, and he capitalized on every event they were both attending by bringing it up to her. With a fake smile stretched across her face wide enough to hurt her cheeks, Maggie nodded before sliding her eyes to the right.

The annual awards banquet was at one of her favorite Massachusetts hotels. The Hawthorne Hotel was situated in downtown Salem, not far from the Salem Witch Museum, the Witch House, and the House of Seven Gables. Maggie loved the food they served in the restaurant and the ambiance of the tavern. She was looking forward to indulging after the ceremony concluded. Helen would be joining her in an hour, and after dinner they were planning to stroll around Pickering Wharf. The dichotomy between the hotel's character and the blathering idiot beside her was marked. Maggie did her best not to lose her patience.

"I was under the impression you were happy with the added services." Maggie speared the congressman with a look. "Didn't you tell me at our previous meeting how happy your constituents are with the additions to the blue and purple lines?"

"Well, yes, they are, but the fares have increased again. You can understand how that causes additional financial constraints on them."

"The increases are not directed toward them. They are uniform throughout the state. And they can apply for several discounts and subsidies. I'm sure you know all about those, Charles." Maggie patted his forearm. "I appreciate how fervently you advocate. Keep up the good work." She was relieved when she heard someone at the front podium, the microphone amplifying the person's welcoming words.

"Thank you for being here today. We here at Healing Abuse Working for Change provide comprehensive support to those who have experienced domestic abuse. Part of our goal is to break the cycle of violence and teach others better ways to communicate, to react, to think. Throughout the year we raise money and accept donations to support those who need help rebuilding their lives. We do more than provide food, clothing, and shelter. We offer counseling, support groups, legal services, self-defense classes, and career training. We want to help those who feel afraid, who feel powerless, and who feel trapped to break out of those mindsets and step into a better future. With the help of local, state, and national political figures, such as Senator Ambrose, Congressman Knaff, and Salem mayor, Maria Kostan, we've made great strides with shining a light on domestic violence. Let's thank them all for being here today."

The speaker was the executive director of HAWC and an attorney at the law firm where Maggie used to work more than twenty years ago. Terri Lovitz's specialty was domestic relations, and her support of HAWC spanned from her own family tragedy while in high school. HAWC couldn't ask for a better advocate and staunch supporter. Maggie had made a point of keeping in touch with her after leaving the firm.

The next hour passed in a blur as three other speakers took their turns at the podium to discuss new programs, community outreach, and funding. Maggie showed her support through these banquets and other publicized events, but she did most of her work behind the scenes.

A hand on her arm stopped Maggie from escaping after the speakers concluded their remarks. She stifled a sigh and turned, breaking into a smile when she saw it was Terri. "I didn't think we'd have a chance to chat," Maggie said as she waved her hand around. "Lots of possible donors."

They chuckled.

"I wanted to thank you for coming. I know how jam-packed your schedule is these days. Also, thank you for steering Sammy Wilkins our way."

"Oh, no problem. He was looking for a new way to give back to the community and he's a wiz at social media. He'll help you get a more robust media presence in no time."

"We're excited about that. Where's Helen?"

"She's spending time with her sister." Maggie checked the time on her watch. "She should be back soon, and we'll go wandering around. How's Jacob?"

"He's doing great. The doctor gave him the all-clear this month."

"That's great news. I'm so glad for you both." Maggie thought about the long road they'd traveled while her husband battled colon cancer. "Please give him my best."

"I will. It was great seeing you, Maggie. Tell Helen I said hello."

"I will." Maggie leaned in and exchanged air kisses before making her way out of the conference room.

Once in her hotel room, she propped some pillows against the headboard and sank into the bed's soft mattress with a sigh. She closed her eyes, allowing her thoughts to wander.

Hearing the click of the hotel door, Maggie opened her eyes, surprised to find the room in shadow. She felt the bed dip next to her and smiled as Helen ducked down to deliver a kiss on her cheek.

"I was hoping you'd be back." Helen lay on the bed and Maggie scooted down to join her, back twinging.

"I shouldn't have fallen asleep that way. Now my back's going to act up." Maggie stretched, reaching her arms up before flopping back on the mattress. She twisted her neck, sighing as it cracked.

"I hate when you do that. Why don't you schedule a massage?"

"Oh, I'm fine. Don't fret." Maggie shifted on her side and ran her fingers down Helen's cheek and neck, circling back to pull on her earlobe. Helen's hum encouraged her to graze her lips down her jawline. She felt Helen turn her head and changed direction to snag her lips. Helen wrapped an arm around her, pulling her closer. Smiling against her lips, Maggie opened her mouth to allow their tongues to rub together. With each slow swipe, Maggie felt her body heat up. Helen knew how to kiss her, how to wind her up with slow, thorough kisses and wandering hands. When the kiss broke, Maggie untucked Helen's shirt to run her hand up her back, delivering light scratches in a circular motion.

"Oh, you know just what I like."

"I'd hope so after twenty years." A thrill ran through Maggie. She knew if she were still married to Timmy, she wouldn't be happy. Although she wasn't one to dwell on the past—the what ifs and roads-not-taken—it didn't take much imagination to visualize a much different life than the one she lived. A less fulfilling one.

"Sweetie?"

Grimacing, Maggie realized she'd stopped moving her hand, stopped paying attention to the woman next to her. "I'm sorry." She delivered a short kiss. "Where were we?" She moved her hand to the front of Helen's shirt, intent on unbuttoning it. A hand on top of hers stopped her.

"What's on your mind?" The caring look Helen gave her made Maggie's heart quiver.

"Nothing as important as you. Now help me get these clothes off."

She yelped when Helen pushed her on her back and hovered above her. Sharp teeth nipped at her lower lip before well-known lips sucked on it to soothe the small hurt. Helen leaned back, thighs bracketing Maggie's hips. She watched Helen unbutton her white linen shirt while she moved her fingers in circles on Helen's knees.

"We've come a long way, haven't we?" Helen grinned. "Remember when I used to turn the lights off before I removed my clothes?"

They could laugh about it now, but years ago this was a sore point. Maggie had no qualms about undressing in front of Helen. Not that she felt she had a perfect body. Maggie believed feeling insecure was a wasted emotion. That didn't lessen Helen's apprehension. It took time and trust before Helen became comfortable having sex without a stitch of clothing on.

"And here I was going to suggest turning one on," Maggie said.

Helen reached across her body, her lacy bra rubbing against Maggie's arm as she switched on the bedside lamp.

Maggie wrapped her up in her arms with a chuckle. "Tease."

"No way. I plan on delivering."

Maggie helped Helen remove her blouse and bra before unbuttoning her shorts. "Lift up." She removed Helen's shorts and panties, not surprised when Helen returned the favor by stripping off the rest of Maggie's clothing before resettling on the bed. They kicked the covers off the bed, leaving only the flat sheet at their feet. When Helen leaned down to kiss Maggie, they moaned together. This was Maggie's favorite part, the first full-body contact before they made love. It felt decadent and sexy and perfect. Helen's curves molded against hers, and Maggie was quick to massage her ass as their lips met again. Maggie rolled them over, chuckling at Helen's squeak of surprise. It was rare for Maggie to take control.

She paused for a moment, gazing at Helen's mussed hair and half-closed eyes, heaving chest and dark brown nipples. She was a vision. Maggie supported herself on one arm and took a nipple in her mouth. She licked and sucked, allowing her mouth to encompass more of the breast. Helen's moans encouraged her, and she voiced her own moan when Helen sifted her fingers through her hair. She released the breast, blowing cool air on the glistening nub, hardened and red from her attention, before showering the same affection on the other breast. When Helen was in the mood, she could be tipped over the edge by breast-play. Although tempting, Maggie wanted to touch her, be inside her.

"Don't stop, babe. I love how you touch me." The husky quality of Helen's voice sent a thrill through Maggie.

"I won't, love." Maggie ran her nails across Helen's ribs, her pelvic bone, and her thigh as she released the breast and captured Helen's lips. Her fingers touched Helen between the legs, playing in her wetness. She swallowed Helen's gasp, as she spread the wetness up to her swollen clit. Knowing how Helen liked to be touched, Maggie made random patterns with two fingers, not touching her clit directly. Helen went after her orgasm, thrusting hard and fast. Maggie felt her desire rising. She moved in counterpoint against Helen's thigh, resting her head above Helen's heart. She heard it jackhammering.

"God damn it, yes! Fuck, yes! That's right. Give it to me! Holy shit. Here it comes, that motherfucker." Helen's body jerked hard underneath Maggie, throwing her into her own orgasm. They moved against one another, Helen's litany of expletives petering off as the aftereffects faded.

Maggie rested on top of Helen, sated. After several seconds of silence, she chuckled. "That was some inventive narration. Your Boston roots were showing." She felt Helen's body shake and looked up to see eyes full of mirth. "Was your dad a fisherman or something? The potty mouth you have, woman."

Helen rolled her eyes. "Please. I read an article that said people who swear a lot are intelligent."

Guffawing, Maggie propped herself up on her arms and smirked. "Not quite. The article said intelligent people are more likely to swear. Not quite the same thing."

"It also said people who swear a lot are more likely to be happier, and I can tell you that while I was swearing, I was the happiest person alive."

"Well, how can I begrudge you your fleeting happiness?" Maggie kissed the tip of her nose and rolled into a sitting position. "We should get up. It's getting late."

"What time is it?"

"Six fifteen." Maggie rose and pulled Helen in for a hug. "I think I'll take a quick shower." She released Helen and turned toward the bathroom. "How was your visit with Angela?"

Not receiving an answer, Maggie looked over her shoulder. Helen sat with the sheets pooled around her waist, hungry eyes trained on her. Her chest was flushed, eyes glazed. Maggie raised an eyebrow. "Sweetie?"

"I'm, yeah. Fun." She rose. "Need a hand washing your back?"

"Just my back?" Maggie placed her hands on her hips, watching with amusement as Helen pulled her in for a kiss, her hands roaming as far as she could touch. Not just her back.

"Did you want my hands somewhere else?" Helen's sexy smile sent a thrill through Maggie.

"I'll leave that choice to you." Maggie turned on the shower, humming when Helen hugged her from behind and nuzzled behind her ear. "You feel good."

When she felt Helen's arms loosen, she entered the stall and allowed the hot water to course over her. Her muscles may not be as defined or her body as firm as she once was, but she was strong and fit. She grinned when she felt Helen join her. Holding out the soap, she reveled in the feel of loving hands smoothing soap on her torso, stalling on her breasts before moving to each arm.

"Open. We need you to be clean everywhere."

Maggie widened her stance, chuckling. Helen made it her sacred duty to clean every inch of her. She turned when directed, leaning forward to grab the bar of shampoo. She lathered her hair before placing it on the soap holder.

"Rinse."

Leaning into the water spray, Maggie tipped her head back enough to get the shampoo out. She pivoted in place to rid herself of the soap covering the front of her. Stepping back, she opened her eyes to gaze into Helen's eyes. With a smile, Helen stepped in and raised her hands, the bar of conditioner in one hand. She ran it over Maggie's head several times before placing it aside and running her fingers through Maggie's short locks. Maggie sighed, contentment stealing across her.

"Okay. All set."

Maggie watched Helen grab the soap, sliding it across her body.

"Hey. Not fair. That's my job." Maggie frowned while stepping into the shower spray to wash out the conditioner.

"Next time, love. I'm getting hungry, and I know you are, too." Helen washed her hair with quick motions. "Go ahead. I'm right behind you."

"Okay." Maggie got out of the shower and grabbed a towel. After drying off, she grabbed another towel and held it open for Helen, who stepped into Maggie's embrace. They shared a short kiss.

"Thank you. Now let's get dressed. Some haddock gave its life for my happiness. We mustn't keep it waiting."

"You're ridiculous." Maggie slapped her arm lightly.

"Yup. But I'm your ridiculous."

"That you are." Maggie felt a pleasant tingle down her spine. She was hers. And vice versa. Twenty years ago, she could never have imagined being so happy and fulfilled.

Am I willing to risk it by running for president? she thought suddenly.

"I can see the storm clouds gathering above your head. Let it go for now. Let's enjoy ourselves. We can figure out the rest tomorrow."

Nodding, Maggie returned to the bathroom to dry and style her hair. Helen was right. Tonight was for them. The rest could wait.

Chapter Seven

1978

THE WIND AND TRAFFIC vied for dominance, each loud enough to drown out the other. Maggie hunched as she plodded down the street, ignoring nature's attempt to freeze her. With her faux-fur lined hood pulled over her ears and distorting the sounds, they meshed into a discordant whoosh. Maggie had walked this route many times during the school year. It was thirty-five minutes from school to home. Although she took the public bus in the morning, waiting for forty-five minutes in the cold for a ride home wasn't attractive. Better to be moving forward instead of stuck in one place, freezing her ass off. Nor was she tempted to take the school bus. She didn't like the kids on it. They were loud and rowdy. Although Mike didn't mind taking the school bus home, he often agreed to walk with her.

Mike whacked the snowbanks with a long, thick stick he'd found near the school. The thwacks resounded off the dirty ice every few steps. Hearing Mike's voice, Maggie peered at him. "What?"

"Do you want to stop for pizza or chicken fingers?"

Food did sound good. The school lunch had been a baked pasta dish that was cold and half-cooked in the middle. They were approaching Wyoma Square, which meant they needed to decide. They could continue straight to reach Nicky's for a slice of pizza or veer to the right to get chicken fingers at Mino's. It wasn't a hard decision. Nicky's took less steps. In twelve-degree weather, the extra distance to Mino's wasn't worth it.

Stumbling into the fast food place, they found a small table in the back. Mike shucked off his jacket and looked over. "I'll get it. The usual?"

Nodding, Maggie emptied her pockets and pulled out five crinkled one-dollar bills and a quarter. "My treat."

She'd gotten paid a few days ago at her shadow job, set up by the local Boys & Girls Clubs of America, where she filed paperwork at a law firm near the courthouse. Plus, the lawyers often paid for her lunch on the Saturdays she worked, handing her money and telling her to keep the change once she picked up the food.

Mike came back a few minutes later with two paper plates. He deposited them and left to get the drinks. The plates held large, steaming pieces of gooey cheese pizza. The pieces were large enough to fold over the edge of the plates, the pointed ends dripping oil on the checkered table. Maggie flipped the pizza tails onto the plates and grabbed some napkins to sop up the mess.

Once Mike returned, Maggie picked up her slice and bit off a huge chunk, pushing the bite around in her mouth to dissipate the heat. It didn't work. Feeling the burn on the roof of her mouth, she opened it to allow some air in. "Hot." She fanned herself while Mike grinned. She swallowed and grabbed her drink. "How was school?"

"Same as always." Mike shrugged and lifted his slice of pizza, blowing on it before taking a bite. He hummed with pleasure.

"Are you trying out for basketball?"

"I haven't decided. Maybe."

"Did you hear what happened to Donna? Two boys cornered her after school and were touching her. She said one of the teachers heard her screaming and the boys ran away."

"No." Thunderclouds gathered above his brows. "Does she know who they are?"

"Some eighth graders. Her mom's picking her up from school now. Donna said she didn't know who they were, but I think she's just too scared to admit she does."

"If anyone tried that on you, I'd kick their asses."

"Nah. I wouldn't want you to get hurt."

"You know Chris and Joey would help. I'll always protect you, Maggie. That's what older brothers are for."

Maggie flashed a smile. "Thanks."

"I have some English homework. Can you help?"

"You mean will I do it." Maggie sighed. "I'll help you, but you have to learn this stuff. It's your language. You need to know it."

"Who cares about the structure of a sentence?"

"Um, anyone who doesn't want to sound like a shithead." Maggie bit into the thick crust, ripping a piece off to chew. She washed it down with the rest of her soda and wiped the oil off of her hands, watching Mike finish his piece.

"Ready?"

"Yup." Maggie rose, donning her black puffy coat and pulling the zipper up. She felt like the Michelin man, waddling around in it. The length ended above the knees, and when she had the hood on, she couldn't see anything other than what was in front of her. She shouldered her backpack and picked up her trash. Noticing Mike near the door, she picked up his refuse, too.

"You don't have to do that. Leave it. They'll get it." The thunderclouds were back, but Maggie ignored him.

Maggie heard a murmur of gratitude from the girl behind the counter and she waved before opening the door. She was blasted by a stiff wind. They fell into step, crossing Lynnfield Street before the street widened as it got closer to the highway. Traffic was getting heavier, the constant hum of passing cars filling their silence. Maggie kept her head down, the cold seeping into her bones. Her legs felt numb, her nose was running, and her eyes leaked tears.

Next year she'd be doing this alone as he attended high school and she the eighth grade. For now, she was glad she had a walking companion to eat up the miles in silent solidarity. They reached the cemetery, and Maggie perked up. They were walking past the street that led to the neighborhood elementary school, and soon they would round the bend toward the final straightaway. She saw their house, about a quarter mile away. By tacit agreement they sped up, thoughts of defrosting their frozen bodies a great incentive.

She didn't always walk home from school. Sometimes she went to a friend's home. They were always picked up by a parent, sheltered from the New England wind chill by warm cars and warmer homes. When she was lucky, she was invited to stay for dinner before being dropped off at home.

It took a moment for Maggie to realize it was snowing with the windy gusts. She pushed back her hood and looked around. The snowflakes were big and fluffy. "It's snowing."

"Better than yesterday when it was sleet."

When they reached the sliding glass door that led to the breezeway, Maggie was happy to note it was unlocked. Sometimes their stepfather, John, locked it. Although they lived in Ward One, some of the homes had been broken into. Maggie's frozen fingers were too clumsy to remove the house keys from her belt loop, so she stood in the breezeway, a five-foot space which connected the house to the garage, waiting for Mike to open the side door.

A loud screeching sound filled the air, and Maggie jerked. She looked at Mike, whose eyes were wide. He tried to pull the key out of the deadbolt, twisting it back and forth until the key came loose.

"What do I do?" Mike held the key in a loose grip.

"We have to turn it off. Where's your alarm key?"

"I don't have it." He rushed toward Maggie, as the door swung open. The alarm became louder, loud enough that Maggie had to read his lips to understand what he was saying. "Where's yours?"

Unzipping her coat, Maggie pulled at her keys on her belt loop. She fumbled with the metal ring, trying to part it enough to slide it off the fabric. Seeing the problem, Mike bent close and took over. It was no use. The alarm sounded like a panicked person screaming for help, urgent and desperate.

"I'll lift you." Mike wrapped his arms around her waist and hoisted her up toward the alarm panel. It was near her neck when she was standing, so he lifted her at an angle while she lifted the keys up.

"Closer." Maggie could hardly hear herself shouting. The alarm seemed to drown out all other sound as it drummed into her head. She was sure the police would arrive at any moment. Mike released her and bent down on all fours. She got the hint. Balancing on his back, Maggie got as close as she could to the alarm panel and lifted the keys, slotting the alarm key into the panel. Once she turned it to the right, the sudden silence sounded deafening. She stepped down, watching Mike climb to his feet. "Good thinking."

He laughed, and she felt her nerves settle. As they walked into the house, she glanced around the kitchen. It had a motion detector in the corner, which turned on whenever they moved. They liked to pretend they were secret agents, making their way across the room with slow, fluid movements.

Maggie looked around furtively, half expecting her stepfather to appear, arms crossed and mouth spewing recriminations about stealing food from the refrigerator. They weren't allowed to touch any of their stepfather's food. In fact, they weren't allowed even to be in the kitchen when he was home.

Mike made his way into his bedroom down the hall as Maggie pushed one of the kitchen chairs more snuggly under the table. With a sigh, she unpacked her bookbag. With any luck she'd be done with her homework well before her mom got home.

Chapter Eight

SIPPING HER COFFEE, MAGGIE skimmed the paragraph she'd written about her college years. It seemed too pedantic, like a checklist of achievements. Feeling two hands squeezing her shoulders before strong thumbs dug into her scapula, Maggie moaned. "Feels good, babe."

"How's the writing going?" Helen squeezed her shoulders one more time before sliding into a chair at their kitchen table.

"Slow." Maggie smiled. "I'm hoping to submit the chapters on my childhood by the end of the month. Now I'm tackling my college and law school years."

"Ah, all the fun you had before meeting me."

"Yeah. Life seemed so much bleaker back then. No color."

"Speaking of bleak. I read your chapters on your childhood." She stopped, a pensive look on her face. "You know, it's pretty depressing." She chuckled. "Do you think you could add a few good experiences? I mean, the reader will get the point pretty quickly that you had a shitty childhood. I'm wondering whether it's necessary to include a traumatic experience in every chapter."

"Those are what I remember."

"Of course. That's natural. However, you make it clear you were neglected when you talked about the phone incident, so why include the time you nearly floated out to sea?"

"Because it underlines how we were left alone all the time to fend for ourselves."

"Right, but the alarm incident also indicates you were a latch-key kid. Plus, that happened when you were older. Do you have a timeline for the events?"

"A what?"

"Here." Helen rose and grabbed some paper and pens from a drawer. "Let's list the ages for the chapters. You didn't go in chronological order, so the first event was when you nearly floated out to sea. How old were you?"

"About ten. I know the chapters are out of order, but it's hard to remember my childhood. To be more exact, I don't really want to remember it. It wasn't until I got to college that I was able to stop living in fear."

"I know, honey. Writing the chapters in non-consecutive order might confuse the reader, though. Maybe if you list the year for those events, it will help the reader keep track."

"That might work. The next chapter was the bike. I was seven. And chapter three was the phone call when I was five. The chapter on the alarm going off was when I was twelve. Then I had two chapters about my high school years. Stephanie advised me to write six chapters on my childhood, six on college and law school, six on political life, and six on my romantic relationships."

"Okay. Well, even the two chapters on high school were about traumatic events. You need to intersperse some good memories. Why not get rid of the chapter on falling off the bike? You already have chapters which reflect neglect. Your childhood sucked, but you don't need all those chapters to get the point across. Show how you found happiness even during your childhood years."

"Yeah, but people will want to know why I champion the causes I do. Writing about the neglect, the violence, the struggle—those will act as a window to my motivation." Maggie propped her chin on her palm, drumming her fingers on her lips. "I want to keep the phone and floating sections, but I suppose I could get rid of the bike and the alarm. I'm not sure which traumatic high school memory to keep. The first one is when my stepfather waved a gun in Mike's face after he found out Mike stole some pot from him. That's when we found out he was working for the Mafia. He was hiding a lot more than pot in the basement."

"And the second one was when your stepfather pulled your half-naked mother down the stairs and threw her out the front door while she was getting ready to go to a dance club with her friends. That was rough. Which one are you leaning toward keeping?"

"Yeah. He's a piece of work. No wonder Mike's so messed up. He wasn't a good role model. Maybe the second one. Better not to talk about his illegal dealings. The wrong person might become upset. I know for a fact Mike still has dealings with those guys, particularly since he's in prison with several of them. There's a reason his family is being looked after. Mike agreed to be the fall guy for a deal gone wrong. In exchange his family is taken care of, and he has a job waiting for him when he gets out at the end of his bid."

"How much longer does he have?"

"He's trying to get in a halfway house. From there, he could get parole after nine months. Otherwise, he'll have to finish out the two years."

"Have you been in contact with him?"

"Not in a while. It's not like he writes back. I try and visit every few months, you know that. But with all the traveling, I haven't seen him since May."

Helen placed a hand over Maggie's, intertwining their fingers. "Four months isn't a long stretch. You do a lot for him. You always have. I think you treat him better than he deserves."

Maggie looked up, mouth opening to argue. She stopped when Helen raised her free hand.

"I know. Sorry. I worry about you."

"No need. Let's get back to the memoir." Maggie gazed at Helen, noticing her worry. "It's okay."

Helen nodded. "Right. Well, then. Now that we've narrowed down the three traumatic childhood memories, let's brainstorm three chapters on good memories. Do you have any ideas?"

"I could write about going Christmas caroling with my friend and her family, and spending Christmas with them. Or about learning how to swim at Brown's pond one summer with another friend. We'd bike over to her grandparents nearly every day, and a lifeguard taught us. After swimming we'd drink Shirley Temples her grandmother made for us. Although instead of grenadine, she used cranberry juice. Oh, I could write about when I was appointed president of the National Honor Society in high school, and I had to MC the awards assembly. I got so nervous that instead of asking everyone to be seated after pledging allegiance to the flag, I told them to sit, like I was talking to a dog instead of an auditorium filled with teachers and classmates." She chuckled.

"Those are three great memories. Maybe you can think of one from when you were in elementary school and use the swimming lessons and award ceremony for the other two. That will be a good mix for the ages."

"I could write about how I and another girl would go to all the second-grade classrooms to read our poems in the morning. Or how elated I was when I won prizes like Silly Putty for rhyming the most words within thirty seconds."

Helen covered Maggie's hand, squeezing it. "The writing itself is wonderful. It's an unflinching, direct look into your life. Keep going. I'm glad to talk out the next part of your book once you're done with it. I'll help in any way I can."

"Can you—"

"No." She smirked. "I won't write it for you."

"You're no fun."

"Oh. Well, I guess I'll cancel the harbor cruise I booked for us as a surprise." Helen rose, eyebrow cocked.

"You do know we live in DC, not Boston. Right?"

"Another good reason to cancel then. No need to view the monuments lit up at night or dance the night away."

Reaching out, Maggie grabbed Helen's hand. "Don't you dare." She got up, pulling Helen closer. Leaning in, she delivered a soft kiss. "Thank you. I love you."

"I love you, too." Helen closed her eyes, and Maggie took the hint, kissing her again. "Now, finish your work so we can play." She wiggled her eyebrows.

With reluctance, Maggie released her and reseated herself. "Will do. I'm going to rework those chapters while they're fresh in my mind."

"I'm going to get a few errands done. I'll text you later."

Maggie noted the bright sunlight filling the kitchen nook and bouncing off the computer screen. Deciding to relocate to the living room, she unplugged the computer and closed the top, stacking her notes on top and balancing her coffee cup in her other hand. The kitchen, with its stainless-steel appliances, white cabinets, and large granite-topped center island, was one of her favorite spots in their home. She loved how bright and comfortable the room was, but it was hard to read the computer screen early in the day.

Walking through the formal dining room, Maggie entered the living room. She sank into the comfortable, overstuffed couch with a sigh. They had purchased the two-story, brick colonial on a quiet, tree-lined, cobblestone street in Georgetown, near some of the pricier restaurants and boutiques, after she'd become a US Representative nearly twenty years ago. After moving, she'd packed the past into a box and shoved it to the back of her mind, intent on forgetting. Having to revisit so many painful events was exhausting. At least with Helen's help, she was able to reminisce about the good times, too.

When she talked about the memoir with Helen, everything seemed clear and straightforward, but as soon as she tried to type it out, it was like trying to capture shadows. When she was young, she loved to write stories and poetry. Loved to draw. Loved to act out scenes with her friends. By the time she graduated law school, all her creative tendencies had fled. Or perhaps they were quashed. She wished now that she had worked on retaining her artistic mien. This lack was never as apparent as it was now. It was like looking at an empty room and being asked to decorate it. She didn't know how. Should she paint the walls or apply wallpaper? Use traditional or modern furniture? Rugs or hardwood floor? Monochrome or vibrant colors?

That's how she felt while attempting to write the memoir. She knew every choice would introduce shades of color and nuance. Would people jump to the conclusion that she didn't have children because of her horrible childhood? Would they think she rejected heterosexual relationships after her disastrous marriage to Timmy and failed relationships with male figures? Would they connect the dots and decide she was too damaged to lead the nation?

I'm not damaged goods. I came from a tough childhood, but so have many others. Who am I to compare? It could have been worse. Much worse, she told herself. The vicissitudes of her childhood had shaped who she was.

She had seen casual cruelty every day—the hairpulling and head slapping, the shoving and pinching—and Maggie had lived in constant fear of being on the receiving end of such abuse. It wasn't only in her home. When visiting her aunt and uncle, she was the unwilling witness to a verbal fight which progressed into a physical altercation. Her uncle slapped her aunt across the face and wrapped his meaty hands around her throat, screaming into her face while she pulled futilely at his grasp. Maggie had no idea what the argument was about, but she would never forget the look on her aunt's face. The fear, the shame.

Chapter Nine

MOVING TO COLLEGE EQUALED reinventing who Maggie was. She could present herself however she wished. She had enough money to buy new clothes, and food was included with the scholarships she'd earned. She had everything she needed to succeed. Best of all, she knew no one.

She'd worked hard for this opportunity. In high school, she mastered all her classes, joined clubs, played sports, and helped her teachers and peers in any way she could. She befriended people in different cliques, traveling from group to group with a smile and the promise to be fun, loyal, and supportive. All so she'd have the chance to leave home, and with it the constraints of an abusive atmosphere.

This past year she'd spent countless hours researching scholarships and grants and ended up receiving sixteen for her first year of college, a school record. Only four were renewable, but that was okay. She'd received a full boat from Boston University, as well as from several other colleges, including Boston College, UMass Amherst, Tufts, and Emerson. She decided on BU because it was known for its diversity and located in the heart of Boston. She had a plan. She intended to become an attorney and work in Boston. She would rise in her profession and leave her old life behind. People would see her success and know she wasn't like her family. Nor was she weak. Or afraid. This was her launchpad, and she would rise so high that no one would see her humble roots.

Her two best friends, Lizzie and Kevin, were attending Boston College, and it was a deciding factor in Maggie's decision to attend BU. She didn't want to compete with them for grades. They'd had a friendly competition in high school, but she had no interest in continuing the rivalry. She knew their friendship would suffer, but it was for the best. Also, the two had begun to date, and Maggie had no intention of being the third wheel. Although they were known as the three musketeers in high school, she knew that was no longer true. She had hoped they would keep in touch, but she'd learned early in life not to depend on anyone. Or anything.

During her freshman year, she struggled to take notes during the large classes. The professors lectured for sixty to ninety minutes, often using jargon she didn't recognize. She was good with time management and self-motivated to study, but her classes were hard, harder than any classes she had taken in high school. Each week she read three books, wrote two essays, and attended two labs—one for French and the other for chemistry. At first, she found it hard to roll out of bed for an eight o'clock class three times a week, but she adjusted. By January, she knew where to grab food in between classes, how to cut five minutes off her walk by crossing through the back parking lots, and how long it took to type out a five-hundred word essay on the latest book she'd read. Often, she ran to class with the newly typed essay, stopping at a cork board to pry off a staple and push it through the two pages before pressing the ends in to secure them as she entered the classroom.

Maggie's fear that her friendship with Lizzie and Kevin would lessen went unrealized. They kept in touch throughout their first year in college, even meeting to watch the Beanpot hockey games in February.

Maggie's thoughts were interrupted by the screeching of metal wheels as the train entered Copley Station. Lizzie had directed her to meet them at this stop, although she wouldn't tell her why. She watched as people streamed off the B train, and when she saw her friends, she didn't try to hold back her smile. Their answering smiles made her feel as if no time had passed between visits.

"So, what's the surprise?" She looked at them, noticing their excitement.

"Not yet. You have to trust us." Lizzie grinned. A strong flow of wind signified a car was arriving. "Come on. We can catch this train."

They moved forward with the crowd, jockeying for position, guessing where the doors would open. With so many people pushing to get into the cars, Maggie focused on not falling and ignoring the less savory smells close to her. She felt hands wrap around both forearms, and a moment later she was propelled through the car door. Since no seats were available, she wrapped her fingers around a pole. People of all ages wore baseball caps and shirts reflecting their support for the Boston Red Sox while they chattered about the upcoming game.

"You have to put this on." Kevin held up a bandana. "Don't worry. We'll make sure you don't fall."

"You're kidding." She stared at their dancing eyes and sighed. "Okay. Fine."

Kevin leaned in and secured the red cloth around her head, covering her eyes. They each kept a hand on her arm as the train swung into a turn. She swayed, laughing. Various conversations flowed over her, but Maggie didn't try to engage her friends in conversation. The train stopped, but they remained standing. By the time the doors closed again, Maggie was leaning against the pole with others pressed against her.

"When the train stops next, we're getting off." Lizzie's words were shouted so she could be heard.

"You both better not let me trip."

"We won't. Don't worry." Kevin's voice held laughter, and Maggie supposed they must be having fun seeing her like this.

A pull on her arm had Maggie stepping forward onto the platform. They walked at a brisk pace, and Maggie feared she would stumble at any moment. They kept in step with the lively crowd up an incline and exited the T-stop. Maggie had a good idea of where they were taking her. She'd traversed this route several times since moving to BU. They were in Kenmore Square, walking toward Fenway Park.

The cacophony of voices became louder, announcements on the loudspeakers merging with the general racket in a joyous way. Vendors tried to entice them with roasted peanuts, hot dogs, and sausages—the smells made Maggie's mouth water. Others hawked available tickets and autographed memorabilia. Maggie knew they would soon reach whichever gate they needed to find to attend the baseball game, and her blindfold would be removed.

"And we're here. Happy late birthday!" Lizzie removed the cloth from Maggie's eyes with a flourish, as Kevin slapped her on the back. They were standing in front of Gate B of Fenway Park.

"Woohoo! This is an awesome surprise." Maggie leaned in to deliver a quick hug to each of her friends.

"We knew you'd like it." Lizzie pushed back her curly hair while flashing a smile.

They stood for the national anthem and shouted with the crowd when the Red Sox ran onto the field. Vendors came around, and Kevin waved a hand while shouting to him. Once the vendor was looking their way, Kevin ordered hot dogs and peanuts for all of them. He caught each bag of peanuts as they were tossed over a dozen cheering heads from ten feet away. The hot dogs were passed down the row to them in exchange for the bills Kevin sent back the vendor's way.

Roger Clemens struck out three batters, and Boston trotted off the field. The crowd roared, and Maggie noticed that the crowd had started the wave. As it gained speed, more people participated. Maggie jumped up with her arms extended and hollered joyously before plopping down. She glanced at her friends, and they all laughed together. She loved the feeling of togetherness they shared during that moment. She'd missed spending time with them.

In the bottom of the third inning, as a Red Sox player trotted to home plate with a bat in hand, Maggie cupped her mouth with both hands. "He's a batter! He's a battaahh! Saaa-wiiinnngggg, battaahhh!" She inhaled another big breath, ready to yell out again when she happened to look to her left. Lizzie and Kevin were staring at her, eyebrows raised and smirks covering their faces. She lowered her hands, feeling her face heat up. "Um, what? You've never heard anyone cheer for a team before?"

Their resulting laughter was infectious. Lizzie patted her arm. "That's unique, Maggie. Just like you."

"Pullease! You're not a true Red Sox fan unless you yell out your support."

Lizzie rolled her eyes, but with the next batter both she and Kevin yelled as loudly as Maggie did. The afternoon sun felt like a caress on Maggie's skin. It was the perfect day, a welcome reprieve from the pressure she usually felt. Final exams were around the corner, and she'd have to figure out whether she was going to stay in Boston or return to Lynn for the summer.

The Red Sox won, and the crowd cheered. Maggie was sad the game was over, sad their time together would soon end, and with a heavy heart, she followed her friends as they exited the bleachers. They followed the crowd as it spilled out of the stadium, walking back to Kenmore Square.

"Do you need to leave, or do you want to grab something to eat?" Maggie peered at her friends, hoping they could stick around for a while. She lived close by, a mere five-minute walk from Kenmore Square, and she knew the perfect place where they could eat.

"Actually, we do need to get back to campus. We have an early class tomorrow."

Maggie frowned at Lizzie's words, but she understood. "Bummer."

They reached the Kenmore Square stop and stepped away from the crowd.

"Well, thank you for this awesome gift. I had a great time." She hugged them. "I'll talk to you soon."

Her eyes followed them as they descended into the bowels of the subway station before she turned to walk to her dorm on Beacon Street, steps from Mass Avenue. She shook her head at their failed attempt to confuse her by making her take the subway to meet them. For the first time, Maggie wondered whether she should have attended BC with them.

Chapter Ten

A LOUD BOOM RESOUNDED off the walls, awakening Maggie from a deep sleep. Her heart raced as she lay as still as possible, listening. She heard no voices, no movement, no additional booms. She opened her eyes, staring at the ceiling until she could make out the well-known hairline crack around the edge of the molding. It was still dark outside, but the streetlights helped her eyes adjust enough to focus.

She turned her head to identify the items in her room. Her dresser situated across the room was a dark blob. Helen's dresser was in their walk-in closet. She waited until she saw the indentation of the drawers, counting each one. Once she could identify all four, she swung her eyes to the left. Several pieces of clothing were draped on a chair. She was only able to get away with such sloppiness when Helen was out of town. To the right was a desk, and behind that a bookshelf in between two windows. It was stuffed with an assortment of reading materials—books, journals, magazines, and paperwork. Knickknacks were haphazardly placed on each shelf. She sat up, looking toward the bedroom door. She was relieved to see it was still closed.

Another boom made Maggie flinch, and she rose, crossing the room to peer out the window. Nothing seemed out of place. No one walked down the street, no cars drove by, not even a cat prowled through the city jungle. Looking beyond her neighborhood, though, she saw a plume of smoke, its ominous mushroom causing her to shiver as her stomach dropped.

"Well, that can't be good."

As if she'd summoned the devil, her cell phone lit up, and she sprinted back to her bedside to answer it.

"I'm sorry to disturb you, but we have a situation," she heard.

"So I gathered. Tell me." Maggie placed the phone on speaker and shucked her sleepwear before reaching for the clothes draped on the chair. She wasn't surprised Alice was the first person to call her. She was her bulldog, the one who wrangled her schedule. Anyone who wanted to get to her had to go through Alice.

"Two bombs. One on Capitol Hill, the other at the Mall."

"Where on the Hill? Surely not the White House."

"No. It was in the basement of the Capitol building. We don't have many details. The bomb squad is still sweeping the building for any other explosives while other details are searching the surrounding federal buildings."

"At least everything was closed. I'm assuming since it's three in the morning, no one got hurt."

"Correct. However, I'm sure it's no coincidence with the new network going live, or supposed to be going live this morning."

"Dammit!"

"Indeed. I'm going to the Hill now. Jeremy is gaining intel on the Mall and will text me in five minutes. You have a car coming to you, ETA three minutes."

Grabbing the phone, her shoes, and her sanity such as it was, Maggie wrenched open the bedroom door and ran down the staircase, counting in her head the number of steps since she couldn't really see. "Good. Thank you. I need some—"

"The driver will have coffee for you. See you soon."

"Right. Okay. Bye." Maggie grabbed her wine-colored messenger bag, checking to make sure her laptop was inside, before grabbing her housekeys, reading glasses, and wallet. Pausing in front of the small round mirror in the front hallway, she blanched. Dropping everything, she ran to the bathroom to straighten her bedhead and brush her teeth. Smoothing some lotion on her face, she sighed. The puffiness made her eyes look ten years older. And wiser. With a smirk, she turned off the light and gathered her belongings. As she locked the front door, she watched a car pull up in front of her. Sliding onto the backseat, she nodded her thanks when a large, steaming cup of coffee was thrust toward her. "Thanks."

As soon as the car stopped, Maggie was out the door, striding toward the group of security personnel off to the side of the front entrance. She noted FBI, DC police, and Secret Service. When she was a few feet away from them, she heard her name called. Swinging her head to the right, she saw Alice. Without slowing her gait, she altered course. She glanced at her cell phone as a text came through. It was from Helen. She sent a quick reply that she was okay and would contact her later and stopped next to Alice, who was also firing out a text.

"What's the latest?" Maggie was glad to see the front of the building looked no different from several hours earlier when she'd left for the day.

"They're still sweeping for more explosives, but they did confirm the bomb in the basement destroyed the computer banks, backup drives, and Wi-Fi. Although we have remote servers, it will take time to implement the new email and server protocols. We'll have to share information the old-fashioned way. Anything sensitive can't be shared via the internet, or really through any electronics. Certainly not by unsecured cell phones."

"I see." Maggie's mind raced.

During the past few years, the use of technology had become a double-edged sword. While it facilitated communication and research-gathering, hackers became more talented at breaking through their so-called secure networks. The new system that was supposed to be launched today would have provided a tighter security web with several platforms and redundancies coded into email, internet, and cell phone access. This would set back their timeline. Maggie squeezed the bridge of her nose.

"What information did Jeremy give you?"

Alice grimaced. "The second bomb was at NTIA."

This was bad news. The National Telecommunications and Information Administration controlled internet access for the government. It dealt with a good deal of sensitive information, including the latest threats to the internet. It was a goldmine for hackers or really anyone who wanted to trade government secrets on the black web.

"Anyone hurt?"

"No. It was isolated to their databanks. They're hoping to retrieve the video surveillance. It was stored at an off-site location."

Noticing several media vans pulling up, Maggie sighed. "What a nightmare. Our bold initiative to strengthen internet security will seem like a joke now. I'm sure the media will be quick to highlight this as yet another example of how unsafe we are."

"Well. It's not Wikileaks."

"True, but it's an attack on information technology. It's possible the attackers retrieved information on our security protocols before destroying the servers."

"Ah, good. You're here. What a shitshow," said a voice behind her.

Maggie turned to see the harried figure of her mentor, Ted Stapleton. He was the chairman of the Homeland Security Governmental Affairs committee. Maggie had served on the committee with him for the past five years.

"That's an accurate assessment." Maggie studied him.

Wisps of gray hair covered his balding dome, his face was scruffy, unshaven, and his eyes were bloodshot. His jowls seemed more pronounced, although Maggie guessed that had to do with his tired appearance. At least his clothes were as pristine as always. His overcoat hung open, revealing a sharp navy-blue suit with white pinstripes, a starched white Oxford shirt, and robin-blue tie. He kept his hands in his pants pockets as he surveyed the people grouped around the entranceway to the building.

"I'm surprised to see you here," Maggie added.

"The president asked me to head the investigation on this. Looks like there was a coordinated cyberattack on our systems before they were blown to smithereens. He's worried this was a terrorist attack, mining for sensitive information—things that could endanger our nation. Now, before you jump all over me," Ted held up his hands as if to ward off Maggie, "I'm not overstating the potential danger if the information is leaked."

"But we don't know what information was stolen, if any." Maggie looked around at the groups of security, media, and government officials. "That's pure conjecture at this point. Look, I may not be an expert, but I know it will take time to determine whether our systems were hacked before they were destroyed. Let's not jump to the worst-case scenario."

"I'd rather be prepared for the worst now than scrabbling to deal with it later, when the world's watching. As it is, I'll have to speak to the press soon—give them something."

Maggie felt a hand on her arm. Alice stared at the cell phone in her hand, a frown taking up residence on her face. "Jeremy confirmed the second bomb was at the National Archives, more specifically at the Rights to Privacy and Sexuality exhibit."

"Why would someone want to destroy that?" Maggie felt a headache forming behind her eyes. All she could envision were the countless emergency meetings on implementing more stringent security measures in DC while sifting through inventories of what was stolen, destroyed, and in danger of being leaked. Add on her looming deadline of submitting her completed memoir, and Maggie feared her bed would become a fond memory.

"It seems a bit on the nose, don't you think? Destroy an exhibit on privacy rights while stealing sensitive information?" Ted sighed. "All right. I'll let you know once we receive information on what was stolen. I better get started with calming the rabid press corps."

"Do you want me to come with you?" Maggie was hoping Ted wouldn't need her. She glanced at her phone. It was way-too-fucking-early o'clock.

"Not for this one. Once the information starts rolling in, we'll need to determine what types of data breaches we're facing and how they may affect our constituents. I expect we'll need to address what steps we'll be taking to protect against this happening again. The fact that explosives were detonated in our nation's capital does not bode well. We've become too lax."

Maggie had to agree. It boggled her mind. How were two bombs planted in DC? It seemed preposterous. "Do you think a group will step forward to take credit?"

"I don't know. It doesn't seem like a terrorist attack, but we need to get more facts. I can tell you that we're going to get the answers we need. I'll call you later."

Maggie nodded, thoughts racing.

She felt helpless, and it made her question whether she was ready to run for the presidency. She wondered how she would respond if everyone was looking to her for guidance. She crossed her arms, one hand rising to tap her index finger on her lips. If she were the president, she would be gathering her resources, asking them to find answers. She'd want to know why this happened. How they got close enough. What the fallout might be. If she were the president, she'd want countermeasures executed as soon as possible so she could reassure the populace. Was this the action of an extremist group? A foreign threat? A cyber-terrorist? What was their endgame? She'd need to rely on others to get those answers, people she could trust. A leader was only as good as her team. She turned toward Alice, eyeing her as she stared at her phone, tapping away.

"Whatever you're thinking, stop worrying," Alice said. "We can get a jump on the day while we're waiting for the reports to come in. I know you were planning on meeting with the representatives from GLAAD this afternoon, but maybe we should postpone it."

"I'd like to keep that appointment, if possible. Like you said, we need to wait for the reports to come in. Might as well try to keep to my schedule as much as possible."

"All right. I'll confirm with them." Alice concentrated on texting while Maggie took note of the various groups around her.

"Let's go." Maggie strode to the car idling at the curb, sliding in far enough for Alice to join her. Curling up in a ball and hiding away from the world wasn't an option. She had work to do.

***

Stepping out of her car one morning a few weeks after the bombing, Maggie was surprised by a horde of reporters, their microphones flung in front of her face. The bright flashes of their cameras blinded her.

"Senator, do you have any comment on what was leaked from your memoir?"

Maggie didn't like being taken by surprise. Abhorred it. She did everything in her power to be prepared before she walked out the door each day. Not only did she skim the internet to take the temperature of her constituents, she listened to NPR and watched CNN. Alice even emailed her soundbites she believed Maggie would want to see. She studied all the information as if she were about to take an important test, and she took pride in knowing what was happening in her world.

None of that mattered now, for none of her actions had prepared her for this moment. Despite all her efforts, she found herself flatfooted. "No comment for now."

She pushed forward, anxious to find out what the hell they were talking about. Was her entire manuscript leaked or only parts of it? She hadn't even warned anyone mentioned in it of its contents, excluding Helen. Some sections were extremely personal and if not handled with care, Maggie feared the fallout could prove disastrous.

Just a few more steps. Maggie's spirits lifted, knowing she would soon be able to find out what was leaked. Once she knew, she could create a plan to spin any sensitive information, maybe use it to her advantage. Some free publicity on her impending memoir could be beneficial. She could build on it. Stir interest and, depending on which parts were posted, provide some background information. By the time the book was published, she'd have a large audience frothing at the mouth for the rest of her book.

It will be okay, she told herself.

The reporters didn't let up. Although she hadn't bothered to answer their questions, one reporter's words made her steps falter, her raised hand stopping short of grasping the door handle.

"Have you spoken to your brother about your chapter regarding his incarceration?"

Shaking off her stumble, she imagined looking in the mirror while making what she dubbed her political face.

"Is he why you've been a vocal advocate for the legalization of marijuana and abolishment of mandatory minimum sentencing laws?"

Pressing her lips together in a hard line, Maggie flung the door open and nodded toward the security guard who stepped forward to block any reporters from entering. She passed through security to where Alice waited for her.

"I'm so sorry. Documents were leaked about twenty minutes ago to all the major media hubs. We believe there's a correlation between the cyberattack and today's leaks." Alice handed her a cup of coffee while synching their steps to the elevator. "We're meeting in Ted's office."

"Was my entire manuscript leaked?" After three weeks of silence, she was surprised the leak occurred now. Why the wait?

"No. Only about twenty pages, but…"

"But?" Maggie looked at Alice, who twisted her hands together. She couldn't remember ever seeing her this anxious. "Spit it out. I need to know the damage."

"Three chapters. One about your brother's arrest, another about your marriage to Tim, and the final one's your romance with Helen."

"Great." Maggie shook her head. She'd have to get in touch with Mike. Probably go visit him. That meant an unexpected trip to Massachusetts. Although she'd told him about the memoir the previous time she'd visited, she hadn't written his part yet. She was planning to visit him after she received feedback from her editor and knew what would remain in the memoir.

As for her disastrous marriage to Timmy…well, she didn't even want to guess at how he might respond. She squeezed the bridge of her nose, leaning against the elevator railing. She felt as if she hadn't slept in a million years. She felt as if a boulder had settled on her chest. She felt as if her head was being squeezed by a vise.

"There's more. The group that posted the memoir is the XY Institute. We leaned on the media to take the chapters down, but they were up long enough for it to be copied, downloaded, and shared. The FBI is working to link them with the bombings."

Maggie groaned. "I'll need you to contact Middleton jail so I can get in there for a visit. I need to talk to Mike, and a visit will be the best way. Maybe tonight."

"I'll take care of everything. And what about the other subject matters?"

"I have no idea what Timmy or his family will say. I think it will be best if we meet with the team later today to troubleshoot and come up with a plan of action."

"Right. I'll coordinate it." Alice's fingers danced across her phone.

Maggie took some deep breaths. She needed to focus. She could deal with this. Everything in that book was going to come out in a few months, anyway. Now any backlash would come out earlier and be a vague memory by the time she announced her presidential run. This didn't need to be a catastrophe. She'd scrabbled all her life, and she knew how to pivot.

The elevator door opened, and Maggie marched toward Ted's office. "Did the XY Institute take responsibility for the leak?"

"Yes. They posted it on their website." Alice's scowl brought a grin to Maggie's face.

"Well, it's not as if I had national secrets in the book."

Maggie was not surprised to see several people already in Ted's office. With a sigh, she nodded toward him as she entered the room and sat on the couch. The others rearranged several office chairs as Ted rolled his desk chair closer. Alice took the available space next to Maggie.

The office always seemed crowded to Maggie, with its overflowing bookcases, multitudinous array of framed photos, the large wall of shame displaying the endless accolades Ted received throughout his political career, and the files stacked on his desk. The furniture and rug colors were dark and masculine.

She glanced at the liquor cabinet, smirking at the half-empty bottle of Macallan whisky. It was a rare cask batch received as a wedding present from Timmy's brother, Ron. She'd felt a delicious sense of vindication when she was awarded it in the divorce. It was one of the few times she'd fought for something purely because she knew Timmy wanted it. After receiving it, she'd gifted it to Ted on some weak pretext—an event of no importance. They'd shared a drink and toasted to new beginnings. It was easy to see he'd dipped into it a few more times.

Besides Alice, Ted, and Ted's aide, Sean Cummings, five other politicians crowded the room. All were on the Homeland Security Governmental Affairs committee. Across from her was the Washington State Senator, Beverly Chandler. She was in her sixties with a short gray bob, washed-out blue eyes, and a perpetual frown. To her right sat the Virginia Senator, Paul Johnson, a former linebacker who entered politics after blowing out his knee in college. To her left sat Stacey Gibson, the senator from Missouri who won her spot after the former senator, her husband, died. Beside her, Jackie Anderson, a dark-haired, brown-eyed politician out of New York, stared at her phone, a pensive look on her face. Next to Ted sat Winston Fitzgerald, the Pennsylvania senator who was best-known for destroying Philadelphia's public school union on the pretext that the state must be able to terminate the employment of teachers who were, he said, taking up space and treading water until retirement.

"Thank you for coming on such short notice." Ted opened a folder and passed out several documents to all the HSGA committee members. "We've established a link between the XY Institute and the information breach which occurred shortly before the bombings. We have enough to prove they were behind the cyberattack, but we need to gather more evidence for the bombings. Evan is in the process of getting a warrant to search their headquarters, affiliate offices, and the homes of their key players. We'll pull in the employees for questioning, but I can tell you now, this is going to take time."

"They're claiming responsibility for posting personal information for twenty-three politicians. The link between them is...well, each person is part of the LGBTQ community." Sean, a gaunt twenty-something who looked like he would cry if anyone raised a voice in his presence, stared at the document in his trembling hand.

Maggie wondered whether the shaking was due to stress, lack of sleep, or too much caffeine.

"This was a coordinated attack, and we believe their objective is to turn the public against those they exploited." Ted tapped his finger against the document. "The rhetoric the XY Institute published with the leaked documents push their agenda of healing America by not allowing—and these are their words, not mine—immoral, psychologically damaged individuals to serve as leaders. They believe sexuality is a choice, and children raised by same-sex parents will experience emotional problems, become promiscuous, and break the law."

Maggie read the documents, tasting bile in the back of her throat. She swallowed with difficulty, feeling eyes on her bowed head. Taking a deep breath, she looked up at Ted, the hardness she saw in his eyes no doubt caused by knowing how this affected her. "I didn't have my memoir on the government server, which means they used it to access my personal accounts. How was that possible?"

"Once they got access to the government server, they could use it to access anyone's personal servers. They basically created pathways through IP addresses, cell phone connections, any electronics." Sean's answer was disturbing. Every email written or received, every website visited, every document viewed—all could be accessed? Her chest tightened. The invasion of privacy was staggering. She crossed an arm over her stomach, hunching as she reviewed the documents.

"So if this is a terrorist attack, why aren't we passing this off to the local authorities? Or the FBI?" Stacey asked.

"The president wants us to keep abreast of all developments and report to him. The fact that our federal servers were hacked, and politicians were attacked, is ringing all sorts of bells. It's within the realm of possibility that the XY Institute has formed a partnership with a larger, more formidable group to influence the general populace. If the bombing is linked to them, then we're looking at a terrorist attack."

Ted's answer confused Maggie. Although the XY Institute was reprehensible and abhorrent, she'd never seen any indication that it used violence to further its agenda.

"In what way?" Winston's scowl made his eyebrows look like dark clouds.

"The elections, of course. Next week we have the midterm elections for our senators and representatives. The leaked documents could hurt anyone on this list who's up for reelection," Ted answered.

Maggie was grateful she didn't have to deal with the reelection. Looking at the list, she saw how sabotaging these candidates could cause a change in who held the majority for Congress.

"How many on this list have an election?" Beverly's question echoed Maggie's thoughts.

Some of these people hadn't been in politics for long. This could jeopardize their runs if the wrong people used the information to further a smear campaign.

"Eighteen." Ted's answer surprised Maggie.

"But what's the point of leaking the information on those who aren't up for reelection? It seems like a wasted opportunity." Maggie shot a glare at Stacey, who shrugged. "You know what I mean. If you ask me, they overplayed their hand. If they were smart, they would have attacked each politician separately, beginning directly after the bombing instead of all at once."

"Hurray for incompetence." This was Jackie's first year on the committee, and Maggie appreciated her sardonic humor and sharp wit.

"It's likely it took this long to decode the information. President Sugarman is bringing in some IT guys to see what they can uncover. Until then, we are acting on the assumption that although the bombings didn't kill anyone and the leaks don't consist of state secrets, the perpetrators were more lucky than skilled. This could have gone sideways fast. We need to shut it down and mitigate any damage as soon as possible."

"Why would this hurt them? I mean, I'm sure their constituents are already aware." Paul's question had Maggie shaking her head in exasperation.

"You'd be surprised what they don't know. What they're willing to ignore unless the information is pushed in front of them." Maggie exhaled loudly. "This comes back to bringing people's personal lives into the limelight instead of the hard work they've done while in office."

"I can see how this could hurt them on a national scale. They may be supported in their home states, but if they try to broaden their base, this might prevent them from even getting a national campaign off the ground." Jackie had a good point.

"Once I receive more information, I'll call another meeting. I'm sure it goes without saying that none of this information should be shared outside this room." Ted rose, closing his folder.

As everyone prepared to leave, Ted approached Maggie. "Can you spare a minute?"

"Sure." Maggie remained seated, turning to Alice. "Go ahead back to the office. I'll join you soon."

"Okay. I'll start organizing your schedule and text you when everything's confirmed."

After everyone filed out, Ted took Alice's spot next to Maggie. "I realize the leaked documents have affected you. Are you okay?"

"We'll see. I'll have to put out some fires. Maybe put out some feelers to see what the reactions are." She shrugged. "I'm preparing for the worst while hoping for the best."

"This probably won't help with your presidential run, but you have a few months to get it back on track before you start your campaign."

Surprised by his words, Maggie looked up and noticed Ted watching her closely. She cocked her head to the side. *Act cool,* she told herself. "Presidential run?"

His chuckle made her bristle. "Come on, Mags." He patted her on the knee. "We both know you're going to run." He sat back and crossed an ankle over his knee. "I have to admit, I'm a bit hurt you haven't confided in me. You know I can help you."

Shaking her head, Maggie tried to decide whether to confirm or deny, whether to stroke his ego or laugh it off. "Ted, it's early days. I haven't decided anything, but when I do, you'll be the first to know. After all, you're my mentor. I trust you have my best interests at heart." She grinned. "Thanks for checking in with me."

She rose, walking toward the exit. "Gotta run. I'll catch up with you later."

As she passed his desk, her gaze snagged on a partially hidden document with the XY Institute letterhead.

She paused at the door and turned toward Ted. "Tell Nellie I said hello." She hated Ted's wife and her condescending attitude, but she always attempted to remain civil, if only due to her respect for Ted.

"Will do."

Maggie walked to her office, her mind on Ted's words. He seemed sincere, but something about his behavior seemed incongruous. It didn't sit well with her. She hadn't told Ted she was running for the presidency on purpose, wanting to have a solid plan before letting anyone outside of her team and family know. It was possible he knew her well enough to have guessed her intentions, but her gut warned her someone might have told him. That meant someone on her team.

And so it begins.

She thought she'd built a strong, loyal team. Now she'd have to weed out whoever was reporting back to Ted. And why did he need a mole, anyway? She knew knowledge was power, but they were friends. Weren't they? Her stomach churned at the thought that Ted might have a hidden agenda, one at odds with her own plans. She shook her head, as if to shake loose such ridiculous thoughts. The best she could do was be more judicious with who received what information in the future. Maybe share some inaccurate information to determine who was feeding Ted information. If anyone.

She hoped she was being paranoid. It would be better than being proven right.

Chapter Eleven

1987

COLLEGE WAS A REVELATION. She got into school politics in her freshman year, and by the end of her sophomore year, she was tapped to become a student tribunal. It was the student union's judicial branch, on par with a judge, for all student political affairs. She resigned her position of dorm senator, thrilled she wouldn't have to deal with annual re-elections, and took the new position. She no longer had to back anyone's political agenda. The two other tribunals were quick to show her the ropes, and she earned one of the coveted gold student ID stickers which allowed her access into any dorm on campus. Moreover, she could also use it to allow others into any dorm she chose. The power was heady.

Besides working hard to become a recognized figure in the student union, Maggie mastered a successful study regimen for her classes. She figured out how to navigate life, and she loved being seen. No longer did she hide in the corner, afraid to move while she watched her stepfather manhandle her mom, or her brother slap his girlfriend, or her uncle throttle her aunt. She didn't need to freeze in place or slink away from the danger. She was powerful and confident and safe in this new life she created.

Needing to earn some money for summer expenses, Maggie took a job at a department clothing store in her sophomore year. She'd returned home for the summer after her freshman year, and she'd vowed to find somewhere else to live during the summer months. Her stepfather had thrown away all her belongings—her clothes, books, even her bike—and she'd spent the summer months doing her best to not capture his attention. This year would be different.

Dragging herself up the steep stairs to the third floor, Maggie sighed once the door swung open to Nancy's smiling face.

"I thought I heard you," Nancy said.

Maggie passed through, closing the door behind her before plopping onto the couch. She closed her eyes, listening to the steady hum of the upright fan in the corner. Above her the ceiling fan was on high, circulating the warm air. Maggie contemplated moving into her bedroom to change into shorts, but she needed a few minutes to gather her energy.

"Here."

Opening her eyes, Maggie grabbed the cold bottle of hard apple cider with a smile. "Thanks." She clinked bottles with Nancy and watched her sink into the old stuffed chair next to the couch.

The thing was ancient. It had a flower pattern Maggie imagined was popular about thirty years ago. It had been included with the apartment along with the couch, kitchen table, beds, and dressers. She couldn't complain. Although the furniture was old, the pieces were sturdy and comfortable. She hummed with pleasure as the cold beverage slid down her throat. She kicked off her shoes, wiggling her toes.

"Long day?"

"Yeah. It was busy. There was this one woman who wanted to try on every pair of shoes in her size. And I had to put each one of them on her feet. At least she bought three pairs."

"Well done. You should come with us tonight to Paulie's house. He's having a party."

Paulie was Nancy's boyfriend. They'd met in the Philosophy 101 class. Nancy was a soccer player from California, a powerhouse with a compact, muscular body and bubbly personality. That day she had her long, chestnut-colored hair pulled back into a ponytail, although several escaped tendrils framed her glistening face. She closed her eyes as she held the cold bottle against her forehead. Maggie admired her natural insouciance, often finding Nancy revived her spirits after a stressful day.

"What time are you going over?"

"Not for a few hours. We can get something to eat beforehand if you want."

"Emily coming?"

"No. She's working until closing."

"Bummer." Maggie liked Emily. She was a hard worker, but she liked to have fun. On the odd night all three roommates were together, they played games—cards, Scrabble, Trivial Pursuit, backgammon, whatever caught their fancy. Emily was a tall, willowy blonde, her Norwegian heritage shining through light blue eyes and ivory skin.

Maggie took a long sip from her bottle. "Yeah, we can go to Charlie's." She glanced at Nancy as she nodded. "Are you staying at Paulie's tonight?"

"No way. If I do, I'll have to deal with all his wasted friends sprawled around the house or worse, throwing up. Last time I got stuck cleaning up."

"Gross." The thought of cleaning up puke made her stomach roll. She shook her head, as if that would clear her mind. "Thanks for this." She raised her cider. "I needed it."

"You probably need water, too."

"Probably." Finishing her drink, Maggie pushed up from the couch. "I'm gonna take a cool shower."

"Don't forget—"

"I know. Getting water now." She chuckled as she grabbed a water bottle from the refrigerator before entering her bedroom.

Nancy was a student at Sargent College, and she loved to use her knowledge about the human body whenever possible. She often reminded Maggie she needed to drink more water during the summer to remain hydrated.

After taking a cool shower, Maggie donned some pleated tan shorts and a navy-blue tank top. She found Nancy sitting in front of the fan, eyes closed. "You didn't fall asleep, did you?"

Hazy hazel eyes focused on her. "Just waiting for you. I was afraid you'd drowned."

"Ha. Not likely. I grew up playing in the ocean. I won't be taken down by a shower." Maggie pulled her hair back, knowing that once it dried it would be wavy and thick. "Ready to eat?"

"You know it."

Charlie's was a hole-in-the-wall pizzeria on Commonwealth Avenue located in the basement of a brownstone. They did no advertising, relying on word of mouth.

They placed their orders and sat down at one of the two-person tables. Maggie sat facing the rest of the restaurant, watching the steady flow of college students. "I wish they accepted points."

"Yeah, that would be awesome." Nancy worked at the main food court on campus. "I heard the school's in negotiations with several restaurants, so it's a possibility."

Once they received their food, they sat in companionable silence. Maggie watched a bit of the Red Sox game as it played on the overhead television. She heard the roar of the crowd as Roger Clemens struck out a batter. It took her a moment to realize she was hearing the crowd not only through the television but also from Fenway Park. The pizzeria was close enough to the ballpark to hear the echoing shouts of the spectators. "We should go to the game tomorrow night."

"Sure. I think Emily's off, too. We can get some tickets from the GSU tomorrow." Nancy had a knack for keeping track of everyone's schedule.

Once they finished eating, they made their way outside. "Let's take the T," Nancy suggested.

With a nod, Maggie fell into step with Nancy. They crossed the street to catch the outbound Green line B train. Paulie lived on the westside of campus, about two miles away. Maggie was happy to find the car nearly empty. It was still hot and being pressed against a crowd of sweaty commuters wasn't her idea of fun. Once they hopped off the train, they walked the two blocks to Paulie's apartment. People were sitting on the stairs leading into the apartment, chatting. Maggie didn't recognize anyone she knew, but when they greeted her, she made sure to smile and nod her hello.

They were greeted by more partygoers as they made their way up three flights of stairs. The apartment door was open, at least forty people jammed into the living room. Music blared from two large, black speakers situated on the hearth. It was loud enough that the floor vibrated with the bass.

Nancy sang along to "Addicted to Love," and Maggie chuckled. Whenever Nancy couldn't remember the words, she made them up or hummed. They made their way to the kitchen, weaving through the dancing bodies.

Paulie's familiar voice cut through the discordant sounds. "There you are. I was wondering when you'd show up." He pulled Nancy into a sloppy kiss, liquid sloshing out of his cup. "Oops. Did I get any on you?"

"No. I'm fine." Nancy pulled him close for another kiss. "This is quite the turnout."

"Yeah, baby." He looked over Nancy's shoulder. "Hey, Maggie. Nice to see you. And guess who's here?" He waggled his shaggy eyebrows. "Brett-boy. He's been asking about you."

Biting back a grimace, Maggie did her best to appear excited. "Cool. I haven't spoken to him in a while." One glance at Nancy's face, and she knew her response hadn't convinced her of any desire to see Brett. Not that Paulie seemed to notice.

"Yeah. He's here somewhere. Let's get you girls some drinks." He twirled around, swaying a bit. "Woah." Nancy held on to the back of his shirt. "Thanks, babe. I'm good."

He made his way to the kitchen table, which was pushed against the wall. It was covered with a keg, bottles of wine coolers, and large tubs filled with ice and soda. Bags of opened chips, popcorn, and pretzels were propped up or partially spilled across the surface. "What'll you have?"

"I'll have a beer."

"One beer coming up. How about you, Maggie?"

"Coke."

"Not drinking tonight?"

"Nah. I have an early start tomorrow." That wasn't true, but she always felt as if she needed a reason to refuse alcohol. All her friends drank. The change in the drinking age did nothing to slow down their consumption of beer and wine coolers. Since she'd had her one bottle of booze after work, she had no intention of drinking more.

Once Paulie handed her the dripping can of soda, Maggie held it against her forehead and the back of her neck. "Oh, that feels fabulous."

"Beer pong in five minutes. Pick your teams," a sonorous voice announced.

"Babe, let's show these amateurs how it's done." Paulie led the way to the living room, a dopey smile on his face.

Several brawny guys pushed two wooden coffee tables toward the middle of the room and covered them with a long board of plywood while people continued to talk above one another and the blaring music. Maggie found a spot on the ratty couch. It would provide her with a good view of the game since it was behind one of the ends, but at an angle.

Maggie felt the couch sink next to her as someone sat down.

"Hey, Maggie." Taking a deep breath, she turned her head, knowing whom she would see. She shot a smile at Brett.

"Hi. Aren't you going to play?" She waved toward the game.

"Nope. Maybe later. How ya been?" His pearly white teeth gleamed.

"Fine. You know. Working. Going to class." She shrugged.

"Cool. Glad it's only one more week. I'm going home after it ends. Thought I could get a bunch of friends to join me and we could catch a show on Broadway. You interested?"

Maggie pushed down her first impulse to reject the offer. She was worried about the cost involved. She knew New York was expensive. Attending a Broadway show, though, might be worth the expense. She could probably work extra hours to raise the funds. "I've never been to New York before. Where would we stay?"

"My place. Well, my parents' place. We have plenty of room. We can fly in for a long weekend."

"I don't know—"

"What's up?"

Maggie looked up at Nancy. "Did you lose already?"

"Of course. Paulie can hardly stand up. What are you guys taking about?"

"Brett was inviting me to New York to catch a Broadway show, but I don't think I can rationalize spending that much money for airfare and a show."

"You and Paulie can come, too." Brett swallowed some of his drink. "We have plenty of room, so no one will have to pay for a hotel. I was about to tell Maggie my dad can hook us up with tickets to *42nd Street*."

"That's wicked awesome! I'm in," Nancy said. "I've been dying to see it. We can take the bus from South Station to New York. I heard it's easy, and we can get around Manhattan by subway."

Maggie found herself nodding. She wanted to go, and that seemed a lot less expensive than flying to Manhattan.

She glanced at Brett, who was frowning as he awaited her answer. "I suppose that can work."

His face cleared. "So, a week from Friday? We can go in the morning and return Sunday night. Catch the Saturday show. Oh, we can have dinner at Sardi's. You'll love it."

Maggie wondered how expensive the restaurant would be. With a sigh, she pushed back her worry. She had some money saved, and she could forego eating out for a while by using her points at school for meals. This would be a great experience. She nodded. "I'm in."

"Great." Brett clapped his hands together, his lips pulling into a broad smile.

He was attractive with his dirty blonde hair curling at his collar and long eyelashes. He reminded her of George Michael, but he couldn't dance to save his life. He had no rhythm, although she assumed he was fit since she often saw him jogging across campus.

She studied him, noting that he was wearing his usual rich-boy preppy tan khakis and polo shirt. She knew he could be arrogant at times, but he seemed unaware. Maggie believed his upbringing had taught him to take his wealth for granted. She doubted he had ever experienced hunger or the anxiety that came with not knowing whether he could pay his bills. He had a job waiting for him once he graduated college, whether it was next year or after earning a master's degree.

She hadn't given him the opportunity to talk to her about his future, or anything else for that matter, but she decided this trip would be a good time to find out more about him.

"Hey, let's dance." Nancy pulled Maggie to her feet as Janet Jackson's well-known voice floated through the air. Maggie began singing the lyrics to "When I Think of You," bopping to the beat. She loved this song. Although she'd never felt the way the song described, she had high hopes that someday she would fall in love. For now, she was content to spend time with her friends.

***

Getting to the bus terminal in time to make the trip to New York City wasn't as easy as Maggie had anticipated. She'd arrived home late the night before and waking up had proven challenging.

Switching shifts so she could have the weekend off made for an exhausting week, but she knew the excitement of being in Manhattan would counteract her tiredness.

The six of them sat toward the back of the Peter Pan bus. Besides herself, Nancy, Paulie, and Brett, they had been joined by Emily and her friend, Stella. Maggie stared out the window as they drove down I-90, wondering whether she could take a nap. She was a light sleeper, but maybe if she put her Walkman on, she could be soothed by the slow music she'd copied onto the cassette.

"What's that guy doing?"

Hearing Brett's question, Maggie looked at him and followed his eyes to an unkept man stumbling toward the front of the bus.

"You need to sit down." The bus driver sounded annoyed, and Maggie couldn't blame him.

Paulie kneeled on the seat, his focus on what was happening at the front of the bus.

"Sit down." Others added their voices, as the man mumbled about needing to get out.

"I can't stop right now. You need to sit down." The driver was getting louder. Maggie wondered whether this happened often.

When the bus swerved, several people screamed.

"Oh, my God! He's pulling at the wheel."

"Someone, get him!"

A man in his thirties near the front grabbed the guy in a headlock, as the bus driver regained control of the wheel. Before Maggie quite knew what was happening, the bus was on the side of the road and two state police cruisers were pulling up.

"I'm sorry, folks, but we're going to be delayed for a bit while I talk to the police. They may want to talk to some of you. Just sit tight."

"Good thing we weren't planning on seeing the show today." Emily sighed, looking past her friend to Maggie. "It figures this happened to us. We always seem to get into trouble."

"You mean you always get into trouble. Sometimes I'm with you when it happens." Maggie raised an eyebrow, waiting for Emily to argue the point. It was a conversation they'd shared several times. Trouble was Emily's best friend. It followed her around like a puppy. Emily was anything but boring.

"Okay. Yes. I'll own that." Emily scrunched up her nose. "Maybe it's because I was born on Friday the thirteenth."

Maggie laughed. "Yeah. That must be it."

They arrived at the Port Authority Bus Terminal two hours later than scheduled. By then, Maggie wanted nothing more than to eat and sleep. She knew it was only four in the afternoon, but the whole getting-nearly-killed-thanks-to-a-steering-wheel-grabbing-lunatic had shot her nerves.

"Well, thank God. I thought we'd never get off the bus." Nancy pulled her hair back and used the blue scrunchie she was wearing on her wrist to secure it.

"I was about to write a will bequeathing my college books to my sister," Paulie said.

"Well, at least they're in pristine condition since you've never opened them."

Maggie chuckled as Paulie pantomimed being shot in the heart after Nancy's acerbic comment. "What's the plan? Anyone hungry?" She hoisted her travel bag on her shoulder, adjusting the strap to a comfortable spot before looking around.

"We have options. We can take the subway to my house and order some Chinese food, or we can find something to eat around here."

Although Maggie wanted to go straight to Brett's house, she refrained from voicing her preference. She wanted to do whatever everyone else preferred. She could rest later.

"I'm starved, so I vote food. As soon as possible." Emily looked at her friend. "How about you, Stella?"

"Yeah. I can do food." Stella, a psychology major from Atlanta, was a soft-spoken, dark-skinned girl. Whenever Maggie was around her, she felt warm, as if she were sunbathing at the beach. She half-expected to hear seagulls crying.

"Food for the win!" Paulie raised his hands in a winner's clasp, shaking them above his head while imitating the roar of the crowd. "Let's do the tourist thing and eat in Times Square."

"No way. I can take you to a much better place, somewhere only locals know about. Burgers okay for everyone?"

Maggie's stomach growled at the thought of eating one. "Sounds perfect." It had been a while since she ate a burger, the last time being at the fast food chain located on campus. She hoped wherever Brett was taking them was good.

Once they ordered, they stood to the side to wait. No tables were available, but Brett said the turnover tended to be quick. By the time they had their burgers a group of tourists were leaving. Maggie nabbed a seat and bit into her cheeseburger. She moaned. "So good."

"I knew you'd love it. I was thinking that after we eat, we can drop our stuff off at my house and explore Central Park. If you guys want, we can catch a comedy show tonight. There's one pretty close to me."

"Where do you live?" Nancy leaned forward as she directed her question toward Brett.

"Upper Westside. It's about forty blocks uptown, close to Central Park." He ran his fingers through his hair.

"That sounds like a plan, my man." Paulie popped the rest of his burger in his mouth and wiped his hands with a napkin.

The streets were clogged with visitors, but Maggie didn't mind. She was enamored with Manhattan. She wondered why she'd never thought to visit before today. She'd had opportunities, but they hadn't enticed her. She was certain being with her friends made the experience more enjoyable. Even taking the subway was fun, although the strong smell of urine was prevalent in the hot subway station. She wanted to learn more about the city. Perhaps spending more time with Brett wasn't such a bad idea.

The rest of the day flew by. Maggie couldn't remember a time she had laughed as much. Once they returned to Brett's home after the comedy show, they had drinks and talked about their day.

"You know, we could do standup comedy ourselves and tell them about the psycho who tried to get us all killed on the bus," Paulie said and pretended to pull a steering wheel to the right. "Ahhh! We're gonna die."

"No, babe," Nancy said. "You have to play it off like it's just another shitty thing that's happened in your life. All monotone like, 'yeah, today I decided to visit New York City by taking the bus. I almost died on the way. But I view it like the in-flight entertainment.'"

"Not to criticize, but you need to work on that."

"That is a criticism." Nancy flung a napkin at Maggie, who blocked it.

"That's like when someone apologizes and tacks on a 'but' with some half-assed reason," Emily said.

"Is it a cute butt?"

Maggie's eyes widened at Brett's remark. Was he flirting with Emily?

"Shut up, ya loser." Emily shoved Brett out of his seat, where he sprawled on the floor as the rest of them guffawed.

"That's my cue. I'm going to get ready for bed." Maggie rose, taking her glass to the sink and rinsing it off.

When Brett joined her, she did her best to suppress her desire to get away from him. She wasn't sure how she felt. Before this trip, she had no interest in dating him. Watching him flirt made her uncomfortable, but she wasn't sure whether she was jealous, possessive, or hurt.

"Hey. I was just kidding. You know that. Right?"

"We were all joking around. Don't sweat it." Maggie flashed a smile. "Today was a lot of fun. I'm looking forward to tomorrow." She was glad to see him smile back at her. "Good night." She patted his arm as she walked past him.

She would let the weekend play out before she made any decisions about dating him. It was possible he might want to date Em, and she had no intention of standing in the way. It's not like she was in love with the guy. She wasn't sure she was even attracted to him. He was funny and intelligent, but so were many other people she'd met at college. She certainly didn't miss him when they didn't see one another for several days. She didn't light up when he was near. She didn't think about kissing him or holding his hand.

Up until today his best quality had been his blatant interest in her. Maybe she'd waited too long to reciprocate. If that were true, though, she was glad she waited. Someone else, someone better suited for her, would come along. Until then, Maggie was determined to enjoy spending time with all her friends.

The next morning, Maggie woke up late. She stretched her arms above her head and sat up before looking at her bedmate. Nancy was still asleep. Emily and Stella shared the other bed, while Paulie and Brett slept in Brett's room. She didn't hear anyone moving around. She glanced at the alarm clock, surprised to see it was ten seventeen. Since she felt well-rested, she didn't think she'd be able to go back to sleep.

Rising, she tip-toed around the room as she gathered clothing and necessities for a shower. The door stuck when she tried to open it, and it made a loud noise as she pulled it open. Maggie froze, checking to see whether she had disturbed anyone. She was thankful to find everyone remained asleep.

Brett's home was an old townhouse on the Upper Westside. It had five levels with hardwood floors, carved moldings, fireplaces, and chandeliers. The house oozed wealth and privilege. She couldn't imagine growing up in such a place. On the first floor was a den filled with bookcases, old leather tomes, and various knickknacks Maggie wanted to explore. She wished she could spend her time discovering the stories behind each memento, each dog-eared book, each framed photograph attached to the back wall. Brett hadn't seemed interested in the room though, and after a cursory tour, he led them into the other areas of the house.

After taking a quick shower and dressing, Maggie wandered downstairs to the kitchen. Brett's mother was sitting at the kitchen table, reading the *Wall Street Journal* and drinking coffee.

"Good morning, dear. If you're hungry, we have an assortment of bagels and toppings on the counter and some fruit. If that doesn't suit you, I can make you eggs or oatmeal."

"A bagel sounds great." Maggie cut an onion bagel in half and popped it in the toaster.

"Feel free to get yourself some juice or coffee."

"Thanks." Maggie poured orange juice into a tall glass. She leaned against the counter, sipping the juice while waiting for the bagel to toast.

"How are you liking the city?"

"I love it. We're going to walk around today and explore. Maybe go to the Empire State Building. Paulie wants to go to Coney Island."

Maggie heard the toaster pop up and busied herself with smearing cream cheese on the pieces. She carried her food and drink to the kitchen table and sat down across from Mrs. Spanner. She was a small woman with frosted blonde hair and a tanned face. She reminded her of the actress who played Goose's wife in *Top Gun*. Petite, cute, and kind.

"I'm sure you'll have fun. Lots to explore. Is this your first time in Manhattan?"

"Yes. Definitely won't be the only time, though." Maggie took a bite of the bagel, enjoying the chewy texture. These bagels tasted much different from what she'd eaten in the past. The ones she ate before didn't even compare to the real thing.

"Brett mentioned you're going to see *42nd Street* tonight. You'll love it. We've seen the show a few times. Majestic Theater is beautiful."

Brett's father had gotten rear mezzanine seats for free through his company, and it would be Maggie's first Broadway musical. She was dressing up in the most expensive thing she owned, a black velvet gown with gold fringe. It was a winter dress, but she was hoping the temperature would drop before they made their way to the theater. "I'm sure I'll love it."

"Morning." Stella strolled into the kitchen, her damp ebony hair pulled back in a French braid. She wore white shorts and a red, sleeveless cotton top.

Maggie was blinded by all the skin on display. She shook off her reaction and flashed a smile before taking another sip of orange juice. "Hi. Are Em and Nance still asleep?"

"Nope. Em's taking a shower, and Nancy's talking to Paulie. I haven't seen Brett." She grabbed a plain bagel and cut it in half, spreading a thin coat of cream cheese on it. After filling a glass with bottled water, she joined them at the table.

"How'd you sleep?" Sitting back in her chair, Maggie crossed one leg over the other and gazed at Stella.

"Great. That bed is as soft as a cloud. I felt like I was in a warm hug all night."

"Yeah, I fell asleep right after my head hit the pillow." It was possibly the best night's sleep Maggie had ever experienced.

"Have you visited New York before?" Mrs. Spanner lowered her newspaper, eyes inquisitive as she waited for Stella's answer.

"No, Ma'am. I'm loving every minute of it." Stella's southern drawl seemed to caress each syllable she uttered.

"I'm sure. We're glad to have all of you as our guests. Please let me know if you need anything, but now I'm going to get ready for the day." Mrs. Spanner rose, leaving the newspaper folded on the table.

"Thank you." Maggie chuckled as she and Stella said those words at the same time. Their eyes connected, and Maggie smiled. "I'm glad we decided to do this. Even though I'm going to have to work some overtime to replace the money I'm spending, it's totally worth it."

"I get you, girl. I'm doing the same. Sometimes you just gotta take the leap and figure out how to pay for it later. I'm having a hell of a time. My mama isn't gonna believe all the things I've seen."

"Wait. Don't you live in Atlanta? That's a big city, too."

"Well, I tell everyone I'm from Atlanta, but I'm about an hour southwest of there in LaGrange. It's pretty small."

"What made you decide to go to BU?" Maggie took the opportunity to study Stella's face. She was beautiful. Her dark eyes, smooth skin, and enticing lips captured her attention.

"I wanted to live in a big city. See what all the fuss is about. What about you?"

"I grew up north of Boston near the coast. Like you, I wanted to live in a big city. I like having so many choices of what to do and where to go. I picked BU because it has such a large, diverse student population. I wanted to meet all types of people."

Movement near the doorway signified the arrival of the boys.

"Morning. I'm starved." Paulie grabbed two bagels while Brett opened the refrigerator and pulled out apple juice.

Maggie watched them gather their breakfasts before joining them at the table. "Nance and Em aren't here, yet?" Paulie asked.

"Can't put anything past you, Mr. Observant."

"Hardy-har-har. You're so delightful in the morning, Mags."

"Don't call me that, caveman."

"All right kids, break it up." Nancy hugged Paulie from behind, delivering a kiss on his cheek. "Be nice to Maggie, babe."

"Yeah, yeah." He turned his head and delivered a short kiss to her lips. "Only for you."

Emily sat down next to Maggie, yawning so hard her jaw cracked.

"That sounded like it hurt. Didn't you get enough sleep? Did I keep you up?"

Waving her hand in a dismissive gesture, Emily yawned again. "No, no. You didn't keep me up. Once I get some caffeine in me, I'll perk right up."

"I think mom made coffee." Brett sat at the end of the table, his plate loaded with bagels, fruit, and hard-boiled eggs.

"Yuck. No thanks. I'll get a soda later."

"Aren't you eating?" Maggie got up and brought her plate to the sink before retrieving the orange juice to refill her glass. It was fresh squeezed, not the nasty concentrate she usually drank.

"Oh, right. Der." Emily got up and grabbed a bowl, scooping some of the cut fruit into it. She eyed the bagels before picking out an everything bagel and popping it in the toaster. She crossed her arms and leaned against the counter. "What are we doing today?"

"I think we decided on Coney Island. We have reservations for Sardi's at six-thirty, so we have plenty of time. We can leave after we finish eating," Brett said.

Everyone picked up the pace, and they were soon on their way. It took a little less than an hour to make the trip to the amusement park by subway. Maggie enjoyed watching kids run through the crowd, laughing and shouting. Their enthusiasm was contagious. They made their way through the park, playing games and riding the rollercoasters. Maggie loved the bumper cars and the carousel. Brett had brought a camera with him and was capturing their silly poses on the hand-painted horses. Maggie tried a corn dog for the first time. She wasn't sure she'd have one again, but she was glad for the experience. By the time they returned to Brett's house, she was sunburnt and happy.

"Looks like we're a bit behind schedule. Me and Paulie can use the showers upstairs, but the four of you will have to buck up to see who uses the two showers on the third floor first. We have forty-five minutes before we need to leave."

Stella and Maggie volunteered to take showers after Emily and Nancy. Maggie had perfected her routine and could be ready within fifteen minutes when needed. After a quick shower, Maggie dressed and used makeup to emphasize her cheekbones and eyes. It was rare for her to wear makeup, but this was a special occasion. She stepped into the kitchen to join everyone with five minutes to spare. She took stock of how everyone looked. Brett wore a light-blue Oxford button-down shirt with khaki pants and a patterned navy and gold tie. He was freshly shaven, and it looked like he'd tried to tame his mane of hair with mousse. Paulie was dressed similarly, only he wore black pants and a God-awful black tie with Boston terriers on it.

Switching her attention to the females, she recognized the pale-yellow sundress Nancy wore. It was her go-to outfit when she went somewhere fancy. Her dark hair was pulled back by a silver barrette in the shape of a butterfly. Emily wore a long white dress with black polka dots, a large black ribbon holding back her blonde hair. When Maggie looked at Stella, her heart stuttered before speeding up.

Stella's tight, black curls framed her face and flowed loosely over her bare shoulders, a thick gold ribbon holding back the riotous mass from her face. She wore a pale lilac halter top and flowing white slacks with matching sandals. On her collarbones sat a thin gold chain. Hanging off it was a star and the letter S in the middle. Maggie's fingers twitched with the desire to touch the charm where it rested on her sternum. Taking a deep breath, Maggie realized she was staring and redirected her gaze.

Stella's chocolate-colored eyes were fastened on her, a smile flirting on her parted lips. "Don't you clean up well."

Heat raced through her at Stella's compliment, and Maggie couldn't hold back her smile. She smoothed her hands down her dress, loving the feel of the black velvet under her fingertips. "Thanks. I like your top. That's a nice color on you." With effort, Maggie looked at the others. "Ready to go?"

Brett stepped forward. "We are." He leaned in. "You look really pretty."

Pressing her lips together, Maggie turned away, moving to the refrigerator to grab a bottle of water. She held it to her forehead before chugging half of it down, her back to the group. With a deep breath, Maggie placed the bottle on the counter, pasted a smile on her face, and turned toward her friends. "Let's go, then. I'm starving."

At Sardi's they were seated in the back, the booth's signature red leather more comfortable than Maggie expected. Rows of celebrity faces lined the walls, providing Maggie with a good excuse for not paying close attention to Brett. Or Stella. She allowed the conversation to flow around her as she studied the menu. The prices were astronomical. They were double what she paid in Boston. Her chest tightened, and she told herself to calm down. This wasn't the end of the world. She had enough money with her. *It's part of being a grown up. Pull up your big-girl pants and suck it up, buttercup.*

"I'm going to order a bunch of appetizers for us. My treat." Brett waved the server over. "For appetizers we'll start with the shrimp Sardi, some mozzarella, the crab cake, and the prosciutto with melon." Once the server left, Brett looked around. "You guys are going to love their food. I've been coming here since I was a kid."

"I've never had crab cakes before." Nancy tapped the menu. "Or prosciutto."

"You're in for a treat," Stella said.

Surprised, Maggie glanced at her, eyebrows raised. She watched an attractive blush suffuse Stella's face.

"My dad's a chef. He likes to try his new creations on us. Prosciutto is just fancy Italian ham. It tastes awesome with the melon. The crab cake tastes like a mixture of stuffing and pieces of seafood. Like shrimp or lobster." She shrugged.

"I've never had lobster before." Maggie was a bit embarrassed to admit it, but when she looked at everyone, she didn't see any judgment. "I know you probably have." She waved her hand at Brett. "Has anyone else?" Everyone besides Brett shook their head. "Well, maybe that can be our next great adventure."

Their beverages arrived with the promise that the appetizers would be coming right out.

Paulie raised his glass of lemonade. "To new adventures with cool friends." Everyone picked up their glasses and clinked them together before taking a sip.

Their appetizers arrived, and Maggie's eyes widened. Each dish looked too good to eat. She was tempted to take pictures of each plate. Brett grabbed the dish of crab cakes and cut off a piece before passing it to his left. "Take a piece of each appetizer." By the time all the plates were passed around, everyone's plates were filled.

Deciding to play it safe, Maggie speared pieces of mozzarella and tomato, smearing it with olive oil and balsamic vinegar. She moaned as flavor exploded in her mouth. Everything was fresh. As she ate the appetizer, Maggie allowed her taste buds to revel in the different textures. She tried the crab cake next. It did remind her of stuffing, except for the chewy pieces of crab. She wasn't sure whether she liked it. She knew she loved shrimp though, and she gobbled up the piece on her plate, the garlic hitting her nose. After sipping the lemonade, she picked up the prosciutto and melon. The combination of salty and sweet made it her favorite appetizer.

"Okay. Let's take a vote on what each person liked the best." Nancy looked around at everyone. "I'll go first. I loved the mozzarella. How about you, Stella?"

"I'd go with the shrimp because the garlic sauce is yummy, but the prosciutto is a close second."

"I'm all for the crab cakes, but since I ordered it, you probably already figured that out. How about you, Paulie?" Brett asked.

"The shrimp, for sure. The rest are all foo-foo, uppity stuff."

Maggie chuckled with everyone else. "I liked the prosciutto best. What about you, Em?"

"Mozzarella and tomatoes. So good." Emily flashed a smile.

"I knew you'd all love it here. Let's order our meals so we have plenty of time to eat." Brett seemed mighty pleased, and Maggie couldn't blame him. She could get used to eating this type of food.

Once they arrived at the Majestic Theater, they made their way to their seats in the upper balcony. They were seated next to the back row, but it didn't matter to Maggie. Not only did she prefer the bleachers at Fenway Park, but she'd sat in nosebleed seats several times while attending Patriots' football games. She sat with Brett to her left and Stella to her right and felt a delicious thrill race through her. If someone asked her about the musical, she'd be hard-pressed to remember any of it. Instead, all she could remember was the feeling of Stella's arm rubbing against hers on the armrest, her distinctive flowery scent, and her gleaming smile.

They remained in their seats as the balcony emptied after the show. Once the crowd cleared, Maggie moved to the balcony railing and peeked over it. Noticing movement in her peripheral vision, she cocked her head to watch an older couple leaving one of the opera boxes. She imagined they'd been married for forty years, navigating life with the knowledge they were loved and supported. Nothing like her mom's relationships.

Mom talked about getting a divorce, but Maggie doubted that would happen any time soon. She liked the restaurants and vacations too much, enough to stay even when she was roughed up by an inebriated John. That happened on a more frequent basis nowadays. In her less charitable moments, she believed they were perfect for one another—two miserable souls who seemed to like torturing one another.

"Hey, Maggie, let me take a picture of you." Brett stood with a camera pointed toward her.

Leaning against the railing, Maggie posed with one leg bent and a hand on her hip. She smiled for several seconds, glad when Brett lowered the camera.

"Okay, how about one with all the girls?"

The flowery scent Maggie was beginning to love wafted over her as an arm slid around her waist. Stella whispered in her ear. "Is this okay?"

Maggie nodded, swallowing several times. Her throat was so dry.

"Everyone, get closer. Pretend you like one another." Brett pantomimed with his hands before lifting the camera.

Turning to her side, Maggie inhaled a ragged breath as she felt Stella's breasts pressed against her shoulder blades, her hand resting on Maggie's hip, unseen by the rest. Maggie held her breath, her entire focus on the thumb which rubbed small circles in a distracting, hypnotic way. She turned her head toward Brett, her body on fire, and smiled at the thought of no one knowing how close she was to spinning in place and pulling Stella into a kiss. The camera flashed in succession several times, as she caught up to her thoughts. She stiffened, not sure what to do.

"You okay?" Stella's breath tickled Maggie's ear. She nodded and stepped toward Brett as he approached them.

Placing her hand on his chest, Maggie leaned in to deliver a lingering kiss on his cheek. Drawing back, she grinned. "Thanks for getting these tickets for us. I loved the show." She turned toward Nancy. "What was your favorite part?"

Maggie felt Stella's eyes on her. Felt the imprint of burning fingers on her waist. She kept her eyes trained on Nancy as she answered, pulling Emily into the conversation. They made their way toward the exit, traversing the many steps down to the main atrium. She kept close to Brett, allowing him to place his hand on her lower back under the guise of directing her through the diminishing theater crowd. She laughed louder than she needed to, fluttered her eyelashes each time her gaze connected with Brett, and kept as far away from Stella as she could without drawing attention. She wanted to push aside the attraction she felt for her. It confused her. Frightened her.

By the time they returned to Brett's home, Maggie was exhausted. All she wanted to do was go to sleep. When it was her turn to use the bathroom, she removed her makeup and stared at herself in the mirror. "Get it together." She opened the door and jumped back as Stella crowded the doorway. "What are you doing?"

Stella closed the door and turned toward Maggie with measured movements. "Why are you upset with me?" She stepped toward Maggie, arm outstretched, but Maggie stepped back.

"I'm not. I'm tired. It was a busy day. Let me get out of here so you can get ready for bed." Maggie stepped around her but stopped when Stella placed a hand on her arm. Not able to look directly at her, Maggie waited.

Whispered words drew her in. "I know you felt what I did. You don't have to be afraid."

Fingers under Maggie's chin directed her face up, and before Maggie knew what was happening, soft lips brushed against hers. She gasped, not sure what to do. She lifted her hands to push Stella away but found herself clinging to her instead. Her luscious mouth asserted gentle pressure, inviting her to accept the connection between them. Maggie stepped back, chest heaving. She felt as if she had been running for miles, her breath labored and body hot.

"I can't...we can't. I'm sorry, Stella. Truly. But this isn't what I want." She looked into mocha-colored eyes, fascinated by the specks of gold. She shook her head, much like a confused dog would. "I'm sorry."

Maggie flew out of the bathroom and through the bedroom door, focused on getting away from Stella, from her plush lips and soft skin and sparkling eyes. From the confusion and desire and disappointment. She had no time for romance. Not with Brett and certainly not with Stella.

God, why did I kiss her? What's wrong with me? She didn't know anyone like that. *Am I a lesbian? Do I like girls? Or is it only Stella?*

With a muttered good night to the others, she pulled the sheet over her head and lay on her side. Tomorrow was another day. Tomorrow she would put aside these inappropriate urges Stella stirred in her. She would let them fade away like a bad dream.

Chapter Twelve

BY THE TIME MIKE was escorted into the small room, Maggie was seated on the uncomfortable metal chair, her tablet on the table in front of her with the leaked content pulled up. She wanted to give him the chance to read the pages she'd written if he wanted to.

Rising, Maggie rounded the table to hug him. She hadn't seen him in six months and although she wrote to him each month, it was uncommon for him to write back. She'd received two letters in the past two years. He looked more muscular, although scruffier than she remembered. She wrapped her arms around him, squeezing him before pulling back.

"Hey, Mike." She grinned.

"Hi." He smiled widely before ducking his head. A moment later he looked up again. "You look good, sis."

Mike sat in the other metal chair as Maggie nodded to the guard, who stepped outside and took up a station in the raised security office. A glass window allowed him to keep an eye on them without having to remain in the room.

Maggie sat down and straightened her mint-green silk blouse and black pinstriped suit jacket. The matching wool slacks traveled well and were comfortable. She took a deep breath to settle her nerves and studied her brother. He had acne sprinkled across his forehead and chin, no doubt a consequence of his diet. His hair was shorter, making his receding hairline and the gray peppering his hair more apparent. His slate-gray eyes—so like her own, sparkled, his smile creating crinkles in their corners.

"It's good to see you, Mike. I'm sorry it's taken so long."

He waved off her apology. "I know you're busy. Aren't you supposed to be in DC?" He rested his elbows on the chair arms, lacing his hands on his stomach.

"Yes, but something came up." Maggie leaned forward. "You know I've been writing a memoir which is supposed to be published in February. An organization got a hold of the manuscript and leaked some pages from it." She sighed. "They contain things about you. I wanted to warn you in case anyone tried to contact you."

"About me being here?"

"Yeah. I'm sorry, Mike. It's the first draft, so it isn't even edited. The final version will probably look different, but the events I mentioned will probably remain. Things like your arrests, attorney representation, incarcerations, and my efforts to decriminalize marijuana, abolish mandatory minimum sentencing, and expunge certain convictions. I brought a copy for you to read." She pushed the tablet toward him.

"I'm sure everything you wrote is the truth. I trust you, Maggie. I know you wouldn't hurt me on purpose. Don't worry. I won't talk to anyone." He pushed the tablet back to her, his smile small but genuine.

With a sharp exhalation, Maggie slumped in her chair. Still, she wanted to make sure there were no surprises. "Everything I wrote we talked about the last time I was here. Except two sections. I included what happened when Joey and Roxy stormed Pearson, Gunner, Kenny & Associates to get your retainer back." She watched him wince. "Although it wasn't leaked, you should know I also wrote about parts of our childhood, including when we tried to steal candy from Shop Quick."

That was the one and only time she'd tried to steal. She hadn't wanted to, but she felt Mike had drifted away from her after he made new friends in the eighth grade. One of those friends introduced him to the thrill of getting away with shoplifting. She didn't know the first thing about being subtle, and she was caught before she took two steps toward the exit. All three were held until their moms picked them up. They'd been beaten soundly with the gold metal ruler for that one. She was unable to sit for several days.

Plus, it had been summer and they had been grounded for a week, confined to their rooms—his on the first floor and hers on the second. They had to write "I will not steal" hundreds of times. The lesson was costly in many ways, including the gulf that had widened between Mike and her. It grew larger after that fiasco. By the time she entered high school, she had her own circle of friends and spent as much time away from home as possible.

"Why did you write about that?"

"I wrote about how close we were when we were kids, where we began to drift apart, and how all this..." She waved her hand. "Has affected some of my political choices."

Mike rubbed the back of his neck, eyes faraway. They sat in silence, and Maggie did her best not to fidget. Their eyes reconnected, and Maggie fell into his reassuring gaze.

"It's okay. The past is the past. It's not like we can change it. I mean, there's a reason I'm in jail. I haven't always made good decisions."

"True, but I suppose I should have discussed those parts with you before I submitted them to my publisher."

"Well, you're giving me the head's up now. Hey, why do you think they even care?" Mike leaned forward, folding his arms on the table.

"I'm going to be announcing my presidential run in February when the memoir is published." The surprise and bald pride beamed at her washed away her anxiety.

"That's awesome. My sister, the president. Nice ring to it."

"We have a long way to go, but thanks. That means a lot. I wanted to write about you because I know the media will find out, anyway. Their jobs are to dig into my past, and that includes my family." She shrugged. "It's invasive, and I wanted to get ahead of it."

"I get it. With some luck, I'll be outta here by the time you're elected. Don't sweat it. We're good."

They spent the rest of their time catching up. She told him about her latest trips and funny stories about visiting dignitaries, and he told her about the job waiting for him when he got out and the phone call he had with their mom.

By the time she left, she was confident that part of the memoir would not cause any unforeseen problems. She wished the same could be said for the other pages. Although Helen would be fine with the information leaked about their relationship, Maggie was expecting the worst fallout to occur about her first marriage. Although she had drafted several press releases to countermand any negative comments which might come from Timmy's family, she had no idea how they would respond. All she could do was wait.

Tapping her fingers on her desk the next day, Maggie sighed. Damage control was going well, but she still needed to address what Ted had said to her after yesterday's meeting. She buzzed for Alice.

She looked up as her assistant breezed through the open office door, her gaze sharp and expectant. "Close the door, please."

Maggie rounded her desk and sank into the corner of her sofa in front of the non-working fireplace. Although she loved the aesthetic the white marble mantle provided and how it drew the eye to the framed photographs of momentous political events covering it, she'd much prefer to warm the room with a roaring fire.

"I have a problem." Maggie watched a crinkle appear between Alice's eyebrows. "Someone is leaking information about my presidential run, someone on my team." When she saw Alice about to speak, she held up a hand. "I know it's not you." She saw the relief in Alice's eyes and felt her lips turn up. "That's why I'm talking to you. I need help finding out who the mole is."

"Why do you think someone is giving information out?"

"Ted tried to get me to confirm my intent to run. I never told him my plans, though."

"Maybe you said something in passing that tipped him off." Alice clicked at her tablet, her eyes scanning it before looking back up.

"I was careful. Ted has been a great mentor, but he's friends with some people who won't want me as their next president. So, we need to dig into everyone's background a bit. See who might be close to Ted or someone in his office. And don't type anything about this on the mainframe." She nodded toward the tablet. "Or on that. We need to do this quietly and quickly."

"Do you think Ted is against you running?"

"I hope not, but I did a photo search of him and it reflected some interesting meetings between him and a few conservative Republicans." Maggie bit her lip. "I'm hoping this is all nothing for me to worry about. It's possible he pieced things together and was telling the truth when he said he was hurt I haven't confided in him." She shrugged. "But if there's a mole on our team, I need to know, and that person has to be removed."

"If there's a mole, I'll find out." The determined look on her face reassured Maggie. Alice was about ten years her junior with dark brown eyes, short curly black hair, and beautiful cocoa-colored skin. Maggie couldn't imagine not having Alice underfoot. She was like a kid-sister. Even Helen had taken to her like a duck to water.

A chime from her phone alerted Maggie of an incoming message. Maggie looked down and frowned. "Speak of the devil." She looked up. "Thanks, Alice." She waited until Alice left the room before calling Helen.

"I was just thinking about you." Helen's mellifluous voice was a balm to Maggie's soul. "What's up?"

"I just received a text from Ted inviting us to dinner. Nellie's cooking."

"You mean she's catering. I'd be surprised if she can put together a peanut butter and jelly sandwich."

Chuckling, Maggie had to agree. "I doubt she's ever had one. What do you think?"

"I'm sure you're right."

"Not that, silly. About the dinner. I might be able to figure out who gave him the heads-up about the campaign." Not that she would do any snooping. She wasn't a cloak-and-dagger type of gal. She was good at reading people. Good at listening to her gut. Good at reading between the lines. And Helen was an expert at body language. They were a great team, and she trusted Helen's instincts implicitly.

"We should. It's a good opportunity. I'm sure he's intending to use it to find out more."

"No doubt. I'll accept the invitation. It's at six, so do you want to meet me here? I can send a driver."

"No need. I'll take the subway. Have a good day, sweetie."

"You too. Love ya."

"Not as much as I love you," Helen responded.

Maggie knew Helen was teasing her. It was an old, playful disagreement in which they tried to top one another. "Not true, but if it makes you feel better, you can think it."

"I know it." The smile in her voice caused Maggie to grin. "Talk to you later."

The day flew by with no headway on who the mole was. Alice vowed to keep on it, and Maggie knew the woman would uncover the truth. Her past in the DA's office had served Maggie's office well during the years. Alice's web of contacts was extensive. It included several private investigators and detectives who were loyal to her. Alice's integrity and hard work ethic were legendary. Every time someone entered her office, Maggie began questioning whether that person was the turncoat. Not that she had anything to hide, but timing was everything. It was bad enough parts of the memoir were already leaked.

A knock on her door signaled Helen's arrival. Packing up her laptop in her messenger bag, Maggie crossed to the door and delivered a short kiss to Helen's lips. "You're a sight for sore eyes." Before she could step away, Helen cupped her cheek and delivered a soft kiss, lingering. Maggie hummed her approval.

Maggie pulled her into the office and closed the door, not wanting to say anything where others could hear them. "Ready for some major sleuthing? I'll need your observational skills on max tonight."

"I've got you, babe. Even if we can't find any proof on who might have tipped him off, we'll be able to determine whether he's for or against your run."

"Wait. Do you think he won't support me?" Maggie felt as if the wind were knocked out of her. The possibility hadn't entered her mind. Ted had mentored her since she was a junior senator. A hand on her chest refocused her on Helen's golden-hued eyes.

"I'm not saying he won't, but we need to be prepared. Up until now, you've never really acted against him or his interests. Oh, I know you two have debated different issues over the years, but at the end of the day your philosophies have run on parallel tracks. The presidency is a different level. He may have plans that don't include you becoming the president. So let's see what we can find out."

"Okay." She opened the door and led the way through the outer office, nodding to those finishing up their day before pausing in front of Alice's desk. "We're off. I'll catch up with you later."

"Have fun." Alice's smile was more of a tense pressing of her lips, but Maggie appreciated the effort to smile all the same.

The Stapleton's home was in Kalorama, an affluent neighborhood in northwest DC. The townhouse boasted a brick façade, six floors, and a grand foyer which was as ostentatious as it was impressive. They were ushered into the front parlor, where a roaring fire warmed the room. Around the fireplace were two modern leather couches across from one another and two matching armchairs.

If it were summer, they would go up to the rooftop deck. It was Ted's favorite area of the townhouse with a full patio set and stocked bar. Maggie and Helen handed off their coats to Ted before sitting down on the sofa that was perpendicular to the doorway. Maggie preferred not to have her back to the entrance.

"Here we are." Nellie swept into the room with two glasses of red wine, handing them off with a polite smile. "I'm so glad you could join us. Dinner should be ready in about ten minutes." She left the room as quickly as she entered, stopping briefly to deliver a peck on Ted's cheek.

Ted sat in the chair closest to them, a filled wine glass in his hand. "Helen, I haven't seen you in too long. How are you?" He crossed his ankles as he leaned back in his chair.

"I'm keeping busy. We're gearing up for the holiday fundraiser." Helen was the civil rights project director for GLAAD, formally known as the Gay & Lesbian Alliance Against Defamation. She had spearheaded the initiative to change the name to GLAAD to incorporate bisexual and transgender people in their efforts to support the LGBTQ community more fully. Although she didn't litigate much anymore, she had previously litigated in the state and federal courts of New England on discrimination issues, parental rights, free speech and religious liberty, and relationship recognition, leaving her mark and paving the way for same-sex marriages. When she wasn't donating her time and expertise with GLAAD, she was a guest lecturer at several law schools throughout the year.

"Hard to believe Thanksgiving is right around the corner." Ted took a sip of his wine. "Before you know it, we'll be wondering how we got to twenty twenty-three without noticing."

Seeing movement in the doorway, Maggie was surprised to see Ted's son enter. Scott had graduated from West Point the past year and had been awarded a post in DC. He'd filled out since she'd seen him. She remembered him as an awkward beanpole with a laugh that didn't fit. As he joined them, he seemed more self-assured and confident.

"Scottie. I didn't know you'd be joining us. What a wonderful surprise." Maggie smiled at him, holding back a chuckle as she watched a flush climb up his neck. He ducked his head.

"Hi. Yeah. Dad mentioned you were coming by. It's nice to see you, too."

Before Maggie could say anything else, Nellie swept into the room to tell them dinner was ready. They filed into the formal dining room, where another fireplace was in use.

Whereas the parlor mantle was black and white marble, the dining room fireplace had light chocolate tones with eggshell-colored veins running through the marble. Several tall statues occupied the corners, including Maggie's favorite of an eagle in flight. Its talons were extended and the body curved as if it were about to nab its prey. The statue was in brass, reflecting the flames from the fireplace. No doubt it was placed in its spot for that reason. In the opposite corner stood a bronze statue of Alfred the Great, a sword in one hand and a shield in the other. A tapestry in different shades of brown portraying a medieval knight riding past a castle covered the back wall, the colors of the black lion on the knight's red shield popping out.

Maggie sat to the right of Ted, who sat at the head of the polished cherry wood table. The table had been set with crystal and china, the food plates resting on trivets in the middle. Nellie took a breadbasket and passed it around. For a few minutes everyone concentrated on filling their plates with pieces of tenderloin, chicken, vegetables, salad, and bread. Having eaten at their home before, Maggie was not surprised by the sheer amount of food available.

"I read the leaked pages of your memoir today." Nellie's words felt like water thrown in Maggie's face. It shouldn't have surprised her. She'd watched Nellie take the lead with her polite inquisitions many times during the years.

"Most of it, people already know." Maggie took a sip of wine. "Although it's still in its rough form. People will forever believe I love commas, regardless of whether they belong in every sentence."

Helen laughed. "Finally, I can let go of that secret. I must say it was hard to keep silent for so many years." Her grin was infectious. "I've always been pretty good with punctuation, but even after I neaten up her writing, she goes back and adds more." Shaking her head, she lifted her hands to either side of head in a "what are you gonna do" gesture. "Am I the only one here who knows how to use commas?"

Helen's attempt to hijack the conversation was joined by Scott. "I tend to do the opposite. I don't ever use them. I mean, there are more important things to worry about. Isn't that why you have an editor?"

"Editors should get paid a lot more." Maggie jerked her head at Helen. "Not everyone has a master punctuationer in their midst."

"Punctuationer? Really? You know that isn't a word." Helen dropped her head. "You're hopeless, I swear."

"It should be a word. It could be a new career, someone who corrects punctuation for a living." Maggie wasn't serious. She liked getting into these fatuous discussions with Helen.

"That's called anyone who writes or edits. No need for a new word, dear."

"English is a living language. New words are created all the time." Scott wiped his mouth with his napkin. "I mean, look at all the words created with the technology boom. And words that used to be two words or hyphenated are now one word, like fulltime. I'm with Maggie on this one. I think we should promote this word. Use it everywhere and see if it catches on."

"That's enough, young man." Although Nellie said the words in a mild tone with a small smile on her face, Maggie knew she was thoroughly annoyed.

Maggie shot a wink at Scott before placing her napkin next to her plate. "Quite right. We don't want to get the reputation of being trailblazers. That food was wonderful. Mind if I use the powder room?"

"Of course. You know where it is." Ted's answer was all Maggie needed to push her out of her seat. She was thankful Helen and Scott had helped her waylay Nellie's attempt to discuss the memoir. Ted and Nellie often tag-teamed to gather information, and she knew Ted wanted to confirm whether she planned to run for president. She didn't understand why it was essential for him to know. It wouldn't change how they worked together. Wouldn't change what policies she pushed or platforms she championed. It occurred to her that maybe he was asked to support someone else's run, and he couldn't commit until he knew Maggie's plans.

She was tempted to tell him her plans, but until she knew whether someone on her team had already tipped him off, she needed to wait. In fact, once she had a list of possible moles, she intended to leak some false information to observe Ted's behavior. Maybe that a special interest group had agreed to endorse her once she announced her plans to run. She tapped her lips with a finger. She'd have to do a little more brainstorming.

Staring into the mirror, she noticed how dark her gray eyes looked, like burnt wood. The charcoal color glimmered with threads of brown. Her hair remained spiky, a testament to her hair paste. Nodding at herself, she left the bathroom to rejoin everyone. Their plates had been cleared, small bowls of fruit compote with a dollop of vanilla ice cream in their place.

"These look fabulous." Maggie picked up a spoon and filled it with pieces of plum and nectarine, sighing as she tasted it. "This is yummy." She swept her eyes around the table, pausing on Scott. He looked a bit upset. She hiked an eyebrow and glanced at Helen. Her tight-lipped look concerned her. Maggie moved her hand under the table and grasped Helen's hand, squeezing it.

"Will you be staying here for the holidays?" Maggie figured it was a good idea to take control of the conversation before Nellie circled back to the memoir. She allowed her eyes to flit between Ted and Nellie, inviting either of them to answer.

"We'll be returning to Nashville for Christmas. See the family." Ted nodded at Scott. "We're hoping Scott can get time off to join us."

"I put in for the time off, but I'm the low man on the totem pole," Scott offered.

Maggie got the feeling Scott wouldn't be upset if he had to stay in DC. He lived on the fourth floor of the townhouse and didn't have to worry about food or lodging like most people his age. She did worry whether that was worth his lack of privacy. No doubt it curtailed any invitations he might extend to potential love interests.

Come to think of it, she couldn't remember ever hearing that he was dating. In high school and college, he had focused on grades and on sports. Perhaps now that he was settled in a job and on a career track as a mechanical engineer, he could delve into companionship. For a while, she believed he might be gay. Not that it was obvious. He seemed like any other gawky young adult. She'd attributed his shyness to dealing with the pressure of fulfilling his parents' expectations to succeed. She wondered suddenly whether it was more than that.

"Anyone care for a nightcap?" Ted got up from the table, signaling it was time to return to the parlor.

"That sounds wonderful," Maggie said as they entered the room. "Helen, what do you think?" Maggie sat down on the couch once again, one arm extended across the back of it.

"Sure. What are you offering?"

"You can pick your poison. It's fully stocked. Scotch, sherry, Kahlua, brandy, rum."

"Rum neat works for me." Maggie hadn't had anything other than wine in months. Helen chose Kahlua on the rocks, Nellie decided on brandy, and Scott stuck with the same red wine they'd had during the meal. Nellie turned on jazz, the piano tinkling in the background and the saxophone seeming to dance with the crackling fire's snaps. Maggie felt herself melting into the couch, smiling as she listened to Ted talk about a little boy who asked him to autograph his cowboy hat.

"I finally convinced him to let me write him a message on my letterhead, but boy was he disappointed."

"Oh, what a joy." Nellie produced a smile which warned Maggie her next words would be cutting. She didn't disappoint. "You miss so much when you don't have children. Scott is the apple of our eye. Isn't he, Ted?"

"Absolutely. I couldn't be prouder. And when the time comes and you have children of your own, Scott, you'll feel the same sense of pride. I say this with love. Don't wait too long to settle down, son. Have your family while you're young. You'll enjoy your time with them more."

Scott's face flushed, and he looked like a rabbit caught in a trap, the vein in his forehead throbbing in time with his heartbeat. Maggie wanted to help him, but she sensed this was an old conversation and didn't want to get in the middle of it. On the other hand, he'd gotten Nellie off the subject of her memoir.

"Oh, Ted. Before I forget, again," Maggie exaggerated the final word with a flourish, "can you give me the information on that HCA fundraiser you're co-sponsoring?"

"Sure. I have it in my office. Come with me." He placed his drink on a side table and led the way to his study on the second floor. The second floor landing had several overstuffed chairs and tables sprinkled along the hallways. They walked past a small, built-in wet bar displaying several top tier liquors.

Entering the home office, Maggie felt as if she were walking into another time period, one redolent with backroom deals and patriarchal politics. Rough stones surrounded the fireplace and the entire south wall, while the other three walls and the ceiling were covered with a dark walnut wood. The enormous desk displayed intricate carvings of acanthus leaves around the top of the desk and fluted vertical columns on each corner. Two floor-to-ceiling bookcases were filled with leather bound books she was certain he'd never read. She leaned against one of the matching leather visitor chairs while he riffled through paperwork. She took the opportunity to peer at the documents spread across the desk while asking him inane questions about the fundraiser.

"Aha." He raised his hand, a document in his grasp and a triumphant look on his face. "I knew it was here. Go ahead and take it. I can print another one." She reached out to accept it.

"Thanks. I appreciate it." Her eyes swept the room once more, and she moved toward a row of framed photographs. "Who's this?" She pointed toward a group of smiling faces, Ted's young visage in the middle.

"Ah, that's from a long time ago. College." He pointed toward a man and woman to his left in the photo. "Lance and Betsy Allen. Great couple. They moved to California years ago." He shook his head. "I haven't spoken to them in years. She's a pediatrician, and he's a regional manager for Chalkies." He pointed to the woman on the other side of him. "This is Lillian. I dated her throughout college. She introduced me to her friend, Nellie, and...well, you can see how that turned out."

"Ouch. Poor Lillian." Maggie stared at the picture. She had a familiar face. "Is she still friends with Nellie?"

"Yes, yes." He nodded his head. "They talk every so often, and we try to get together at least once each year." He turned off the light and left the room.

"Guess we're done with this conversation." Maggie's muttered words were soft enough that Ted didn't hear her. She was grateful. Sometimes her sarcasm got her in trouble. She hurried after him, the document in her hand. She didn't really need it, but it was all she could think of on short notice. Reentering the parlor, she shot a smile at Helen before sinking down next to her. She reclaimed her glass of rum and sipped it, relishing the smooth caramel taste as it slid down her throat.

"Hon, we should get going soon. I have an early start tomorrow," Helen said quietly.

Maggie knew that wasn't true, but she loved how Helen was providing a socially acceptable way to end the evening.

"Let me text the car service." Nellie looked up from her phone a minute later. "It will be outside in five. I'm glad you could both come by." She stood up. "Let me get your coats."

Finishing her rum, Maggie rose, holding out a hand to help Helen up. Not that she needed it. After years of performing the same action, Helen knew it was an excuse to hold her hand. Turning her head, Maggie saw Scott was watching them, a look of longing on his face. "I'm glad we got to see you, Scottie. If you're ever on the Hill, stop by to say hi."

"Sure. Thanks. It was nice to see you both."

They strolled toward the front entrance and donned their outerwear. "Thanks again for dinner. It was wonderful. You three have a good weekend."

"It was our pleasure." Ted's voice sounded sincere, and Maggie wondered whether her suspicions were unwarranted. She wouldn't mind being wrong about him.

Once their goodbyes were said and they were safely in the backseat of the car, Maggie sighed. Helen took her hand and raised it to her lips, delivering a soft kiss.

"I know. I hope you're wrong, too."

***

Maggie groaned, squinting at the computer screen. It was eleven twelve at night, and the final item on her to-do list was to review the edits she'd received on her memoir. Since the leak, her publisher decided to fast track the release. She figured the edited version would contain the typical notes such as *expand on this* and *we already know this from chapter three,* but what she received made her doubt her ability to form a sentence correctly. She thought she was a proficient writer. She loved the power of a well-crafted speech, loved choosing the vocabulary and setting the rhythm.

Her memoir looked like the battlefield at the Alamo. Not only did it contain blood red corrections, but also blue and green. Besides the cross-outs, corrections, and additions, there were also copious comments on the right side of each page. She read the first comment.

Although not unheard of, most memoirs are not written in third person past tense. It is standard protocol to write in first person present tense. I can live with first person past tense, but third person past tense is the standard for writing fiction. You'll need to change this.

Flashes of watching her seventh grade English teacher reviewing verb tenses by listing them on the chalkboard bombarded her. "Was I supposed to know this?" Maggie pinched her lips together. She scraped a hand down her face before rolling her shoulders. Hurt feelings had no place here. She read the next comment.

With memoirs, it's helpful to assign a title to each chapter to inform the reader what will be covered. Read through each chapter and create a word or short phrase to sum up the chapter.

Well, that sounds horrendous, she thought to herself. *How can one word or a short phrase encapsulate an entire chapter's worth of life experiences?*

She skipped down a few pages, her eyes bruised by the multitude of colors bombarding her. She read a comment at the end of chapter three.

Why did you include this chapter? You already gave the readers some insight to childhood neglect in chapters one and two. Why bring it up again?

"Because the neglect continued throughout my childhood, you numb-nut," she muttered.

And so it went. By the time Maggie finished reading the comments, she was ready to chuck her laptop in the trash. Writing about her life was hard. She hated being this vulnerable, and now she felt incapable of writing a sentence, never mind a book. For years she'd run from her past, distancing herself from those painful experiences. Now she was being told some of those memories weren't worth including in her memoir.

With a sigh, she returned to page one and began the tedious task of changing the person and tense of each sentence, accepting corrections of grammar, spelling, and punctuation when still applicable. She left the comments and highlighted sections alone, knowing it would take longer to sift through them and make the suggested changes. At least she had a light schedule for the weekend. She would use the time to dig into the memoir. She saved the changes she made in the first chapter and powered down the computer.

Glancing at the bed, she watched Helen sleep. Their bedroom was large enough for her to set up a desk near the window which overlooked the street. Helen liked to be in the same room as Maggie, even when she was working.

During their marriage, Maggie had learned to capitulate to Helen's need, even when that meant letting Helen snooze next to her on the couch. Since Maggie preferred her to be comfortable by sleeping in their bed, they'd agreed to the work area in the bedroom, even though Helen didn't like the idea of having electronics in the room.

Changing in the dark, Maggie tried to be quiet. She slid under the covers and rested on her side, counting in her head. *Three...two...one.* An arm snaked over her ribs, as Helen scooted up and spooned her.

"Took you long enough."

"Sorry, love. Go back to sleep." Maggie felt Helen's exhalation on the back of her neck and shivered. Lethargy stole across her, her limbs feeling heavy, as the long day caught up to her. She cleared her mind of the endless tasks demanding her time, glad to have this respite. Glad to have this woman wrapped around her. Glad she had people in her life who were willing to fight with her for a better tomorrow.

Chapter Thirteen

WHEN TIMOTHY PEARSON, JUNIOR, one of the founders of the Cambridge law firm, Pearson, Gunner, Kenny & Associates, took an interest in Maggie's work, she was thrilled. He was known as a top-notch litigator, one who not only knew the law but helped create it through litigating cases of first impression, which became precedent once he won. And he always won. He was as passionate as he was erudite, and people knew to fall in behind him or get out of his way.

One morning, Maggie walked by his open office door, her thoughts filled with how to structure her workday. She heard Attorney Pearson speaking and assumed either someone else was with him or he was on the phone. She didn't dare satisfy her curiosity by peering into the office. Turned out neither was true. His voice sounded much louder a moment later, stopping her in her tracks.

"Maggie. Do you have a minute?" His gruff, no-nonsense voice bounced off the walls and pushed her into the Berber covered floor. As her eyes widened, she twisted her body to face him and pointed at herself. His eyes crinkled as he nodded and waved her inside his office. She retraced her steps and followed him, looking around with interest.

The jet black desk boasted symmetrical lines, its only ornamentation the smooth chrome encapsulating the desktop and drawers. A file's innards, marked up with red pen, was spread across the desk as if they were the remains of some helpless creature picked apart by a vulture. The view behind his desk was spectacular, the sun's rays bouncing off the Charles River, emphasizing the trails left by sailboats and motorboats as they moved across the waterfront, each with its own purpose. In the forefront, cars whizzed down Memorial Drive, the endless bombinating hum reminding her of a swarm of bees.

"One of the best parts of coming to work is getting to watch what's going on out there," he said as he led her to a black velvet sofa and waited for her to sit down before joining her. "It's a far cry from our previous office across from the Boston federal court building. Although it takes longer to get to court, the tradeoff is well worth it."

"I'm sure. I'd be afraid of never getting anything done if I had that view to look at all day."

"Well, I'll keep that in mind when it comes to awarding you an office one day."

Maggie's eyes widened as she looked into twinkling eyes and a telling smirk. "Forget I said that. Please." She smiled when he chuckled.

"How long have you worked here?" Attorney Pearson sat back and crossed his legs, hands resting on his knee.

"A little more than a year. What I've learned has helped me immensely with law school. I'm grateful."

"You can't beat hands-on experience. I heard you attended court last week for the jury selection."

"Yes. That was fascinating. I had no idea how much goes into it." Maggie had spoken to the lead attorney about her strategy for getting people sympathetic to their client picked for the jury. People's interests, background, connections, work, even the types of magazines they read—all were indicators of how a juror might vote.

"Did you take a legal writing course last year?" Attorney Pearson rose and moved toward his desk.

"Yes, I did."

He returned to the sofa with a thick file. "Great. I'm going to pair you with Warren Spencer. He'll assign you some research and motions to draft. I have high hopes for you, Maggie."

Her heart skipped a beat before speeding up. This was an unheard-of opportunity. The firm had enough junior attorneys to take care of all the research and legal writing ever needed by the firm, yet he was giving her a shot. A mere second year law student. "Thank you. I won't let you down."

His face softened for a moment, a small smile making him look much younger than his sixty-odd years. "I know you won't. I have a good feeling about you." He rose. "I already notified Warren, so you can report to him." He placed a hand on her shoulder and squeezed it. "Welcome to the team." He turned toward his desk, a clear sign of dismissal.

"Thank you, Mr. Pearson." She practically ran out of the room, so keen was she to start on whatever assignment she was given. After looking up where Warren, a fourth year associate on the partner tract, had an office, Maggie wasted no time before visiting him. He was nice enough, although the skeptical look on his face warned her that she'd have to prove herself. And she would.

It was no secret that when Attorney Pearson paid attention to an employee, others noticed. So when he began to provide constructive criticism, praise, and useful tips to Maggie, the junior partners took it as a sign to give her more work. That meant more opportunities to learn in ways law school couldn't provide. She received various assignments which took her countless hours of researching different points of law and drafting court documents. Her learning curve was steep. For months she received her drafts back, red slashes bleeding across the type and notes scribbled in the margins. As time passed, though, the red markings slowly tapered off, and Warren gave her harder assignments. Best of all, the junior attorneys became friendlier, and she found herself anticipating the next assignment.

***

Strolling into the elevator, lunch in hand, Maggie was surprised to see Attorney Pearson. She hadn't spoken to him in earnest since their conversation nearly a year ago.

"Maggie, how's law school treating you?" His sincere smile elicited a matching smile on her face. His light brown eyes were focused on her as he leaned against the back of the elevator, hands in his pockets. It was obvious he didn't have court that day since he wore tan khakis, a light blue Oxford shirt, and a simple blue and tan striped tie. On court days he wore tailored Armani suits.

"Great. I had an article on workplace harassment accepted by the law review."

"Really? That's quite a feather in your cap. I look forward to reading it. Did you know Suffolk Law is my alma mater?"

"I had no idea. I love Suffolk. The professors are some of the best litigators, politicians, and judges in the state. And working here has helped prepare me for the practicalities of the law."

"There's no substitute for actual experience. Legal theories have their place, particularly when crafting legal arguments, but they don't teach you how to round up all the details and corral them into a succinct argument."

Maggie nodded. She'd written a few complaints in the past month and plowing through all the perspectives to create a compelling story proved to be the most challenging aspect of the process.

"I'm having a small dinner party this Saturday night. Why don't you come by? My sons will be there, including my oldest son, who will be visiting from DC, so you won't be too bored by all the old people. Say seven?"

"That sounds," *astounding, awesome, scary, incredible*, "fun. Thank you."

"Great." The elevator opened to his floor. "I'll email the details." With a smile and a wave, he left a shocked Maggie.

She didn't know anything about Attorney Pearson's personal life. She wondered how many sons he had. *Are they attorneys, too? What does his oldest son do in DC? Why does he want me to meet him?*

In a daze, she made her way to her cubicle. She had no idea why Attorney Pearson had taken such a shine to her, but she intended to ride the wave. He was her surfboard, and she would do what she needed to glide on the swell all the way to the land of success.

That invitation led to her monthly attendance at his dinner parties. She found out he had three sons, all around her age. None were attorneys. None had any interest in law-related careers. Timmy, the oldest, was a speechwriter for a US Senator. A tall, overweight, short-sighted man, he used to be a star rower in high school, but during his freshman year he suffered chronic pain in his shoulder and lost not only his college scholarship but his drive to exceed in anything. He ended up transferring from Brown University to George Washington University, and then taking a job as a junior program analyst for one of the junior state representatives on the Hill before working his way up to his present position. He was intelligent and awkward.

Normally, Maggie wouldn't have given him the time of day, but he was part of the package for being in Attorney Pearson's orbit. That made it worth her while to at least befriend him. As time passed, Maggie spent more time with Timmy outside of the dinner parties. He visited from DC bimonthly, and she tolerated his adolescent advances. She was receiving better work assignments, most of them from Attorney Pearson's division. Attorney Pearson even worked on some of the assignments with her, pointing out how she could strengthen her argument or evade producing damaging documents to opposing counsel. At least once a week, Maggie could be found working on her assignments while seated in his office.

The first time Timmy kissed her, she nearly called the whole thing off. It was a terrible kiss. A short, wet, noisy kiss, one that landed partly on her cheek. They had gone on a walk at the beach, ice creams in hand. It was a warm summer night, and the promenade was crowded. He told her about DC, a place she had never visited. When she accepted his invitation to visit, she knew he would push for more than friendship. Although she wasn't particularly attracted to him, she did like what he brought to her life. His father was a powerful mentor, and she knew that would propel her career trajectory ahead of the normal path by years. His siblings were funny and witty and caring. They welcomed her into the fold with open arms. And Timmy, for all his faults, seemed to want to make her happy. She could do worse.

The awkward kiss occurred after she drove him home. She hadn't expected him to lean over, deliver his sloppy kiss, and hop out of the car. Outsiders would be fooled into believing their relationship was a whirlwind romance. It was possible Timmy believed it. Maggie wished she did.

The more time she spent with him, the less she enjoyed being with him. It wasn't that he had little experience with romance or that he had terrible eating habits and even worse, bad hygiene. It wasn't that he could be mistaken for an overgrown frat boy. It was his evasiveness, the cagey way he answered her questions about the future, a future he proclaimed wanting to share with her.

If it weren't for the physical part of their relationship, she would be happy experiencing life with Timmy. Even with his horrible habits and dubious behavior, he was fun. He bored quickly, which meant when they had the time, they often explored new areas of Massachusetts, DC, and the surrounding states. Since he wasn't experienced with physical relationships, she was able to slow down that train wreck. She tried to teach him how to kiss without drowning her or overpowering her. He was like an overeager puppy, his saliva-filled kisses repugnant. During the course of several months, his kisses became more tolerable, and she didn't shudder when he came toward her for one.

They spent much of their time in Boston with his brothers and their girlfriends. Sometimes Lizzie and Kevin would join them. Her friends were keen to attend the dinner parties, having heard Maggie's stories for months. It was easy to wrangle invitations for them, and Maggie enjoyed those parties more with her old friends in attendance.

As Maggie prepared to finish law school and study for the bar exam, Timmy moved in with his parents. His father secured a job for him at the law firm as an IT technician. Although he didn't have any formal training, he loved building computers and could write code. The field was growing by leaps and bounds, and Timmy claimed he would be able to make more money than Maggie.

Like their first kiss, the marriage proposal was disappointing. They were watching a television commercial about a cruise. "We should do that." Timmy's voice sounded as excited as it always did when he was concocting a new plan. "It has ports of call in Greece and Italy."

"Maybe someday." Maggie scribbled notes on a products liability case in her notebook, shaking the pen when the ink ran out. With a sigh, she threw it on the table and rose to retrieve another one.

"We could go for our honeymoon."

Turning slowly, Maggie stared at him. He was looking her with a small grin on his face.

"Did you just propose to me while watching a TV commercial?"

He shrugged. "I guess."

"I guess. I guess? That's all you have to say? No planning, no special day, no ring, and you expect me to say yes?" She stomped to him, indignation burning through her.

"Come on, Mags. I moved back to Massachusetts, and we can get hitched after you graduate. I have a friend who's in the travel business. He can get us a good deal." He spread his large hands out in front of him. "We have fun together. Why not make it official?"

Shaking her head, Maggie plopped on the couch with a sigh. He was not Mr. Romantic. This was not news to her, and why was she still with him if they weren't going to get married? She wanted the connection to his family, to the career, to the power, to the feeling of belonging. This was her opportunity to cut the final cords to her upbringing, her family, her loneliness. On his own, Timmy didn't offer much, but when she looked at the entire package, it was attractive. Irresistible. The answer was obvious.

"Okay."

"Okay?" His surprise was surpassed by his joy, his eyes filling with tears as he leapt up and pulled her into a hug. He swung her around in a dizzying whirl of excitement, and Maggie allowed herself to get caught up in his happiness.

She did her best to keep that feeling in the forefront as she purchased her own engagement ring, planned the wedding, and finished out her law school education. She kept busy enough not to question what she was doing or whether she would be happy. She focused on the end goal, ignoring her doubts and dismissing her fears. She could taste success, its sweetness seeping into her heart and promising a life she was deprived of during her childhood.

Timmy's father was more than a mentor. He was the father she'd never had. Timmy's brothers filled the void Mike left when he pulled away from her to spend time with classmates she didn't trust. She might not have the ideal partner, but he checked enough boxes for her to ignore any misgivings.

Studying for the bar exam was a lesson in turning off the world. The law firm suspended assignments to her, and she wasn't scheduled to return until the end of August. Although the bar exam was in July, a week after it, she would marry Timmy. His parents weren't happy about their plans. She didn't think his mother even liked her. Maggie was determined to go through with the ceremony, though. She had a plan and getting married was part of it.

Marrying Timmy would solidify her place in a large, raucous family. She would no longer need to spend the holidays at friends' houses. She would have someone to talk to on the darkest nights. Someone to support her as she reached for the stars. Someone to share all the normal milestones of life. Timmy might not be perfect, but he was malleable and intelligent. Most importantly, he loved her.

With one week left before the bar exam, Timmy arrived at her apartment drunk. She was exhausted from hours of practice exams, taken after watching hours of bar exam prep videos. She needed to get through two more practice exams before calling it a day. His unexpected appearance meant time wasted and less time to sleep. She shook her head at his puerile decision to visit before stomping away from the front door, leaving it open for him to follow.

"Timmy, I told you not to come over. I'm studying." She ran a hand through her unkept hair while continuing to the kitchen. She lived in an attic studio near Harvard Square. It was small but in the middle of everything. She enjoyed wandering around her neighborhood with its restaurants, nightlife, and stores nearby. She poured water for them and sat at the kitchen table.

"I needed to see you. I love you so much." He smiled, blinking several times before leaning heavily on the table, nearly collapsing into himself on folded, beefy arms. "I was having a beer with Tork, and we were talking about the wedding and it made me so happy. I thought to myself, 'Hey, I need to see Mags.' Tork thought it was a great idea. I mean, I haven't seen you all week."

"That's because I'm studying for the bar exam. You know, the reason I asked for you not to come over. I need to study. I have a schedule, and you're messing it up."

"Okay, okay. I get it. But, can't I sleep over?"

"And listen to you snore during the few hours I'll have to sleep? No, thank you." She rose, walking toward the phone. "I'll call you a cab."

"I can't change your mind?"

The whine in his voice grated on her nerves. Gritting her teeth, Maggie squeezed her fists, counting to ten. Exhaling slowly, she picked up the phone and called information. "Yes, please connect me to Cambridge Taxi. Thanks."

She eyed Timmy as he slouched against the wall, wondering whether he was going to slide to the ground. She ordered the taxi and hung up. "Okay. They said five minutes, so off you go. Do you have money?"

"Yeah. Can I at least have a kiss?"

Maggie grimaced. He smelled like a brewery. Leaning in she pecked his cheek, ignoring his disgruntled groan. "I'll call you tomorrow. Go home and sleep it off."

Timmy paused at the door, grinning. "I love you, Mags. I can't believe we're getting married in two weeks."

"Me neither." She kept the smile on her face until the front door closed and the sound of his footsteps faded as he made his way down the stairs. She squeezed her eyes shut, feeling as if she were going to cry. "Me neither."

Chapter Fourteen

ALTHOUGH MAGGIE WAS CERTAIN he already knew, she still had to work to suppress the fear working its way through her after saying the words aloud to President Sugarman. A flutter of nerves made Maggie grimace. She was afraid Frank Sugarman, their illustrious commander-in-chief, wouldn't endorse her, even though she'd been his staunch supporter from the early days when he was a young New York senator with big ideas but little backing. She'd helped him through the ranks, banking his promises and goodwill as he became more powerful. She bided her time, learning the game, making connections, and building a platform which could support her when she decided to take a shot at filling the most powerful position in the nation.

She watched him lean back in his chair, a thoughtful look on his face as he bridged his fingers together. His dark brown eyes were unfocused as he stared at his hands. Maggie did her best not to fidget. She admired how he thought before speaking, even when that meant she had to wait for him to process information. After so many years working with him, she was used to his mannerisms.

"You know Jimmy's planning on running, right? This puts me in a rather uncomfortable position." Frank studied her, his lips twisting. "No chance you could push this off until the next election, is there? Even if Jimmy wins, I doubt he'll last eight years." His hopeful look was all an act. He knew before she walked in the Oval Office what her plans were.

"No. I recognize your position and won't be surprised if you endorse Jimmy. After all, he is your VP. What I'm asking for is your endorsement should he bow out of the election. I've heard he might not run, that he's waiting to see who else is jumping into the deep end. If he does, though, I'm also asking that you not block any endorsements I may attract, regardless of where they come from."

Maggie tried to keep her body relaxed and voice steady, even as her heart pounded. "We go back a long way. I don't plan to call in any markers this early in the race, but when the time comes, I want you on my side."

"I always did like your confidence. Do you think America is ready for you?"

Lifting her chin up, Maggie stared at him. "We're going to find out." His huff of laughter was music to her ears.

Frank rose from his chair, and she knew it was time for her to go. She shook his hand, a small smile on her face. "I'm sure you've seen the same list I have of potential Democrats. If Jimmy drops out or doesn't run, you'll have my endorsement and the full might of this administration. If that eventuality doesn't occur, I wish you luck."

"Thank you, Mr. President. Have a good evening." Maggie strode toward the door, elated by the outcome of their meeting. He was known to be reticent. His words were more positive than she'd anticipated. She nodded to his assistant before making her way through the halls.

Seeing a familiar face as she passed an office, she paused and retraced her steps. Scott Stapleton was standing behind a desk, file in hand. "Scottie?"

His looked up, eyes widening. "Senator Ambrose. Hi." He closed the file. "What brings you to the White House?"

She waved her hand. "Meeting. I didn't realize you were working here."

"Oh, not really. I was lent to the NSA to help with a project."

Maggie's eyebrows flew up. This was the first she was hearing of it, and she had spoken to Ted the previous night. The National Security Advisor acted as the chief in-house advisor to the President for national security issues. Since she was on the HSGA committee, she was normally in the loop for any investigations occurring in the White House. This was rather odd.

"I don't suppose you can tell me what you're working on?"

"Uh, I don't think I can…" Scott shrugged.

"Right. I don't want to get you in trouble. It was nice seeing you." She turned away.

"Wait." He approached her, eyes searching the area behind her. He leaned in so he could whisper. "I was going to contact you. Can we meet tonight? I can't be seen talking to you here, and I don't want dad to know. Eight at Capitol Hill Brewery? I know it's probably not your scene, but that way we won't have to worry about being noticed by the wrong people."

"Sure. See you then." Maggie walked away, her thoughts in a whirl. Once she witnessed his nervousness, she didn't hesitate. She might not know him well, but her gut was telling her that he harbored no ill will toward her. It was a good thing she had a full day ahead. Otherwise, she would end up fretting about the strange interaction and the upcoming meeting.

She stepped into her office and was accosted by Alice, who grabbed Maggie's bag so she could shed her outerwear. Maggie walked into her office and sat down, listening as Alice gave her a rundown of her schedule.

"I'm glad you're here. You have a meeting with the team in ten minutes, then you're catching a flight to Boston for the press conference at eleven, and the book signings at three. Is Helen going to be able to make it?"

"Yes. She's already in Boston." She pulled up the schedule on her tablet, frowning when she saw the meeting at seven across town. "Reschedule the meeting at seven and block out the schedule for the rest of the evening."

"All right. Anything I need to know?"

"Not yet. I'll keep you posted." Maggie shot her a smile. "Do we have an agenda for the meeting?"

"Yes. Let me get you a copy." Alice bustled from the room, coming back with the document. "Here you go. I updated it last night."

Maggie glanced at it before booting up her laptop. She clicked to the *New York Times* Best Sellers list. Her memoir was at number six. She looked up at Alice with a broad smile. "The book's doing well."

"I'm not surprised after the number of calls I've fielded in the past two hours."

Maggie raised her eyebrows, intrigued.

"Talk shows, podcasts, radio, magazines, newspapers, websites...anything you can think of. We can discuss it in the meeting."

As her campaign staff began to filter in, Maggie checked her business email. She'd learned the hard way not to have anything personal on the government servers. The same with her cell phone texts. Anything paid through the government remained business related.

Not that the fallout from the leaked memoir excerpts hurt her in any significant way. As promised, Mike didn't provide any response to the media. More surprising was the silence from the Pearsons. She was convinced they would take the opportunity to rip into her reputation. Instead, they presented a united brick wall, uninterested in discussing her relationship with them, her marriage to Timmy, her work at the law firm, or the aftermath once the marriage imploded.

Even after three months of investigating the security breach, they were no closer to determining who was behind the bombings, the breaches, or the leaks. Alice had every computer used by their employees examined, but she found nothing. Nor could her contacts find any solid leads. It was clear that an insider allowed access to the government's secure servers, but no one could trace it back to the person responsible. Maggie was more worried about the hacker's ability to access her personal laptop, where her manuscript had been stored. She now kept all sensitive documents on external memory drives, but that created its own dangers.

Although new protocols had been implemented to protect government servers and block future hacking attempts, none of those actions would stop a leak if an insider provided access again. According to an update on the investigation, thousands of employees' devices had been examined. At this point, Maggie doubted the person or persons responsible would be found.

Maggie was fortunate her career wasn't affected by the leaks. Several colleagues weren't as lucky. Ten of the politicians singled out by the attackers failed to win their seats, although they had led the polls before the leak. Maggie wasn't surprised since their constituents lived in the Bible Belt. Where they were elected in the past based on their policies, their sexual preferences had become a main topic in those states. She was glad to see the other eight incumbents win their elections, even if their numbers were less than projected.

"Senator Ambrose, we're ready for you." Alice's voice broke through her train of thought. She noticed her team seated, several speaking with quiet voices to one another.

Logging off her email, Maggie locked her computer and made her way toward the group. "Thank you for coming so early. Today's the big day. Let's review the schedule for the next three months. We have a lot of ground to cover."

She was proud of the team assembled before her. They were some of the most experienced campaign runners in the industry. She had even landed Darla Truman, who ran President Sugarman's campaign, as her campaign manager. She bit back a grin, sure Jimmy was upset with failing to secure her for his own run. Darla took control of the meeting, providing early poll results and more details on the timeline they had created to promote the book and attract coverage on a broader scale.

"Alice, where are we on interviews?" Darla asked.

"She's booked to appear on *Good Morning America* and *The Late Show with Stephen Colbert* tomorrow. We have invitations from *The Today Show*, CNN, Rachel Maddow, Ellen, Anderson Cooper, Kelly Clarkson, several late night shows, NPR, some progressive podcasts, and the national print media. We're also finalizing book signings to coincide with political events. That should be done this week."

Alice glanced at Maggie. "I'm sure we have more requests since I looked. The publisher will be in attendance for today's book reading. They took out full-page ads in *USA Today*, *The New York Times*, *The Washington Post*, and the *LA Times*. They also have ads on Facebook, Google, Twitter, and Instagram."

"Okay. We want to spread out the interviews so we can build interest and not oversaturate the news outlets. If we're in the news too much, people will skip over us. Let's discuss the talking points for tomorrow's interviews before we review today's press conference." Darla prodded the team members to brainstorm the topics they believed would play well with the public, fleshing out possible issues.

Taking notes and asking a few questions for clarification, Maggie concentrated on the ideas thrown out from the team. The press conference would be short, a mere formality at this point. It was the upcoming interviews that would introduce her to the nation. Leading up to today, she'd practiced conversing on the main areas which served as her political platform—championing those who could not fight for their rights. They needed help, and she intended to give it to them.

"We don't want to get too specific this early in the race. I suggest you introduce three or four areas you want to have associated with your brand and say a few sentences on each. We don't want to get cornered into a policy war this early, but we do want to signal our stance in broad strokes." Zack Baxter was her lead strategist. He kept an eye on the pulse of the nation, watching the polls and news cycles to determine how receptive the nation was on the issues Maggie championed.

"All right. We have a good working plan." Maggie glanced to her right where Michelle Polinski, her national finance director, sat. "Where are we at for funds?"

"We have seed money from the Ambrose Foundation and early support through the LGBTQ+ community. I'm working with Jamie to set up rallies, fundraisers, and appearances across the nation. Now that you're officially declaring your run for president, I'll be able to kick this up into high gear and secure dates."

Nodding, Maggie closed the meeting. "Send updates to Alice and Darla. We'll be seeing a lot more of one another during the campaign. Make sure you're ready. Thank you all for your hard work."

She rose, returning to her desk as everyone filed out. Darla and Alice stayed in their seats to coordinate their calendars and discuss how best to use Maggie's time. Her life was no longer her own, although she had the final say. Unlike when she was younger, though, she felt good about the direction of her life. She had a good group to navigate what she imagined would be a challenging election. During the years she'd faced adversity and failure many times. Those experiences taught her to speak up for herself and not merely float along on the currents of others' plans. That's how she built her political career, and it was how she would win the presidency.

"Okay, we need to head out. Car's out front. Looks like the weather will hold, although it's a bit brisk today." Alice pulled on her coat, waiting for Maggie to do the same.

"That's okay. Announcing my candidacy in front of the Boston State House will send the right message." Climbing into the car, Maggie did her best to settle herself. Soon she'd be at her old stomping grounds. She was looking forward to spending time with friends for an early lunch in between the press conference and book signing events. She was hoping for a good turnout at Boston University's bookstore. She would fly back early enough to get some work done before meeting with Scott. It was a full day, but she expected most of her days would be similar. As they made their way to Dulles Airport, Maggie reviewed her speech. She was ready.

***

"I grew up four miles north of Boston in part of its urban inner core. As a latch-key kid in a broken home, I fended for myself, beginning part-time work at the tender age of twelve through the Girls Club's job shadowing program to feed and clothe myself. That job in a Lynn law firm started me on the road to striving for more and looking ahead." Maggie paused to look straight at the cameras trained on her, projecting her confidence and a sense of calm.

"My memoir was released today, and it reveals a childhood not so dissimilar to what many of you listening to me today have experienced. America has various shades of lightness and darkness, and countless individuals are left in the shadows of those who are more powerful, more connected, and more fortunate. I found my way, but not everyone is given the opportunities I received. As a public servant, I refuse to turn a blind eye to the marginalized groups who deserve the same rights, privileges, and support as any other American. I was the first in my family to attend college and law school, and since those days, I've served as a Massachusetts Representative, US Representative, and US Senator.

"For the past twenty-five years, I've dedicated myself to leveling the playing field for every American. I've listened to my constituents and implemented programs to lift those who need support and hold hands in solidarity with those who deserve to be seen. That's you, America. Our founding fathers envisioned an inclusive society endowed with equality, safety, and happiness.

"Today I am announcing my candidacy for President of the United States. It's time to equal the playing field for all families, rich and poor. It's time to protect the middle class, currently under attack by the big corporations who demand more tax breaks than Americans who work hard every day to support their families.

"Our government is supposed to work for all of us. Instead, it's a tool for the wealthy and the well-connected. It preys on the weak and discriminates against those who look, pray, or love differently. This is a path to ruin. Our country was founded by immigrants who brought their cultures, their ideas, their strengths, and their ingenuity to make our nation great. It's time to embrace our differences and strengthen our nation. It's time everyone is given the opportunity to live full, happy lives. So, let's get to work, America."

As the applause broke out, Maggie held her pose, one she'd practiced during the years to seem poised, authentic, and confident. She was used to the camera flashes and the shouted questions. Ignoring all of that, she waved before stepping away from the podium. The brisk wind blew at her scarf, chapping her cheeks. She joined Helen and Alice, accepting Helen's hug with a smile. "How'd I do?"

"Great. I'm so proud of you." Helen wore an Irish-knit white wool cap and matching scarf. Her bright, rosy cheeks were no doubt a consequence of the weather.

Bob Cross, the traveling press secretary, joined them. He was a tall, broad shouldered man in his mid-forties with a head of curly blond hair. "Okay, I've been assured this will run on all major news syndicates. The major media outlets in Boston, New York, DC, and LA are planning to run stories on the memoir and the presidential run announcement. I'm working with Walter and Rachel to circulate ten-second soundbites."

Walter Cramer was the head of communications and one of their deputy campaign managers. He'd worked on several national campaigns in the past ten years, and Maggie trusted his judgment concerning how to spin events. Rachel Tole was her national press secretary. She kept track of the national advertising, rallies, stump sessions, and all the ways to get Maggie's name out to as many people as possible.

"Okay." Maggie looked at Alice. "Is my lunch confirmed?"

"Yes. We should get going for that. You have the back room reserved for quarter past noon, and you'll need to leave no later than two fifteen to get to BU on time." Alice checked her cell phone.

Reaching out to grasp Helen's gloved hand, they hurried to the car. Sighing once they were safely ensconced, Maggie loosened her scarf. The heated car traveled through the city, making its way to the North End.

"Are you sure I can't entice you into coming back to DC with me tonight?" Maggie fluttered her eyelashes, already knowing the answer but wanting Helen to know she'd be missed.

"Are you sure you can't stay in Boston for the night?" Helen tried to form a pout, but she was unable to hold the pose for more than a second before she laughed.

Shaking her head, Maggie joined in. "You need to work on that, babe. No, I have a meeting tonight."

She turned toward the window, noting the dirty slush pushed to the side of the road by traffic. This was her signal to Helen for her not to ask questions while others were nearby. Maggie would speak to her when they were alone. In fact, Maggie was hoping Helen might have insight into why Scott wanted to meet.

"Are you nervous about the book reading?" Helen squeezed Maggie's hand.

"Not really. I've practiced enough so I won't stumble over the words. I'm more anxious about any possible questions which may arise. I mean, it's one thing to reveal my past, and another to have to talk about it."

"You'll do fine. I know you're prepared, and people will be curious."

"If anyone asks a question you don't want to answer, you can always tell them they'll have to read the book." Alice flashed a smile. "And if it's not in there, you can hint that your next memoir may cover it. Even if you have no intention of doing so, it will push the question off."

A chime indicated Helen had a text. She looked down to read it, her lips quirking up. "Looks like Christine and Evan are at the restaurant. They're ordering appetizers and drinks."

Maggie glanced out the window and saw they were turning onto Hanover Street. "Tell them we'll be there in two minutes."

Once they arrived, Maggie and Helen made their way to the indicated private room tucked in the back of the restaurant. They were met with loud exclamations and tight hugs from Helen's oldest friend, Christine, and her husband, Evan. They sat down to catch up, glad they were able to meet before the election grind prevented them from finding the time.

"We watched your election announcement. I like your message, Maggie." Christine's eyes crinkled as she smiled, her green-tinged brown eyes lighting up. The restaurant lighting hit her shoulder length brown hair, revealing red highlights.

"Thank you. I'm sure as we get closer to the election, you'll become sick of seeing me everywhere." Knowing she shouldn't, Maggie dipped fresh bread into olive oil and took a bite. She was a lover of bread, cheese, and wine—all of which she intended to have today. She was aware she'd have to adjust her eating habits, particularly in the face of endless workdays and extensive traveling she expected to experience between now and the election. It was a long road ahead of her. She needed to stay healthy and strong.

"I'm surprised you're announcing it so soon. Is there a strategy involved with that decision?" Evan was a financial advisor at Merrill Lynch in the Boston financial district. His wavy, dark brown hair gave him a boyish look, even though he was in his mid-fifties. He wore a maroon cotton sweater and a white collared shirt underneath it.

"I need time to meet with people around the country and build momentum. Plus, we have about fifteen Democratic candidates. We'll be jockeying for position and trying to stand out. It's four months until the first debate, and I need that time to gain support."

A server came with shrimp scampi and Caesar salads for everyone. "May I tell you the lunch specials or would you like more time?" He was a college kid with a bright smile. At their urging, he told them the daily specials, each one sounding delicious.

"Any chance I can have fettuccini alfredo with shrimp?" Christine's eyebrows rose as she asked, a small smile on her face.

"Heck, yeah. We can do that."

After Evan ordered the jumbo lump crab cakes and Helen decided on the mushroom ravioli, the server turned to Maggie for her order.

"I'll have the lobster, but instead of spaghetti, can I substitute it for angel hair pasta?"

"Heck, yeah. No problem." He reminded Maggie of a life coach, one of those always positive, gosh-shucks-we-can-do-this, happy-go-lucky people who made major challenges seem like small anthills. It was endearing.

As soon as he left, Helen chuckled. "Boy, I need some of his positive vibes. Talk about happy."

"He does put a smile on your face." Maggie sipped her wine before giving in and taking another piece of bread. She saw Helen cock an eyebrow. "I know. Don't say it. I'll exercise for an extra twenty minutes tonight."

"Getting old does suck as far as gaining weight. I only need to look at an éclair to gain five pounds." Christine patted her belly.

"Oh, please. You're beautiful." Evan kissed her on the cheek. "All I care about is that you're healthy and happy. Besides, you're always in motion. Extra calories don't have a chance at hurting your waistline."

"You all heard it here first." Christine squeezed his forearm. "Remember those words as it gets harder for me to keep off the weight. My metabolism is already slowing down."

He looked at Helen and Maggie. "Any help here? I feel like no matter what I say, it'll be the wrong thing."

Maggie held up her hands. "No way. I have speechwriters to help me come up with the perfect words, and even they wouldn't be able to placate a woman who believes she'll become less attractive as she ages. All we can do is reassure and prove our love as often as possible."

"She's right. Actions speak better than words. That's coming from someone who's married to a wordsmith. Maggie's career is based on using the right words to communicate. That means nothing if her actions don't back them up." Helen smiled. "She's the real deal, though. And Evan is, too. Christine, you got a good one."

"Don't I know it." Christine finished her salad and reclined in her seat. "When are you heading back to DC?"

"After the book signing. I have an evening meeting. Tomorrow I go to New York for television appearances. The next day is a radio show. Next week I'll be heading to LA."

"Basically, I'll never see her." Helen's smile took the sting out of her words.

"Sure, you will. Anytime you turn on the TV or search the internet, I'll be front and center. At least that's the hope." Maggie bumped Helen with her arm before intertwining their fingers. "Plus, you get to skip the Bible Belt and conservative states. That's not something most spouses of presidential candidates get to do."

"That's hardly a good thing. It's difficult to believe people still discriminate against same sex couples."

"I agree with you, Helen, but in some ways, America hasn't evolved at all. We face some of the same struggles we did a hundred years ago." Evan swept his hand toward the front of the restaurant. "People discriminate, take advantage of the weak, abuse the very people who work hard every day to make the world a better place. That's why we need someone like Maggie as president." He held his glass up. "To making our country one we can be proud of."

Everyone raised their glasses and clicked them together in the middle of the table. "Thank you. I've always wanted to be of service. To help those who can't help themselves. To show them it doesn't matter where they come from. It doesn't matter what their backgrounds are. All that matters is that they want to move forward.

That they want to help make a better world, one where everyone gets a fair chance."

"All right. No more pontificating. You'll have plenty of time later." Helen patted Maggie's hand.

"Oh, I don't mind. I feel lucky to know you." Christine laughed. "And I'm one of the fortunate ones to know you from the beginning of your political career."

"With all my missteps and less-than-stellar speeches." Maggie scrunched up her nose. She shuddered, remembering the early debates.

"Well, you've come a long way from that. Most importantly, you champion causes for the right reasons instead of because big business is funding you." Helen looked at their friends. "It's one of the qualities I love about her. She doesn't sell out."

The food arrived, their server plus three others delivering it. Everything smelled divine. They ate without much conversation, each focused on their lunch. Once they finished, Maggie was disappointed to find it was time to go.

"I'm glad we were able to have lunch. Sorry I have to scamper out." Maggie stood to hug Christine and Evan. "We're off to BU." She donned her outwear and led the way out of the restaurant, stopping next to the car double-parked out front.

"Good luck on the reading. I'm sure you'll do great." Christine looped her arm through Evan's and waited as Maggie and Helen climbed into the car. As the car pulled away, she saw them waving.

"I'm glad we were able to fit that in." Maggie looked at Alice. "Any updates?"

"Just the logistics for the reading. Where in the bookstore the reading is taking place and who the contact person is. Lunch was good?"

"Yes. Did you eat something?" Alice was known to skip meals, and Maggie needed her healthy and focused. Once Alice nodded, Maggie let it go. "Good." She knew she should take the time while they drove to the bookstore to review emails or look through the paperwork that she had with her, but she chose to close her eyes. She held Helen's hand on her lap as she breathed evenly, clearing her mind of all the responsibilities she had. For a few minutes, she wanted to think of nothing. Not the election, not the memoir, not the road ahead. She visualized floating on the ocean, her body warm and loose. She felt the sun on her face, smelled the salt carried by the breeze. Her body was pushed by the gentle swells of the waves. And when she felt the car slow down, Maggie was ready. She opened her eyes and smiled.

***

By the time Maggie entered Capitol Hill Brewery, her energy was flagging. She was coming off the high of announcing her run and having a large crowd attend her memoir reading. She'd like nothing more than to curl up in bed, preferably spooned by Helen, but that wasn't in the cards for today. She swept her eyes around the large restaurant, noting the clientele consisted of twenty-somethings, most in jeans and sweatshirts. She felt overdressed. Older patrons in business attire sat at the bar, although they were decades younger than she. She felt a presence at her elbow.

"Thanks for meeting me." Scott pointed toward the back. "I have a booth in the back. Follow me."

He weaved his way through the restaurant, leading them to a small wooden booth with black leather seats. It was shadowed, which would help preserve their identities but would make it harder for her to interpret Scott's facial expressions. She took off her coat and sat down.

"I'll get our drinks from the bar. What would you like?"

"White wine. Anything except chardonnay. Here, let me—"

"No, no. I've got it." Scott flashed a smile and left.

Maggie checked her cell for messages while she waited, replying to Alice's confirmation of the flight details. Tomorrow would be another long day. When she saw Scott returning with the drinks, Maggie placed the phone on her lap.

"I got you a pinot blanc. Hope that's okay." Scott placed the drinks on the table before sliding into the booth. He wrestled his coat off and placed it next to him. "I'm sorry for dragging you out here. I know how busy you are. Oh, I saw your memoir's in the top five. Congratulations."

"Thank you. Scottie, I realize I don't really know you well. The last time I saw you was when you were thin as a rail and too shy to meet my eyes. Yet my gut tells me you're a good person, and I always listen to my gut. So, tell me why we're here." Maggie made sure to maintain eye contact, wanting him to know she was willing to listen to whatever he had to say.

He took a steadying breath, spreading his hands out in front of him before returning her gaze. "As you know, I was trained as a mechanical engineer and am stationed in DC. What you don't know is that I had a secondary concentration—cyber security. I learned how to spot weaknesses in network security, how to trace IP addresses, how to bounce signals all around the world, how to find and access backdoors in the systems. Things like that."

Maggie nodded, understanding most of the jargon he tossed around. Although she wasn't particularly adept with technology, her years in HSGA had helped her learn about the security threats it presented. "Does that have something to do with being in the White House today?"

"Yes. Look, my dad doesn't know about this, but I was assigned to a task force to trace who was involved with the security breach on the government servers. Because my father is the chairman of Homeland Security, the FBI organized an independent investigation and tapped me to be on the team, thanks to my professor. They asked me to trace the hacks, which includes studying my father's laptops. At first, I was against it. I mean, I couldn't imagine him having anything to do with it."

"But you found something." Maggie felt as if a heavy cloak were sitting on her shoulders, pushing her into the seat. Foreboding filled her. It seemed inconceivable that her mentor, someone she'd worked with for years, someone she trusted, could have taken steps to tank other politicians' careers. Worse, his actions were focused on politicians who had same sex relationships. That included her.

"Yeah." Scott shook his head. "The truth is, I'm freaking out. I found the proof on his personal laptop—emails with someone high up in the XY Institute. They were deleted, but I was able to recover them. And that's not all." His face was pale, hands trembling enough that he pressed down on the table to stop them.

Not able to imagine how it felt to find out a family member was behind such an abhorrent plot to single out and hurt those who had done nothing other than follow their hearts' dictates to love someone of the same sex, Maggie felt the strong urge to comfort him. She placed a hand on his, squeezing it before she let go. "You can trust me."

"I know. That's why I decided to tell you. I mean, information was leaked about you, too. And that's the other part. I saw an email yesterday talking about your memoir and campaign run for president. They were planning a smear campaign against you. Someone in your office named Valerie was forwarding information about your scheduled appearances, campaign timelines. Everything. She's the daughter of one of dad's college friends. Lillian."

Maggie's eyes widened. The ex-girlfriend in the picture she saw. She wondered whether it was Ted or Nellie who enlisted her help. Grinding her teeth, she pulled out her cell phone and tapped out a message to Alice.

Val's the mole. First thing tomorrow, confiscate her electronics, revoke her privileges, and fire her. We can look into lodging formal charges.

Maggie reviewed her message and sent it before she refocused on Scott.

He was rubbing the back of his neck. "I'm going to report everything tomorrow. I have to do it before they cause any more damage."

"I can't imagine how you feel. All I do know are my feelings. I feel angry. Hurt. Disillusioned. I trusted him. He's been like a father to me since I became a senator." She felt her eyes burning, tears lining up to express her grief. She sniffed, willing herself to keep her emotions in check until she was alone. "I'm sorry."

"No, I'm sorry. Maybe if I'd said something sooner, none of this would have happened." His face was flushed, the vein in his forehead making an appearance. He was getting worked up, and Maggie was at a loss to understand what he was thinking.

"I don't understand."

"I'm gay. I've never told my parents because I was afraid, but maybe he wouldn't have done these things if he knew." Scott dropped his head, his hands turning into fists. She saw his shoulders shaking, repressed whimpers cutting into her heart.

Leaning over, Maggie used her hand to lift his chin enough to see his face, letting go once he looked at her. "You need to listen to me, Scottie." His reddened eyes were heartbreaking. "This is not your fault. He knows I'm married to a woman, yet he is taking specific steps to derail my campaign, specific steps to hurt me." She shook her head. "I've been in your home at least fifty times. Gone to hundreds of functions with him. Worked side by side to develop national policies. He's always asked about Helen, always treated her as if he had no problem with my sexual identity. So no, I don't believe you telling him would have made a difference, at least not a favorable one. No one is going to blame you, and you shouldn't either."

"I don't know what to do. I can't keep living in their home. Just the thought of seeing him…" He covered his face with his hands before rubbing his eyes with choppy swipes.

"If you want help getting out of there, I can arrange it for you. All you need to do is say yes, and I'll help you. And I can do it in a way that only the people you want will know where you are." Maggie was mentally calling forth the people she could contact to find him a place to live. Her connections would ensure discretion. His courage with revealing all he had tonight impressed her. She wouldn't mind having him on her election team. She wouldn't discuss that with him tonight, though. First, she wanted to protect him.

"Thank you. If you can help me, I'd appreciate it. I want to leave as soon as possible. I only need one bedroom. I earn enough that I can afford it, and I have money saved. You know how hard it can be to find a place."

"I do." Maggie took out a business card and scribbled her number on the back. "This is my personal cell. Only use that number to call or text. As a matter of fact, text me now so I have your number."

She sipped her wine as he tapped at his cell phone. A moment later the text came through, and Maggie saved his number. "Good. If you're serious about getting out of there, we can probably get you out tomorrow. So, finish whatever you need to do and pack up. Either I or my assistant, Alice, will contact you tomorrow with options. We're going to get through this."

His small smile lit up the booth. "You don't know what this means to me. I'll never forget it. If there's anything I can ever do for you…"

"I would never capitalize on this. I'm not that kind of politician. And I'm the one who's thankful. Your actions are protecting me. Your bravery and integrity are trumping your loyalty to a family member, and I know how hard that is. Do me a favor and text me tomorrow once you submit the report. That way if Ted contacts me, I'll be ready. I'll be in New York tomorrow for interviews, but I'm sure he'll be scrambling, trying to shore up his defense and mitigate any damage the report causes. I strongly suggest you pack up tonight. In fact, can you delay filing the report until the day after tomorrow? That way we can get you out of there, and I'll be back from New York."

Taking a large sip of his beer, Scott took a moment to think. He placed the sweating glass down and nodded. "That will probably work better. I can do one last sweep of his computer tomorrow morning. Do you really think I can move tomorrow?"

"Absolutely. Give me one sec." She called Alice, staring at the bar as she waited for her to pick up.

"Don't tell me you're in the office." Alice sounded a bit cranky, which pulled a grin out of Maggie.

"Does that mean you aren't? What a slacker." She chuckled at the squawk Alice emitted. "I sent you a text about the mole. We can sort that out tomorrow. We have another pressing matter. I have a favor, and it has to be on the downlow. We need to move Scott Stapleton out of his home tomorrow. So, we need to find a one-bedroom apartment close to the Hill. Avoid Kalorama. And I'm texting you his number so you can contact him directly, but I want to be kept in the loop."

The marked silence was no surprise. She knew Alice was thinking of which contacts to use and where to look. They knew several real estate brokers, although not all of them were discrete. "How much can he afford per month?"

"Good question." Maggie relayed the question to Scott and nodded at the amount.

"Up to twenty-five hundred. That should be enough to give him some choices."

"I know just the person to handle it. I'll send possibilities tomorrow morning and arrange the movers for early afternoon."

"You're the best. Thank you. I'll see you tomorrow bright and early for the flight."

"Good night."

Once the call disconnected, Maggie smiled at Scott. "It's in motion. You'll receive a text from Alice tomorrow morning with some possibilities. Is there anything else you want to tell me before we call it a night?"

"No. I never expected this. I was just planning to warn you of the conspiracy."

"I know, and it's a testament to your character." Maggie finished her wine and stood. "I'll touch base with you tomorrow. I advise you to avoid your parents and not let on that you're moving. That will give you more room to maneuver without worrying they'll find out where you're going. After you submit the report, things will get messy. I want you safely away from it."

They made their way to the front of the brewery. "Let me leave first, and after a few minutes, you can leave. We don't need to be seen together right before the shit hits the fan."

"Yeah. Okay. Thank you for everything."

"You're welcome." With a wave Maggie left, hurrying toward her car. She had a lot to think about. She knew alliances would shift once she began her campaign, that some people she counted as supporters would distance themselves while others would come out of the woodwork to strengthen their connections. It had occurred throughout her political career. What shook her was how blindsided she felt with Ted's betrayal. It made her wonder who else she counted as a friend was actually a threat.

Chapter Fifteen

THE WORST PART OF the divorce was losing the closeness she shared with her two oldest friends, Lizzie and Kevin. Oh, they still invited her over. They still went through the motions of contacting her to see how she was. They forwarded funny emails and met her for walks on the Lynn Shore Drive promenade and talked about all the milestones their toddler was reaching. While they were together, it felt like old times. Like donning her favorite sweater. Comfortable but frayed at the edges—the perfect description for their friendship.

When Lizzie invited her for dinner, Maggie had mixed feelings. She didn't want to discuss Timmy, but she knew it would come up in conversation. How could it not? Still, she missed her friends and wanted to spend time with them. Hoping for the best, she arrived with a bottle of wine and a small smile. Dinner was better than she anticipated, filled with lighthearted teasing and rehashing of past escapades they shared. It wasn't until Kevin left the room to put Gemma to sleep that uneasiness crept across Maggie.

"Let's sit in the living room. I can clean up the dishes later. Oh, let me refill our wine."

Maggie sank into the soft, smokey gray chenille fabric-covered cushion, resting her arm on top of the rolled backrest. She loved this sofa, having spent many nights tucked into its corner while they chatted. She smiled as Lizzie approached with a glass of wine, handing it to Maggie before taking a seat in a plush overstuffed chair.

"How are you doing?" Lizzie leaned toward her, tilting her head.

"I'm okay. As you can imagine, work is challenging. And the campaign has taken a hit." Maggie drank the wine, trying not to gulp it all down. She sighed, spinning the stem of the wineglass slowly with her fingers. "The timing for the breakup couldn't be worse. Next week we're meeting with our attorneys to parcel out our personal effects. That ought to be fun."

"I can't imagine. I'm so sorry. Is there anything we can do?"

"Not really. I'm just trying to get through it. I mean, I'm losing more than my marriage. I'm losing my family. His mom never warmed up to me, but his father took me under his wing years ago. He helped me with learning how to practice law. He introduced me to the right people and provided opportunities for me I never would have gotten. He's the one who talked me into running for office. So, I'm losing more than a husband. I'm losing a father. I'm losing brothers. And I'm losing traction in my careers—the law firm and the election. I'm entirely adrift. I have all these decisions I need to make and I feel too overwhelmed to do anything."

"Is there any chance you might reconcile? You never told me why you're getting a divorce. Maybe you can go to a marriage counselor and work through your problems."

Maggie was already shaking her head. She leaned back against the sofa, allowing her eyes to slip closed for a moment. She grimaced, not wanting to think about all the reasons. "Lizzie, there's no way to come back from this. It was a lot of things, and each on its own may seem small, but they all added up."

"You said it yourself...this is destroying your life. Why not try to stay together? At least until your career settles down. I mean, if you knew you were going to file for divorce, why didn't you plan for it to happen after changing firms or after the election?"

"He punched through the bathroom door while I was getting ready for work. He could have hurt me. I had to file a restraining order. Once that happened...well, there was no point waiting."

"You know he wouldn't have hurt you."

Maggie looked at her friend, her face twisting. She felt a bolt of incredulity mix with anger. "You can't be serious. Who pounds down a door with their bare hands? I was afraid. And now he intends to take everything that's important away from me. Those aren't the actions of a man who loves me."

"He could take an anger management class to learn control."

"And what about the trust issues? He lied to me for months about getting fired. His father didn't even know, and it's his firm. I found out by accident. And it's not like he was even looking for a job. I came home from the firm early because I was sick, and there he was on the couch, eating chocolate and watching a game on the television."

"I would have been pissed off about that, too. But he said he was afraid to tell you, and—"

"He was afraid? Of what? Admitting he was late to work so many times that he got fired? He's not a little boy. He needed to admit his mistakes and learn from them. Wait. When did he talk to you about it?"

"We saw him on Friday." Lizzie was looking down at her lap as she pulled on her fingers.

Maggie sat up, placing her glass on the coffee table. She stared at Lizzie, modulating her voice as she fought to contain her anger. "Do you mean to tell me you went to the Pearsons' dinner party?"

"We did. Listen, Maggie, I know that might seem weird, but we've become close with the family. We don't want to lose that."

"Are you serious?" Maggie's voice rose. Her body pulsed with heat, the feeling of betrayal fueling her anger. "Do you know how that will look? You're my closest friends. They'll think you're taking their side, that you believe I'm in the wrong."

"No. I don't think they will." Lizzie's eyes skittled off to the side. "You know this isn't easy for anyone. We don't want to lose what we've built with them, and Kevin isn't close to many people. He wants to remain friends with Timmy."

Maggie thought of the other reasons for the divorce and bit her tongue. She refused to tell Lizzie how she found him more than once masturbating in their home office while reading smut or his unwillingness to learn how to please her in the bedroom. It was confusing and embarrassing. He seemed to prefer his own hand to being intimate with her. She thought of all she was losing, and mentally added her closest friends to the list. Sorrow welled up, sweeping through her like a tidal wave. She needed to get out. The betrayal felt like a hot-tipped knife slicing through her heart. She couldn't listen to another word out of Lizzie's mouth. She stood, grabbing her purse from beside the sofa before moving toward the door.

"Wait. Where are you going? Let's talk about this." Lizzie followed, stepping in front of the door before Maggie could open it. "Please. I wanted to tell you about the celebrations for Gemma's christening. We're having two—one for family and one for everyone else. You can come to either or both. Timmy's coming to the one open to everyone, but you can come on the other day. I wanted to make sure you knew."

"Timmy's coming?"

"Yes, but that's why you can come to the other party." She placed a hand on Maggie's shoulder. "You're the only one we're inviting to that one who isn't a relative. We're doing the best we can to navigate this, but it's not easy."

"Then don't. You're my friend. You met the Pearson's through me. I don't understand why you can't get this."

Lizzie shook her head. "I'm sorry."

Maggie pressed her lips together, understanding bitter in her mouth. "You don't want to lose the connections. The power. The perks of being associated with them." Maggie made a sound in the back of her throat. "Well, let me clue you in. It's all fine and dandy until it isn't. So, watch out. One day they may turn on you, and you'll be left in the cold. Or even worse, you may end up selling your souls to remain a part of their group. At least I still have my dignity."

She grabbed the doorknob and pulled, not caring whether the door hit Lizzie. As she passed through the entrance, Maggie swallowed down her despair. "One day you'll regret this choice." She hurried down the stairs, gritting her teeth as the tears came. She was able to drive around the corner before having to pull over, the tears obscuring her vision. She felt betrayed and alone.

Her mind shied away from dwelling on her own role in the mess called her life. She couldn't. Couldn't think about why she entered a romantic relationship when she felt nothing but friendship. Why she agreed to marriage after finishing law school. Why she decided being a part of the Pearson dynasty was worth losing any possibility of finding personal contentment. Or love.

In many ways, the weakening in their friendship was much worse than her divorce. She couldn't understand why they continued to spend time with Timmy. They were her friends. Their friendships were forged during the formative years of their lives. They learned and grew and shared and loved together. They worked on their friendships while attending different colleges and began their professional careers while making plans for future adventures. Their friendship spanned seventeen years. She thought they would support her, help her as she navigated the changes in her life.

After nine months, the divorce was finalized. Maggie rented an apartment in Lynn, across from the ocean. The sound of the waves pounding against the sand soothed her, and she spent much time wandering the beaches from Nahant through Marblehead Neck. She took the opportunity during these walks to contemplate what happened, why she'd married Timmy in the first place, and all that she'd lost.

Exiting Pearson, Gunner, Kenny & Associates wasn't as hard as she anticipated. Once word got around of her impending divorce, she received several offers from other firms. It surprised her that many came from opposing counsel, attorneys she'd faced in court. She feared they were looking for insider information, but that wasn't why they extended offers of employment. She was told time and again that she was fierce in court. She knew the law and had a way of gaining the jury's trust. She exuded wisdom and scrupulousness.

She ended up accepting a job offer from a firm located near Ashburton Park, mere steps away from the courthouses. Schwartz, Litman & Associates offered her a large signing bonus and an office with a paralegal. She packed up her office and made the transition to the new firm, slipping away as if she were a wraith, and in many ways, she felt like one. Although she knew she would rebuild and move forward, she felt dead inside, a shadow of the confident, driven woman who rose to the challenges presented in the law firm where she'd worked for seven years.

Sitting at her desk on a sunny afternoon, Maggie had a decision to make. Before her life went up in flames, she had announced her candidacy for the Massachusetts House of Representatives, 10th District, representing Lynn and Nahant. Even though she no longer had the support and financial backing of her former law firm or the Pearson connections to help her win, her campaign had attracted a following from her hometown, and the latest poll projections indicated she was in the lead. Many of her former classmates remained in Lynn once they graduated high school, and they had surprised her with their support. Since the Pearson's didn't have much clout at the local level on the North Shore, Maggie believed she could win the election. With that in mind, she kept her focus on the new law firm and the election.

As the weeks passed, Maggie found a new rhythm. When she wasn't working, she exercised. Each morning she rode her stationary bike and used free weights, and at night she walked along the beach. She used those times to clear her mind and center herself. At work, she refused to allow her mind to wander. As she racked up her court wins, more colleagues asked for her help. By fall, she received weekly invitations to happy hours with the other associates. Her life was quiet and orderly, exactly what she needed while she grieved the loss of her family, her friends, and her job.

Her mother, who was still married to her stepfather, called her several times a week. She was quick to expound on her dislike of Timmy and his family. Although Maggie didn't have the heart to tell her mom, the Pearson's despised her just as strongly. They viewed her as uneducated trash, remaining with John so she didn't have to work. They were polite when in the same room with her, but during the course of Maggie's relationship with Timmy, she'd heard their criticisms about her mom enough that she felt guilty, knowing they formed their opinions after learning about her upbringing.

In a surprising move, Lizzie and Kevin hosted a campaign meet-and-greet at their family's restaurant in September. It was a large turnout, and Maggie used the opportunity to speak to those in attendance and answer questions. The restaurant was in East Lynn near the cemetery on Lynnfield Street. Cars filled the parking lot and lined the main street. The restaurant walls were painted in blues and gold, the well-known Greek key geometric design meandering around the main room. Framed photographs of the mainland and surrounding Greek islands were hung above the tables, and a large portrait of the sprawling family dynasty had a place of honor above the cash register.

Several platters of appetizers and beverages were laid out on a long table against the wall, perpendicular to a small stage, where many a would-be singer had participated in karaoke contests.

Maggie grew up eating at Georgiou's Mediterranean Grille. Their chicken kabob Greek salad with fresh feta special was to die for. Her mouth salivated as she eyed the offerings. It took immense willpower to resist fixing a plate. She had to remind herself that the food wasn't for her. She decided she would place an order to go after the event ended. After Lizzie introduced her, Maggie bounded on the stage and said a few words before opening up the floor to questions.

"How are you planning to address the overcrowding in the schools?" a woman in her late twenties asked. Maggie didn't recognize her. She was tall and thin, her long, glossy hair held back by a gold headband. Her light brown eyes were focused on her, lashes long enough to cause Maggie to question whether they were real.

"Class sizes are a tough issue since the schools are old and the budget was approved for the next fiscal year. That said, I will look into finding ways to supplement the funds and meet with education officials so we can brainstorm how we can ease classroom crowding."

"So in other words, you aren't going to do anything." She stood with her arms crossed, her blouse riding up enough for Maggie to see a strip of tanned skin across her stomach.

Cocking her head, Maggie grinned. "I'm sorry. I don't believe we've met. I'm Maggie Ambrose." She pointed toward herself before sweeping her hand outward. "And you are?"

"Helen Fisher. Look, you sound sincere, but I'm asking for real answers, not pretty platitudes. We need a leader who's willing to do the work and commit to our community, not just use your position as a stepping stone to a more powerful position."

Maggie snickered, not sure whether she was impressed or insulted. "Stepping stone? Really? This is my first election. I can't afford to make empty promises or, what did you call it? Pretty platitudes. I need to be ready to carry through, and that means I need all the information. Now, if you have that information, I'd love to sit down with you to discuss it."

Maggie swept her eyes across the small crowd. "It's citizens like you who foster my desire to make our community stronger, safer, and sustainable." She opened her arms wide. "I'd love to hear what other matters are on your mind. So, while we indulge in the tasty food and drink our generous hosts here at Georgiou's Mediterranean Grille have provided, please come over and say hello."

She waited while the polite applause abated before hopping off the stage and leaning against it. Lizzie handed her a glass of Greek white wine, and Maggie hummed as she tasted hints of citrus and apple. "Thanks."

"Sure. You did great. A lot of people took your information packets. That means they're interested in you." Lizzie sipped her own glass of wine, eyes wandering around the room.

"I appreciate your family hosting this event. I have a few more coffee meets before the election, and did I tell you I'm the attorney coach for a mock trial team at Lynn Classical?" Maggie grinned. "Some of those high school kids are better than actual attorneys."

"That's wonderful. I'm sure they're learning a lot from you." Kevin came to stand next to them, shooting Maggie a smile.

Doing her best not to walk away, Maggie nodded at him. She was, perhaps unjustly, upset with Kevin for maintaining a friendship with Timmy. If it weren't for him, she might be spending her spare time with them, laughing and relaxing like they used to in the old days. Instead, she limited their interactions. It didn't take a genius to figure out this event was Lizzie's attempt to get back in her good graces. She didn't seem to understand that Maggie would never let her guard down with them again. She would never trust them with her innermost thoughts. She would never turn to them when she needed help or a friendly face. That was in the past.

As the silence became stifling a couple joined them, eager to chat about Maggie's plans to help their community. Grateful she wouldn't have to indulge in meaningless small talk with Kevin, Maggie took her time answering, asking them what concerns they had. They talked about their neighborhood in Ward One, the prices of real estate, and traffic. This was the reason why she decided to run for office. She wanted to make a difference, and with her training, she would.

***

By the time Maggie realized the Pearson's were behind a series of op-eds published in *The Daily Item* and *The Boston Globe* filled with derogatory, false allegations, it was too late to implement enough damage control to win the election. What had seemed like an easy win became a firm slap across her face. She cleared herself of the most egregious accusations through several interviews, but the damage was done.

Gulping down her drink, Maggie felt exhausted. Her plans to rise from the ashes like a phoenix had failed. She was a loser, even more than the old man on the stage singing, "Baby Got Back."

The man's hoary appearance emphasized the absurdity of his song choice. He swayed on his feet, microphone catching his spittle as he muttered half of the lyrics, squinting through his spectacles at the words flowing across the karaoke screen.

She slouched in her seat at the back of the Porthole Pub, not interested in doing anything but drinking. For one night she was determined not to care what she looked like or who saw her or how she was abusing her body.

"I should have known better." Maggie pushed her empty glass away, ready to stumble up to the bar to order another one. Next to her sat a teacher she met while coaching the mock trial team. June Murphy was an Irish lass with auburn hair, green eyes, and freckles. This was her first year teaching history, and like Maggie, she wanted to give back to the community which helped her while growing up.

"Come on, Maggie. How could you know? Your ex is a dick, and so is his family. They have no morals and no integrity. They didn't have to drag your name through the mud. That was pure pettiness. You need to shake it off and move on. Be ready to run for the next election. Maybe get someone to help you so this won't happen again."

"Yeah, because it's such a high-profile election. I'm sure people will be lining up to help me." Maggie began to rise, but June's hand on her arm stopped her.

"You stay here and enjoy the entertainment." She jerked her head toward the old guy, now trying to sing "Love Shack." He was sitting on a stool this time, and Maggie was convinced he'd fall off before the end of the song. "I'll get you a refill."

"Thanks." Maggie stared at her Nokia mobile phone, one of the few items she took with her from her previous law firm. It was state of the art, cutting-edge technology, enabling her to receive calls even when not at home or at work. She pulled up Helen's phone number and hit the call button.

After meeting Helen three months ago at the meet-and-greet, she met with her twice to discuss policy. The woman was opinionated as hell, but Maggie found it didn't bother her. Helen backed her words with facts instead of mere opinion. She explained what was needed for adolescents and how certain programs could alter the courses of troubled teens. If such programs had existed while she and Mike were teens, perhaps Mike wouldn't have started to steal. Maybe he wouldn't have drifted away from her.

The cell phone rang several times before she heard a crackling noise and a familiar voice. "Hello?"

"Hi, Helen. It's Maggie." That's what she tried to say. It came out less clear than she wanted, her mouth refusing to enunciate the words.

"Maggie? Is that you? It sounds loud where you are."

"Yeah. Sorry. I'm at the Porthole. Just chilling. Someone's trying to sing. That's probably what you hear." Maggie smiled at June as she deposited a drink in front of her.

"Are you okay? You're not alone, are you?"

"Nah. I'm here with a friend." She exhaled loudly, switching hands as her wrist became tired. "I lost."

Helen was silent long enough that Maggie pulled the phone away from her ear to make sure they weren't disconnected. "Hello? Still there?"

"Yes. I'm here. I'm sorry you lost. Do you want me to come down there?"

"No. It's late. I'm sorry I called. I don't know why I called. I'm gonna go. Sorry." Maggie pulled the phone away, but hearing Helen's voice, she placed it against her ear once more. "What?"

"I said, please be safe. As a matter of fact, send me an email once you get home. Don't forget."

"Email. Right. Wait." Maggie looked through her purse, and not seeing a pen, she dumped the entire contents on the sticky table. Coins rolled on the floor, but Maggie paid them no mind. With one hand she sifted through loose breath mints, tissues, a small notebook, a candy wrapper, and paper clips, crowing in triumph when she found a pen. "You still there? Hold on."

Maggie placed the phone on the table, took off the pen cap, and wrote on her palm, *email Helen*. She stared at the scribbles, cocking her head. She turned her palm toward June. "Can you read this?"

June stared at her hand. "Crawl home?" She raised her eyebrows. "That's not necessary. I'll drive you home."

Grunting, Maggie tried again, writing underneath the two words. Well, she tried to, but her words crossed through the first attempt, making a royal mess. She handed the pen to June. "Can you write email Helen on my hand?" She extended her other hand, relieved when June did as she requested. "Thanks."

Picking up the phone, Maggie stared at it. She heard something on the other end. She looked at June. "Was I on the phone?"

June's eyes widened. She nodded and took the phone. "Hi. This is June. We haven't met. I just wanted to let you know that I'll make sure Maggie gets home safely and that she sends you an email. Okay?" She chuckled. "No problem. Bye."

Blinking several times, Maggie wondered why it was so hard to focus. Maybe the haze of cigarette smoke was obscuring her vision. Or the time of night. Or that horrible singing. She gulped down her drink and smacked her lips. June set the phone on the table before proceeding to place the bag's innards back into Maggie's purse.

"Thanks. Hey, you're a good friend." Maggie smiled, her cheeks stretching. It felt weird. She touched her cheeks. "Hey. I think something's wrong with me. My cheeks are frozen, but they're not cold."

"You're okay. I'm getting tired. Let me drive you home."

"But my car…"

"We left it at your apartment. Remember?" June stood, waiting for Maggie to get up. She placed a hand on her bicep, waiting until Maggie nodded before leading the way out of the restaurant.

"Right. That was smart." She leaned against the car door until June unlocked it.

"Here. Let me." June opened the front passenger door for her. "Watch your head."

Misjudging how low to duck as she tried to slide on the seat, Maggie's head hit the edge of the door and she wobbled. She grabbed the doorframe and waited until the stars faded before attempting once more to climb in.

"Are you okay?" June pushed Maggie's head and feet into the interior before closing the door and rushing around to the driver's side. "Did you hurt yourself?"

"Nah, didn't hurt at all. But I bet it's gonna hurt tomorrow." Maggie guffawed, tickled by how hard she hit her head, how uncooperative her body was, how shit-faced she was. Yeah, tomorrow was going to suck for a variety of reasons, not the least of which would be a horrendous hangover, a raging headache, and shredded pride. Right now, though, all those eventualities were far away.

Somehow June got her inside. She ended up writing and sending the email to Helen from Maggie's computer, letting her know Maggie was home, while Maggie shouted out helpful suggestions. "Tell her about the kara…karoroke…karkero…the singer. Oh, tell her about me hitting my head. That was funny."

June helped her to bed. Maggie flopped on top of the sheets, too tired to get under the covers. She knew what was happening, but she was uncoordinated and logy. So tired. The exhaustion she'd felt earlier washed across her once more. As her body relaxed into her bed, she thanked June for being a great friend. She tried to stay awake to hear June's reply, but she fell asleep within seconds.

Chapter Sixteen

"I LOVE WHAT YOU'VE done with the place." Maggie looked around Scott's apartment. Although a one bedroom, one bath condo, it had an open space concept with a large main room. When he'd moved in, his home was stark with white walls, hardwood floors, and modern appliances. On this visit, she saw how bright pillows on the sofa and side chair, framed artwork, and colored dishware brightened up the place.

Alice had found the apartment in Logan Circle, not far from the Hill. As promised, Maggie made sure Scott was moved the day after she met him at the brewery. He was shielded from the fallout of his father's actions, and the FBI using the information he found to indict Ted and a handful of other people who conspired to carry out their plans. Ted, Lillian, and several officials from the XY Institute were charged with a laundry list of criminal offenses under the Computer Fraud and Abuse Act, Electronic Communications Privacy Act, the CAN-SPAM Act, and the Stored Communications Act.

Ted's trial wouldn't occur for several more months, but it was clear that not only was his political career over, he would likely end up spending several years in prison. He was under house arrest until the trial, and he was no longer the chairman of HSGA. That responsibility fell to Maggie, ironic since she received updates on the trial, details on the XY Institute's role, and a complete report on Ted's actions.

Watching Ted's arrest while he was inside the Capitol Building was an event Maggie wouldn't forget. Scott told her when to expect the arrest to occur, and she made sure she was close by to witness it. The FBI acted with celerity to take him into custody, choosing to make a statement by conducting the arrest in a public forum. Ted seemed flummoxed, leading Maggie to believe he thought he'd gotten away with his heinous actions. She felt a sense of *schadenfreude* and gave herself permission not to feel guilty. This man had betrayed her, and he deserved his comeuppance.

Although Nellie wasn't arrested, she was put on notice that she was being investigated to ascertain whether she took steps to aid Ted and the XY Institute. Warrants were issued to search their house and Ted's offices. Thanks to Scott's help, they had already gathered all the evidence they needed to prosecute Ted. Maggie had a feeling Nellie wouldn't maintain her freedom for much longer. Valerie was also being investigated. She hoped all of them got sent to prison.

"Thank you. Please make yourself at home." Scott smiled at her then turned to greet more guests, leaving Maggie to her own devices. She took her time observing the young crowd of urban professionals before proceeding to the small kitchen area to pour a glass of white wine.

Wandering back into the living room, Maggie paused in front of a bookcase. She spied a novel by an author she admired, Rick R. Reed. Picking it up, she read the title, *The Man from Milwaukee*. The blurb on the back of the book described a young man's mental deterioration as he writes letters to Jeffrey Dahmer, who is in prison for his serial killings. She shivered, wondering how Rick thought up such storylines.

"Are you Maggie Ambrose?"

Pasting a polite look on her face, she turned toward the speaker. "I am. You have me at a disadvantage." She smiled at the muscular man. He was about Scott's age with a tan and sun-streaked brown hair.

"I'm David. Scott's mentioned you." He leaned closer and lowered his voice. "I'm his boyfriend. He said you helped him get this place and supported him while he dealt with the fallout of…" He waved a hand. "You know."

Maggie's smile became more genuine, happiness stealing through her. *Scott has a boyfriend. How wonderful.* "It's a pleasure to meet you. How did you two meet?"

"Uh, uh, uh. No starting that story without me." Scott flashed a smile at Maggie as he wound an arm around David's waist.

"Perfect timing, hon." David wiggled his eyebrows. "He was at the coffee shop down the street, and I knew the moment I saw him that I needed to talk to him. I raced up to the counter, intent on capturing his attention."

"And boy did he. I turned to leave, a large coffee in hand and boom." He clapped his hands together. "Smashed right into him."

"It was awful. Hot as hell, and I'm thinking there's no way I'm gonna get his number now."

Scott chuckled. "And all I could think about as I tried to sop up the dripping coffee from his tight shirt was how in shape he was." His cheeks flushed, eyes shining at the memory. "He asked me out on the pretext of making it up to me."

"That was no pretext. I felt horrible."

"Of course, I agreed to dinner." Scott gazed at David. "It was the easiest decision I ever made. And the best one."

"Oh, my God, you guys. I love your story." Maggie beamed at them. "Oh, before I forget. Helen sends her love. She wanted to make it, but she couldn't get back from California in time. We'll have to have you both over soon."

"I'm sorry she couldn't make it." Scott heard his name called and looked toward the kitchen where snacks were spread across the table. "Let me take care of that. I'll be back."

"Tell me about yourself, David. How do you keep busy?" Maggie rested the stem of her wineglass on her arm, which she rested against her abdomen.

"I work for Brookings."

Maggie felt her eyebrows rise. "Are you a researcher?"

"Yes. I started as an intern, and now I'm a research assistant."

"That's impressive, David. With all the contradictory information floating around, we need think tanks to sort through, condense, and communicate the truth."

She wondered whether she could poach him for her campaign. He'd be a great CIO, culling the topics she needed to address and keeping an eye on how she was coming across as she worked her way through the country, interacting with potential voters. She'd love to get Scottie on her team, too. He'd be ideal for her IT needs. He had the knowledge to make sure she didn't get hacked and all information on the various technological platforms remained safe. She'd have to talk to her team about it. Up until now her core group took care of the campaign, but with the first debate on the horizon and her name becoming known, she'd need to add staffers.

Scott rejoined them with four people in tow. "Maggie, I want you to meet some friends of mine. This is Edgar, Mary, Terry, and Shawnise."

Turning toward them, Maggie smiled. "It's a pleasure to meet you." They were all twenty-something young professionals, at the beginning of their careers. It was hard to remember being that young, filled with energy and opinions and hope. For a while, she'd become disillusioned, losing that hope, but she found herself allowing that light to shine stronger each day, surrounded by people who believed in her. To her immense pleasure, they volunteered to work on her campaign.

Raising her eyebrows, a surprised laugh escaped Maggie. It wasn't often she was caught flatfooted, and yet here they stood offering to reach a demographic she dearly needed to bring the progressive vote to her side. It felt like her birthday, Christmas, and every other wonderful, present-laden day she'd ever experienced. Beating back the urge to pull them all in for a group hug, Maggie settled with smiling wide enough to feel her cheeks protest. "What a wonderful surprise. Let me get your contact information, and I'll have my team contact you to get you set up."

"Here." Scott handed her a piece of paper with names, numbers, and affiliations. "I figured this would make it easier for you."

"Well, I see you had this all planned out. Thank you." She looked around at the group. "Truly. I appreciate your stepping up to help. I want to build a better society, a nation we can be proud of, and your help is going to make a big difference."

Although she knew she would be tired the next day, Maggie stayed for another hour, conversing with most of Scott's guests, although she gravitated back to the group of volunteers several times. The first debate would occur in two weeks, and she knew the campaign would ramp up after that.

***

For months, Maggie met with potential donors, talked strategy with her team, and mapped out a platform she believed in. Qualifying for the first debate was a great affirmation that her name was becoming known, the number of donations from people across the nation increasing daily. The debate was taking place in Orlando, and Maggie would be traveling for two weeks after the debate to capitalize on the surge in popularity she hoped it would generate. She would return home for a few days after being on the road, only to hop back on a plane to attend the second debate in Dallas.

Leading up to the first debate, Maggie's days took on a pattern. Each morning began with a team meeting where she received updates on what the other candidates were saying, the latest media commentary on her campaign, fundraising numbers, and what the schedule after Independence Day looked like for her wide sweep through several states, beginning in Iowa and ending in South Carolina. After the update from all heads, Maggie would prep for the debate with Alice, Darla, and Zack. They did their best to prepare her for any accusations, misinformation, and critiques Maggie might face. After each practice session, they worked on how to word her answers, brainstorming the best ways to connect with voters while promoting the issues which formed the foundation of her campaign. She practiced every day until by the end of the week, she was able to redirect any criticisms about her policies into a more positive spin.

The day of the debate came with Maggie waking to the sound of rain. Taking a deep breath, Maggie exhaled while arching her back and turning to her side. Opening her eyes, she gazed into amused brown ones. Maggie smiled. "Good morning, sunshine." She cupped Helen's face and leaned in for a short kiss.

"Good morning. How did you sleep?" Helen reached out to interlace their fingers, resting them against her chest.

"Not bad." She yawned, ducking her head. "Ready to be seen by the masses?"

Helen grimaced. "If you ever doubted my love, being paraded in front of the media should prove to you that I do, in fact, love you more."

"No way. I love you more. However, I do agree that your willingness to have your privacy invaded and every facet of your life examined does reinforce your assertion that you love me."

"You're not doing yourself any favors by reminding me of the scrutiny I face."

Pulling Helen closer, Maggie leaned in to kiss her jaw, trailing her lips down her neck before sucking on her collarbone. "Perhaps a change in strategy is needed."

"I have always liked the way your mind works." Her chuckle was deep and dirty.

Maggie wanted to swallow it. She hadn't brushed her teeth yet, so she settled for unbuttoning Helen's pajama top and busying her mouth in other ways.

Helen's breathless moans and whimpers were music to Maggie's ears. This was a dance she knew well, one she loved to share with Helen. As she covered every inch of Helen's chest with her lips, she allowed her hand to slide down her belly and slip under the elastic band of Helen's pants. Taking a hardened nipple into her mouth, Maggie paused her fingers on the thatch of hair above her goal, smirking around the nipple when Helen bucked, her impatience plain.

Switching to her other nipple, Maggie sucked it in her mouth while her fingers slid lower to touch Helen's wetness. Swirling two fingers shallowly in her opening, Maggie moved them upward to lubricate the swollen bundle of nerves. Helen moaned in the back of her throat, hissing as Maggie applied pressure. Knowing Helen's body and what she liked, Maggie brought her higher, fingers moving in different patterns. She listened as Helen's breathing sped up, legs quivering and her hands grasping at the sheets.

Maggie pulled on Helen's earlobe with her teeth before licking inside her ear, fingers pressing down firmly on Helen's clit. With a howl, she came, her body jerking. Her body moved in a sinuous motion, and Maggie guided her through her release with soft caresses. She loved the way Helen moved, claiming her pleasure. As her body slowed down, Maggie kissed her breastbone.

"Wow. That was a wonderful way to start the day." Helen chuckled. She looked at Maggie, a small smile gracing her lips. "Now you've made me hungry." Her smile turned wolfish as she moved to hover above Maggie. "And I plan on eating my fill."

Eyes widening, Maggie counted herself the most fortunate woman in the world. Once Helen became focused on an action, she gave it her all. In this case, Helen's ravenous appetite was focused on her pleasure. Maggie had to agree. It was a wonderful way to start the day.

***

By the time they got to Orlando, Maggie's focus was on the upcoming debate. Even with all the practice, she worried she'd forget to work in policy points or would fail to address critiques well enough to shut them down. Her team worked like a well-oiled machine, though, and their belief in her calmed her nerves. She wore a black pantsuit with thin, white stripes and conservative black pumps. She wanted to project a decisive air. In concession to her sex, she wore gold drop earrings and her favorite gold watch with a diamond face.

She was driven to the site for the debate by her team and escorted to the auditorium. A gaggle of producers met her and brought her backstage to be mic'd up and placed in line for the roll call announcement. Before she knew it, her name was called, and Maggie strode across the stage with a smile while waving at the audience. The lights were bright enough that she couldn't make out faces, but she heard the applause and shouts of support. Once she made it to her podium, she glanced at her notes and centered herself. It was time to show the masses why she was the best choice to be their next president.

As expected, Jimmy Thompson, the sitting vice president, promoted President Sugarman's policies, but he tried to emphasize what he contributed to the administration and how he would continue to move forward with promoting American values. His message was centrist, although his political record showed a strong conservative approach. Maggie relished answering questions on her progressive platform, emphasizing equal rights for all, regardless of ancestry, skin color, or who they loved.

Her largest threats were a handful of privileged white men with old boys' club political networks and family dynasties. Although a few other women were running for the presidency, their numbers were flagging. Besides the obvious threat Vice President Thompson presented, she faced Senator Booker Ashford, a youthful forty-three year old man with a chiseled jaw, straight teeth, a full head of hair, and a perpetual tan. He looked the part, although his political record was bland. He was the first to attack Maggie on family values.

"It's no surprise to hear you denounce same sex relationships while implying not having children is another failing, particularly since your voting record has consistently reflected your unwillingness to enact legislation which would protect all citizens, regardless of their backgrounds, their socioeconomic status, or their family makeup. We live in complex times, and we need leaders who will advance inclusivity, equal pay, and gender parity. Every person is important. Every person should get a fair share. Every person deserves to feel safe and supported and heard." She nodded her head at the crowd as they burst into applause.

The debate continued with most attacks centered on the vice president. Since taking office, some of the president's key platform promises were blocked by Republicans, and the candidates were keen to shine a light on how Vice President Thompson was promising more of the same. The New York governor, Thomas Frankel, took a few swipes at Maggie, but she was able to redirect the conversation by pointing at his mostly white administration and its poor reflection of his constituents' multicultural makeup.

"New York is not comprised of only the privileged one percent. Your job is to represent everyone, including the underprivileged, those with racial and ethnic diversity, and the various socioeconomic levels. Your leadership fails to support the actual population, and your office fails to reflect the diverse composition of its constituents.

"Our nation needs a leader who can recognize and utilize the innovation which comes with diversity. Someone who knows how it feels to go hungry and is dedicated to making sure children do not go to bed without eating. Someone who knows how the stress of unemployment, the stress of low paying jobs, and the stress of not having the ability to pay for necessities can wear on a family. Someone who will offer realistic solutions. I am that person. My political record reflects years of pushing through legislation to level the playing field and support the families that need help."

Someone in the audience whooped, his voice stirring others to stand up and cheer.

Once the debate ended, Maggie smiled for the obligatory photographs, glad-handing each person who approached her. Helen stood by her side, keeping the conversation rolling when needed. Eventually, her team spirited her back to the car, and they returned to the hotel. They retreated to a small conference room they had reserved, ready to debrief and celebrate.

"Preliminary polling shows support for you spiked fifteen percent when you talked about inclusivity, and twenty-one percent when you gave Frankel a dressing down." Zack had his tablet out, scrolling the political wags' sites for feedback.

"Good. I'll want to see the popularity numbers for pre- and post-debate." Maggie looked around at her team. "Tomorrow we'll review the results and I'll want to discuss any weak areas in our platform, as well as what we can leverage. For now, I think it's time for a toast."

After Alice and Darla poured glasses of champagne for everyone and passed them out, Maggie raised her glass. "Your hard work is making a difference, and I'm grateful for the endless hours you have and shall continue to devote to this campaign. To the best team a presidential hopeful could ever have." She clinked her glass with each member before turning to Helen and allowing their flutes to touch.

With a smile as everyone finished toasting, she sipped the alcohol, a sense of accomplishment filling her with pride. She knew they had a long way to go. She knew she faced countless late nights, months of traveling, and too many days spinning negative critiques before she could secure the democratic nomination. None of that mattered. In that moment, Maggie knew all the work, all the heartache, all the sacrifices would be worth it. And someday soon, she would make sure other little girls didn't have to go to bed hungry. Other little girls wouldn't witness casual violence. Other little girls would not be condemned for thinking or feeling or acting differently. She might not be able to help every one of those little girls, and her heart ached with that truth, but she planned to do everything in her power to make her nation stronger by implementing legislation which would level the playing field and promote equality for all.

Chapter Seventeen

1997

ALL SHE SAW WAS white. White in the air, on her face, covering her clothes. She clapped her hands together, and another puff of white suffused the air. A white towel passed through her field of vision, and Maggie took the peace offering. Not that it would stop her from exacting her revenge. She wiped the flour off her face, taking time to remove the substance from her eyes before blinking several times.

"Here. Let me help."

Maggie honest to God growled, exasperated by how much flour covered her and the surrounding area. A gentle hand turned her head, and a wet towel was applied to her face, removing the flour from her forehead, nose, cheeks, and mouth.

"Close your eyes."

With an aggravated sigh, Maggie stood still, eyes closed. She felt the wet edge of the towel brushed against her right eyelid, across her eyelashes, and to the outer edge of her eye before the motion was repeated with the other eye. Once the towel no longer touched her skin, Maggie blinked several times. Her gaze met tawny-colored eyes close enough to make her gasp. She stepped back, beginning to slip until an arm shot out to steady her.

"Watch out! Jeez. Do I have bad breath or something?" Helen let go, her smirk firmly in place as she swiped at Maggie's flour-ridden arms.

Grabbing the towel, Maggie took over, dusting off most of the flour covering her torso, shorts, and bare legs. "I can't believe you did this." She kept up a steady stream of grumbles as she moved to the sink to wet the towel more before moving to the kitchen island to wipe it down.

"In my defense, you did say I couldn't cook, and those were fighting words." Helen retrieved the broom and dustpan from the closet and began sweeping up the mess.

"True, but let me ask you this, counselor. Can you make a chicken dish without it becoming burnt on the outside and raw on the inside?"

Stalling in her task, Helen leaned on the broom and glared. "And yet I made those tasty cookies you scoffed up last week."

"That's not cooking. That's baking, which requires an entirely different skill set." Maggie raised an eyebrow, daring Helen to argue the point.

"It's a more concentrated area of cooking. You don't want to acknowledge it since you suck at baking." Helen swept the rest of the flour into a pile and bent to grab the dustpan. Maggie took the broom and swept the pile into the pan as Helen held it steady.

"That wasn't a good enough reason to make my kitchen look like Antarctica. I was expecting to see penguins waddling in." Maggie looked around the room, glad to find the flour whiteout was cleared up.

"On the contrary, it was. Your disparaging remarks felt like a dagger to the heart."

"Ah, experienced many daggers to the heart, have you?"

"Enough to last a lifetime. Just ask my exes."

"Hard pass, thanks." Maggie returned to the kitchen island and continued dipping the chicken tenders through the beaten eggs before dredging them through a panko, oregano, and garlic powder mixture.

"Baking is an art form, which you should know since you've drooled over my concoctions for the past two years." Helen dumped the flour into the wastebasket before returning the broom and dustpan to its place. "Hopefully you learned your lesson. If not, you won't be tasting my sweets anytime soon."

Head jerking up at the peculiar wording, Maggie watched with fascination as a blush crawled up Helen's neck and stalled on her cheeks. This was happening more frequently. The flirting, the light touches, the longer looks. If Helen were a man, Maggie knew she would label the behavior as attraction.

She shook her head, cracking a smile. "Well, that would be a damn shame." Her exaggerated drawl had the desired effect, Helen's resulting chuckle and eyeroll helping them to tiptoe past the awkwardness of the moment. Finishing her task, Maggie moved the plate of prepared chicken to the counter next to the stove and poured olive oil in a deep pan before turning the heat to medium.

"Wait."

Maggie turned partway to watch Helen grab the apron from the closet hook and bring it to her. She reached for it, but Helen shook her head and stepped closer. Maggie ducked her head and felt Helen place the apron strap around her neck. She straightened up and stiffened when Helen's hands rested on her hips. Feeling her fingers tighten before pushing, she took the directive and turned toward the stove.

"There." Helen whispered next to her ear as she tied the apron strings at the small of her back.

"Thanks." Maggie did her best to act unaffected, but it was hard. Helen's proximity was doing funny things to her. She sipped air while placing the chicken fingers in the pan, making sure to avoid splattering the oil.

"I'll, um, I'll make the salad while you cook the chicken." Helen moved away, much to Maggie's disappointment. She heard her rummaging around in the refrigerator, humming under her breath. After a few minutes of silence, she heard Helen clear her throat.

"Tell me about the fundraiser you're having tomorrow."

Thinking about the convoluted journey to what was now a second run for the state representative seat, Maggie wondered where to begin. "As you know, I lost the first time I ran."

She transferred several pieces of chicken onto a plate that was covered with paper towels. She placed a few more paper towel squares on top of the cooked chicken pieces, blotting them to remove the excess oil.

She snorted, waving Maggie away when she looked at her. "Oh, I remember. I wish I had a recording of your call. That would be great blackmail material."

Maggie remembered how mortified she was when she remembered drunk-dialing Helen. She was glad she hadn't said anything too ridiculous. She shook her head to clear those thoughts away. "Well, the next afternoon I was contacted by Victor Cromsby—"

"The man who won the election?"

"Yes. He offered me the solicitor seat he was vacating."

"That's how you got the job? I didn't realize he could pick his replacement." Helen ripped the lettuce into smaller pieces, throwing them into a large glass bowl.

"Technically, the person's supposed to submit a resume and go through the interview process, but he'd had the position long enough to cut through all the formalities. By the time he was sworn into his new position, I had arranged a sabbatical with my firm and had met with my new colleagues."

She placed the final piece of cooked chicken on the paper towel and turned off the burner. Taking another paper towel square, she blotted the top layer of cooked chicken fingers before moving to the kitchen island. Helen was cutting up tomatoes, so Maggie grabbed the block of cheddar cheese and a knife.

"Anyway, I caught on to the new way of things in no time, and to tell you the truth, I'm glad I lost that election. I didn't know shit." She laughed. "But during the past two years, I've made important connections and learned how to navigate the inner workings of the city."

"Then why are you running again?" Helen poured croutons into a small bowl before leaning her hip against the island to watch Maggie cut into the cheese.

"I wasn't planning to. I was prepared to continue working as the solicitor for at least another election cycle before considering it." She smiled when Helen grabbed a slice of cheese and nibbled on it. "And then I saw Victor last month at Lynn City Hall." She shrugged. "I didn't think anything of it at first. We touch base a few times a month. I told you I was calling him all the time when I first began as the city solicitor."

Helen nodded. "Right. You're lucky you had someone to help you navigate the job."

"No kidding. So, seeing him wasn't just a happy coincidence. Turns out it was a bit more calculated. We caught up at lunch while at Brothers Deli, and he presented the idea of my running for his spot while he runs for the federal position."

"Why though? I mean, shouldn't he stay in the state position longer?"

"The US rep position is opening up, and he wants it. I have no idea why he's willing to link our campaigns together or why he wants me to run for his position, but I'm grateful."

"You didn't ask?" Helen's skeptical expression pulled a snicker from Maggie. She hip-bumped her before going to the refrigerator to grab the salad dressing.

"He said he likes my ambition and willingness to swing for the bleachers. He believes we'll make a great team, and I'm inclined to trust him."

"That's incredible. You live a charmed life, my friend." They filled their plates with food, grabbed two bottles of hard cider, and relocated to the balcony where they could watch the tide coming in.

"A few years ago, I would have argued with you, but I do seem to be attracting incredible people into my life." Maggie lifted her bottle to toast. "To kismet, serendipity, and synchronicity. May we never run out of them."

"Hear, hear." They clinked their bottles and drank from them.

Placing the bottle on the side table, Maggie dipped a chicken finger in duck sauce and took a bite. She sighed, a smile flirting on her lips, enjoying the food, the weather, and the company. "The fundraiser is for HAWC. It's to help abused women and children so they can get away from the abuse and rebuild. I became one of their board of directors last year. I'm friends with one of their legal advocates, Terri Lovitz. We worked together before I became the city solicitor."

"Not at your ex-father-in-law's place, was it?"

"No. After that." Maggie took a moment to breathe in the briny air, glad for the longer days. Although it was after six, they would enjoy a few more hours of sunlight. "Anyway, although I didn't end up working there that long, she was friendly from day one, and we clicked. I mentioned the fundraiser in passing, and Victor was interested in helping. So, we're both giving a little speech. We were able to sell out most of the tables, too."

"I'm sorry I can't go." Helen speared a piece of lettuce, chewing on it. "I've heard of the organization. Their mission overlaps with my work's focus on helping underprivileged and abused kids." She reached out and patted Maggie's knee. "You're doing a good thing." She removed her hand and went back to eating while Maggie stared at the ocean, the thunder of the waves seeming to become louder.

Her knee was on fire, the nerve endings communicating how alive and sensitive they were. She half expected to see she had a sunburn on the area, but that was foolish. Her next thought was to check for a handprint, a definite sign that Helen touched her in such a casual manner. Her knee looked the same as always, though, which confounded her. She tilted her head, studying every inch of skin Helen had touched.

"What? Did I get something on you?"

Chest tightening, Maggie cleared her throat. "No. Nothing's wrong. Just thinking." She grabbed her bottle and drank the cider, shoving her thoughts to the side by pure force of will. She glanced at Helen and shrugged. "There'll be other fundraisers. I'm sure I'll find a way to drag you to one soon enough. And you did agree to help with the meet-and-greet next month."

"It'd be hard not to since my company is hosting it." She giggled. "At least I get a say in what type of food is offered."

"Food's important. Thank God we like some of the same things." Finishing her meal, Maggie placed the empty plate on the table and got comfortable in her chair. Her eyes drifted shut, enjoying the moment. She felt the weight of Helen's stare, ghostly fingers running down her face and neck, cupping her breast. Taking a deep breath, she opened her eyes and saw Helen was staring at the ocean. Her breathing was a bit faster, cheeks flushed.

"So, um…" Helen's voice was breathy and weak. She stopped and coughed. "Let's take a walk." She jumped up, moving inside with her plate and bottle.

Not sure what happened, Maggie scratched her cheek, gaze unfocused.

"You coming?" she heard from inside.

Pressing her lips together, Maggie grabbed her plate and bottle, following the path Helen took. Helen was closing the refrigerator when she entered the kitchen. "Oh, thanks for putting the leftovers in the fridge."

"No problem." Helen twisted her fingers before interlacing them together, resting them on her stomach.

Grabbing her keys from next to the door, Maggie held the door open for Helen before slipping the key in the deadbolt to lock it. They descended the stairs and stepped outside, crossing to the large, grassy island sectioning the street. Once the cars stopped at the nearby stoplight, they crossed to the beach promenade. Maggie led the way toward Red Rock Park, veering to the right to circle to the rocky outcropping at the end.

The light breeze felt good. Although it was late in the day, it was humid and warm. Spying the cumulonimbus clouds rising above the ocean, Maggie wondered whether they'd get any storms. She hoped so. She loved falling asleep to the sounds of heavy rain and rumbling thunder. Smelling moisture in the air, she figured it might happen.

"Want to climb on the rocks?" The tide was starting to come in, but it looked like they had at least an hour before most of the rocks would become submerged. "I mean, we can go to that big one and sit down." Maggie pointed to the largest one at the end.

"I don't do much rock climbing." Helen's eyebrows were drawn together as she stared at the rocks.

"It's okay. I'll help you, and if it makes you feel unsafe, we don't have to climb to that one."

Maggie led her through the opening of the seawall and down the stairs that ended directly on the rocks. She picked the easiest path across the first sets of rocks. Once she made it to the edge of a large rock, she stopped to see how Helen was doing. Helen made her way to her and grinned. "This next part isn't bad. Let me get to the next rock, and I'll help you."

A fissure separated the rocks, and Maggie took her time before hopping to the other rock. She pivoted and held out her hand, planting her feet. Helen stared at the crack, the rocks, and Maggie's hand, her face a kaleidoscope of emotions. She took a deep breath and jumped, landing close, so close to Maggie that she grabbed Helen's hips in reflex. They stood for a moment with their breasts pressed together.

Maggie lost her breath, overwhelmed by the feeling of Helen's body flush against her own. Her hold tightened, and she tried to regulate her breathing. Looking up, she was startled to find Helen's focus on her. It intensified as they maintained their connection,

Helen's chest moving up and down with each breath. Maggie gasped at the feeling and loosened her hold, blinking several times as she let her hands fall to her sides.

"Good jump." Maggie rubbed the back of her neck. "This way." She turned, leading the way across the large rocks. She stopped at a tidepool, searching along the barnacled sides for any shells or sea glass. She picked up pieces of purple and green glass, worn smooth. "Look at this." She turned toward Helen, who stood a few paces away. "Aren't these gorgeous?"

Helen's entire expression softened, her lips curled upward and eyes alight. Maggie couldn't interpret the emotion swirling in her gaze. It warmed her from the inside, sent lines of heat through her veins. Helen's long legs were showcased by her tailored shorts, her toned calves the product of daily walks. The breeze tugged at the loose linen blouse, reminding Maggie of the curves she'd felt mere minutes earlier. She cataloged all these details while waiting for Helen to respond.

"Gorgeous. Yes." Helen's voice was soft enough that Maggie strained to catch her words.

Maggie hesitated, not wanting to leave the moment but also afraid to confront it.

Pocketing the sea glass, Maggie flashed a smile. "Follow me." She picked her way to the biggest rock, which jutted out to sea, and sat down. A moment later she felt Helen's warmth as she sat next to Maggie, and they watched the waves hit the bottom of the massive rock. The current pushed large swaths of seaweed toward the shore, and when Maggie concentrated, she saw jellyfish floating under the waves. The breeze lifted her long hair, lashing it behind her ear one moment and across her cheek the next. Before she could push it back, gentle fingers caught the errant strands and tucked them behind her ear.

"Thanks." Maggie faced Helen, noticing how close they were. "I'm really glad we became friends." She snorted. "Even if your bluntness is a bit much to take at times."

Helen leaned into Maggie, a snigger on her lips. "At least you'll always know where I stand on an issue."

They stayed that way for several minutes, listening to the background chatter of people climbing the surrounding rocks and the seagulls screeching and the waves pounding and the tide slapping. It was a moment of peace within a vortex of motion, a time to appreciate all that had brought her to this moment, shared with a person who made her feel more than she'd ever allowed herself in the past. With Helen, she felt safe, safe enough not to worry about what would happen next.

Maggie sighed before leaning away from Helen. "We should get going before the tide gets higher."

She feared Helen wouldn't climb the rocks with her again if they had to jump over too many submerged areas. As it was, more pools were developing on the lower lying rocks. She stood, offering a hand to help Helen. Her grasp was firm, slender fingers interlacing with her own once they were both standing. Maggie led the way, not releasing Helen's hand until they were back at the seawall. Once on the promenade, she pointed at the side of the rocks. "I used to climb up the rocks from the sand. It's a bit tricky, but I think it was a rite of passage for the neighborhood kids."

"No way you'd get me to climb them." Helen's nose crinkled adorably.

"I wouldn't do it now, either. When I was a kid, I did lots of things I'd never do now. It's not even like I was a daredevil. I just didn't know how dangerous they were."

They took a right to remain on the walkway, slowing their walk to a stroll behind an older Russian couple. The patriarch wore a hat and a pair of dressy slacks, his pale yellow short-sleeve, button-down shirt open at the neck. His hands were clasped behind his back, shoulders stooped as he bent to listen to his wife, who spoke in their native tongue.

Maggie's childhood wasn't something she shared with many people, preferring not to dwell on the unpleasant memories. Yet as she aged, she found herself applying her hard fought wisdom to them, coloring them in shades she hadn't seen while younger.

"Like what? Name your top three daredevil adventures."

Maggie waved her hand. "Too many to sift through. How about I name some without categorizing them?"

"Sure. From the tidbits I've heard, I know you've done a few wild things."

"True. Jumping from rooftop to rooftop while playing chase. Creating obstacle courses which included sliding down a bed that was leaning against a wall. That one probably doesn't sound like much but, the bed nearly reached the ceiling, and I was about half my present height. Breaking into my mom's apartment while leaving my car running in the middle of the street during a thunderstorm. That was fun."

"That sounds like a story." Helen's grin was all the incentive Maggie needed to launch into a narrative of the experience.

"Well, it was on one of these side streets." Maggie pointed to her left. "I was driving to my mom's place during a thunderstorm after finishing classes for the day, and I drove up that one-way street." She pointed toward Greystone Park. "Toward the top, I saw a large tree limb blocking the road. I got out to remove it."

"Oh, no."

"Oh, yes. The car door shut. It locked. Of course, it locked. My car was blocking the road, and cars were lining up behind it. What could I do?"

"How far from your mom's home were you?"

"One block. She had left John and moved into a friend's place. Anyway, I ran to the apartment, but she wasn't answering the doorbell. I broke into the basement, ran up the stairs, burst into her bedroom to retrieve the spare set of car keys, and ignored the fact that I'd run into the middle of my mom having sex with a random guy she met at a dance club."

The incredulous laugh was choked off by Helen's hand over her mouth. "That's awful."

"I can't make this stuff up. I ran back to the car, waved to everyone waiting, and drove back to Cambridge." Maggie shook her head. She hadn't thought about that little mishap for years. They passed the Swampscott sign, and Maggie pointed at Red Rock Bistro. "Shall we get ice cream?"

"Twist my arm."

Maggie had discovered Helen's love for ice cream a few months ago when they were on a similar walk. The line was long, but Maggie didn't mind. Helen kept the conversation going, talking about work, the weather, movies, anything and everything that entered her mind. The running commentary amused Maggie, as Helen jumped from subject to subject with no rhyme or reason. Once they got to the takeout window, Maggie ordered two scoops of coffee ice cream in a sugar cone with jimmies, while Helen decided on chocolate chip in a sugar cone. Once they received their ice cream, they walked back the way they had come, sitting on the first empty bench they saw.

"Do you always get the same flavor ice cream?" Helen's smirk took the sting out of the implied criticism.

"Yup. Do you always choose different flavors?" Maggie licked at the top of the cone to stem the path of the melting ice cream.

"Well, I don't like to get bored."

"Bored? Liking one flavor isn't boring. It's knowing what you like and not wasting time looking for something else you might like better. It's being decisive." Maggie nodded her head to reinforce her point before going back to licking her ice cream.

"Are you saying I'm indecisive?"

A glance at Helen reassured Maggie she was kidding, but before she could answer another person sat next to her. Turning her head, she saw Lizzie's smiling face. "Lizzie. Hi. This is a surprise."

"I was taking a walk and saw you. We haven't talked in a little while, so..." Lizzie shrugged.

'A little while' was a blatant understatement. It had been well over a year. As Maggie got immersed in her new job and met new people, she realized remaining friends with people who traded her trust for more powerful friends was a waste of time. She grew tired of wondering why Lizzie and Kevin felt it necessary to remain friends with Timmy, why they continued to attend the Pearson's dinner parties. Maggie figured this was all a part of growing up—saying goodbye to childhood friends.

Maggie turned toward Helen. "Helen, this is Lizzie." She turned back to Lizzie. "Actually, I met Helen at the meet-and-greet you hosted for my last campaign."

Lizzie poked her head forward to make eye contact with Helen. "Right. Nice to see you again." She leaned back and refocused on Maggie. "Too much time has passed since we last caught up. I'll call you so we can arrange to get together for lunch or something."

When Lizzie stared at her, Maggie realized she was supposed to respond. "Oh, sure. I'll talk to you soon, then." She watched Lizzie get up and flash a smile at her. "Bye." Maggie gave a little wave.

Lizzie's smile became more authentic before she reentered the stream of people walking on the promenade.

Letting out a deep breath, Maggie felt ice cream on her hand and swore. She grabbed the napkin Helen held out for her and licked at the melting ice cream before switching hands to wipe her fingers. "Thanks."

"Sure. What was that weird vibe all about?" Helen's eyes held curiosity.

"That's a long story." She gritted her teeth, staring at the ocean. A soft touch on her arm redirected her focus on Helen.

"I have the time. You can trust me, you know."

Placing her hand on top of Helen's, she nodded. "I do know. It's embarrassing in some ways. And painful." Maggie nodded in the direction Lizzie went. "She and her husband were my closest friends from junior high up until a couple of years ago when I broke up with my ex-husband." She glanced at Helen, nervous how she'd respond to that little revelation.

"I don't remember hearing about this." Helen squeezed her arm. "Is it fair to say it was a bad breakup?"

Maggie gave a mirthless laugh. "Yes. I worked for Timmy's father at a law firm in Cambridge. His father was the one who introduced me to his eldest son, took me under his wing, introduced me to the right people." She shook her head. "When it fell apart with Timmy, I had to start over. New job, new home. Lizzie and Kevin chose to remain friends with Timmy, and I felt betrayed. To be fair, Lizzie tried to smooth things over by hosting that campaign event you attended at her family's restaurant. Since then, though, I've found it hard to be around them. I don't know. Maybe I'm being immature about the whole thing. Maybe it's not fair to hold their friendship with Timmy and his family against them. After all, I'm the one who introduced them to the family and brought them to the dinner parties. At the time I was happy to see Timmy and Kevin getting along." She bit into the top of the cone, wondering whether she was too hard on them.

"Maggie, I can't tell you how to feel, and I wouldn't presume to pass judgment on you. All I know is that their actions hurt you during a time you were feeling vulnerable. Your world was collapsing, and instead of supporting you, they did what was best for them. It seems that Lizzie misses you, though. Perhaps getting together with her to hash it out is worth your time since you were friends for so long. Or you may not feel strong enough to do that. Maybe you never will. Trying to protect yourself isn't a weakness. So, think about what you want. If you want to work on getting that friendship back, I'm sure she'd love it. If you feel that isn't a good option for you, then let it go. Whatever you decide is up to you."

"You know, during the breakup and all that came with it, I resented their decisions, but the truth is I made bad decisions, too. Starting with going out with Timmy, beginning a romantic relationship with him when I wasn't really attracted to him, and then agreeing to marry him. Jesus." Maggie ran a hand across her face. "I made so many stupid decisions based on what I thought I needed to do to have a better life. Get away from where I started. I figured the feelings would develop, and in the meantime, I counted the blessings that came with him—the big, supportive family, the connections, the father figure. When I think about it now, all I can see is how I used him to get ahead. How am I any different from Lizzie and Kevin? Depending on the motivation, any action can be rationalized."

She looked at Helen. "And here I am, back in my hometown. I didn't get away from anything. This has been a hell of a learning curve. You know, the whole life thing." She shook her head.

"Don't be so hard on yourself. At least you can see what happened and try not to make the same mistakes with your next relationship."

Maggie balled up her used napkin and rose to throw it out, thinking about Helen's words. She stood before the bench and smiled down at Helen. "You're pretty good at the whole advice thing."

"I'm good at giving advice." Helen chuckled and rose. "Not so great at taking it."

They walked in the direction of Maggie's apartment, the sun inching closer to the horizon. It was partly obscured by the clouds rolling in. They walked in companionable silence, and Maggie loved not having to scrabble for a conversation topic. She did wonder whether Helen dated. She couldn't remember discussing her private life. For all she knew, Helen could be married or divorced or a serial dater. She had no idea.

"I know what you're thinking." Helen's teasing tone broke through Maggie's musings.

Maggie looked at Helen, eyebrows raised. "Is that right?" They were passing the top of Red Rock Park, the waves slapping at the seawall with each surge.

"Yes, it is." Helen linked her arm in Maggie's, her stride slowing to match Maggie's amble. "You're wondering whether I'm in a relationship. For all you know, I could be married with four kids."

Maggie's guffaw took them both by surprise, her body jackknifing as laughter overtook her, dragging them to a halt in the middle of the walkway. "I'm sorry. Sorry." She saw the miffed look on Helen's face and fought to control her laughter, waving her hands in a clearing motion. "It's just, the image of four mini-Helens running around underfoot is hilarious. God, can you imagine debating all the reasons why the bedroom should not be cleaned? I bet a kid of yours not only could but would enumerate them from strongest to weakest points."

She took a deep breath to settle herself and looked at Helen. Her perplexed expression nearly pushed Maggie into another round of laughter, but she bit her lower lip and stared hard at the ground until she felt she could control herself. She patted the arm still linked with hers. "All right. I'll stop teasing."

They resumed walking, climbing the concrete staircase and stopping to lean against the railing overlooking the ocean. Feeling Helen's stare, Maggie shifted to face her. "So, tell me. Are you married? Dating someone? Are you a mom?" She was concerned to see Helen hunched, arms crossed over her chest and eyes flicking over the water.

Helen rolled her shoulders and lifted her chin before meeting Maggie's gaze.

"No kids. I'm not with anyone right now. My last relationship crashed and burned about five months ago when I found myself thinking about someone else. It wasn't fair to her. And although it's quite possible I won't ever be with that person, I knew it was the right thing to do." Helen turned to lean against the railing once more, arms extended before her and fingers laced.

The word "her" seemed to hang in the air between them, as though highlighted in bright yellow. Maggie glanced at Helen and was startled by the fear and insecurity she saw. Drawing herself up to her full height, shoulders back and lips pressed in a straight line, Maggie tried to control her anger. She narrowed her eyes. "Do you think I'm prejudiced?"

Helen's eyebrows lowered enough to create a furrow between them. "What?"

"Do you think it makes a difference to me that you date women? I mean, have I ever given you that impression? Because that's the only reason I can think of for why you never trusted me enough to confide in me before now." Maggie ran a hand through her hair, dragging her gaze away from Helen to watch a seagull careen through the air.

"Maggie, be realistic." The tiredness in Helen's voice surprised her. "People don't always react well when they realize a person's gay. Sometimes people pretend to be okay with it, but they become distant, and suddenly they're too busy to meet. One day you wake up and realize the relationship has disappeared. And I'm not saying you'd do that, but we're still getting to know one another."

Staring into brown eyes ringed with worry, Maggie shook her head. Understanding flooded through her. Helen's reticence had nothing to do with Maggie. Relief coursed through her.

"Nah. I know the real reason you never told me." At Helen's confused look, Maggie allowed a smirk to surface. "You were afraid I'd guess your big secret. I'm the one you're thinking of all the time." Maggie brought her hand to her chest, fluttering her eyelashes several times. "You're in loooooove with me." She laughed when Helen shoved her away, a scowl on her face. "It's okay, Helen. I get it. After all, I'm quite the catch."

"Yeah, right. As if I'd want to be with a pushover."

"Pushover?" Maggie squawked, insulted. "I'm not a pushover. I'm flexible. Easygoing. Besides, someone who argues all the time is contrary." She shrugged. "Totally unnecessary. I'm a great city solicitor because I know how to negotiate instead of fighting for everything."

"Tell me this. When's the last time you made an important decision because you wanted to do it, not someone else? Do you even want to run for office, or is that a leftover idea from the previous time?"

Maggie's first instinct was to say it was what she wanted to do, but she suppressed it. It was true, she hadn't thought of running for public office until Timmy's father talked to her about it. It was also true she wouldn't be running now if not for Victor's proposal that they help one another. However, she was excited about the campaign. She knew more now about her community and what the people needed than two years ago. She cared more.

"Those are good questions." Maggie peered at Helen, unable to read her facial expression. "I do want to run for office, even though it wasn't originally my idea either time. This campaign is different for many reasons. I have a better understanding of what I'm doing. I want to make our community better for others. And I've worked on this campaign every step of the way, developing my campaign platform and arranging to meet people in the community. The last campaign was spoon-fed to me. I was told what to advocate and where to be. That's not true this time."

Maggie indicated the ocean, listening to the roar of the waves. "Although I learned as a kid it was safer for me to go with the flow, sometimes it didn't work out. Sometimes the undertow was dangerous, and I wasn't prepared to deal with the competing push and pull I found myself caught in. Sometimes I nearly drowned. That's how I felt while I was married. What you categorize as a pushover I believed was a necessary course for survival. Leaving that relationship and cutting ties with all that was associated with it was probably the first time I swam against the tide."

She glanced to the side, noting how she had Helen's full attention. "Since then I've made more decisions based on what I want, and I'll admit, it's hard for me. I'm not like you. I don't grab life by the horns and wrangle it into submission. But I'm no longer the girl who floats on top of the waves, following wherever the tide moves."

Helen threw up her hands and exhaled loudly. "Well, great. That was the last roadblock to not falling for you. Now what am I going to do?" She pointed at Maggie. "You need to tell me something horrible about yourself. It's for the good of our friendship."

"Yeah, no. You're out of luck because I'm the epitome of a perfect woman."

Helen's snort was music to her ears. She pulled on Helen's arm to indicate her desire to walk, and they fell into step. Maggie felt a sense of relief after revealing her past to Helen. She couldn't remember a time she'd opened up as much to a friend. Once they arrived at her apartment, she climbed the first two stairs, pausing when Helen remained on the sidewalk. "Aren't you coming up?"

"No, I think I'll get going."

Retracing her steps, Maggie searched her eyes. "Everything okay? I promise I don't mind that you're in love with me. I'm irresistible." She chuckled as she watched Helen roll her eyes.

"Yeah. You wish. Give me a hug, you lug."

Walking into outstretched arms, Maggie snuggled into Helen's neck for a moment, arms wrapping around her. When she felt Helen's arms loosen, she stepped back. "Well, don't be a stranger."

"I won't be." Her features softened, a small smile flirting with her lips. "I'll talk to you soon. I promise."

Once Maggie nodded, Helen walked to her car, waving before she got in. It wasn't until she drove away that Maggie realized she was still smiling.

"You're such a goof." Shaking her head, she turned to enter her building, the shared hug chasing away the effects of the oncoming storm's strengthening breeze.

***

Unlike the first campaign, Maggie didn't receive the election results while watching television by herself. She stood with a small group of volunteers in one of the smaller conference rooms at the Hawthorne Hotel in Salem. A few long tables were pushed against one wall with appetizers and water on them. Two televisions had been rolled in on mobile stands and set up at each end of the room, blaring election results.

The Pickman room was elegant with its heavy, gold embroidered curtains, crystal chandeliers, and a wall-to-wall forest green rug boasting a tessellating pattern of serrated leaves that drew the eye. The fireplace was painted white, its ionic columned pilasters and elaborately carved center tablet in keeping with the refined opulence the hotel emanated.

Hearing someone shout to turn up the volume of the television, Maggie moved toward the closest one, watching the newest campaign results flash across the screen. First the national elections' results were reviewed, a few shouts of approval filling the air whenever a Democratic candidate was declared the winner. Once they switched to the congressional races, Maggie looked around for Victor. She saw him off to the side, his wife and two daughters standing next to him. ABC discussed the results for each US Representative district, and as they got closer to announcing the results for the sixth district, the crowd became quieter. By the time they reached Victor's election, it seemed like the entire room was holding its breath.

As the numbers flashed on the screen, a roar of approval erupted in the room. Maggie clapped in delight, happy for Victor. He beat four other contenders by a landslide. The commentary continued for the other districts, but most turned away from it. Maggie remained focused, listening to the results for each of the state representative races. Her race was for the 10th district. Maggie was surprised when Victor's voice rose above the chattering.

"Quiet down. Maggie's race is coming up."

It felt as if the reporter's words were elongated, each syllable pronounced with infinite care. After five million years, he finished one sentence, leading up to the words she wanted to hear. Needed to hear.

"And in the 10th district, newcomer Maggie Ambrose, who lost the same election two years ago to Victor Cromsby, learned her lesson by teaming up with him. He successfully ran for the US Representative spot and supported her run for his former position. We can confidently call this race as a marked victory for Maggie Ambrose, who captured eighty-four percent of the votes as reported by seventy-six percent of the polling sites. Congratulations, Congresswoman Ambrose."

Anything else the commentator said was lost on Maggie, as supporters shouted congratulations and hands patted her on her back. She looked up to see Victor's smiling face, and she reached out to hug him. She pulled back, euphoria filling her. *This is what it feels like to be a winner*, she thought. The smiles, the exuberant shouts, and the adrenaline coursing through her felt incredible.

"Thank you, Victor. I'm so grateful."

"No more than I am. We make a good team, and we're going to do great things together." He took her hand in his and raised their arms high above their heads. The assembled supporters applauded, whooping and cheering their approval.

Once Victor lowered their arms, the assembly hushed, expectant faces turned toward them. "Today we have won a great victory. Today we have proven how we can help one another by joining forces. We have proven what teamwork looks like. And this is just the beginning. With Maggie in Boston and me in DC, we're going to represent you to the best of our abilities. Thank you for all your help getting us to this point."

As everyone clapped, Maggie spied Helen at the fringe of the group, her face shining with happiness. Victor's family joined them after conversations restarted and people milled about the room.

"Maggie, this is my wife, Anita, and my two girls, Cheri and Sarah."

Anita was a small woman, at least a head shorter than Victor, with light brown hair, dark brown eyes, a button nose, and thin lips. Her narrow face reminded Maggie of a red fox, which was reinforced when she smiled. "Maggie, I've heard so much about you. It's a pleasure to meet you. Congratulations on your win." She held out a hand, and Maggie shook it with enthusiasm.

"Thank you. I have learned so much from Victor. One of the best things I did was lose the last race to him." She grimaced. "And it was so easy."

Cheri and Sarah cackled at her joke, and Maggie flashed a smile at them. "I've also heard about both of you. Your father loves to brag about how well you're doing in school."

"Oh, yeah. He loves to talk about us." Cheri twirled hair around her finger, shifting from one foot to the other as she peered at Maggie. "If he has his way, we'll end up entering politics in a few years."

Sarah elbowed her. "She doesn't care about that. That's years away." She flashed a bright smile. "I voted for you. I like the issues you talked about. I know you don't need a lot of help, but I'd love to be a summer intern. Keep me in mind."

Maggie couldn't hold back a snicker. She liked Sarah's bluntness. "I will definitely keep that in mind."

"We'd love to have you for dinner," Anita said. "We'll figure out a date and let you know."

"Thank you, Anita. I'd love to come over." A hand on her arm pulled her attention to a few volunteers who wanted to say goodnight. "Excuse me, please."

After receiving nods from Victor and Anita, she turned toward the small group and chatted with them for a few minutes. Soon she found herself circulating the room, thanking supporters and accepting their congratulations. Turning toward the next person, Maggie was happy to see Helen.

"There you are. I saw you earlier and got swept up by others. I'm sorry it's taken so long to talk to you." She noticed Helen was wearing an emerald green, long sleeved dress that made her eyes pop. Her hair was pulled back in a tasteful updo, a few curly loose tendrils emphasizing her face. She was wearing high heels that made her taller than Maggie. She liked it.

"Are you kidding? This is your night. There was no way I was going to miss being here. And don't worry about not talking earlier. You needed to do your thing. I didn't mind waiting." Helen pulled Maggie into a tight hug, letting go too soon for Maggie's liking. She stepped back, folding her arms loosely. "Congratulations. You're going to do a great job."

"Thank you. I know if I don't, I'll hear all about it." Maggie smirked. "It's friends like you who'll keep me humble."

"You bet." Helen looked past Maggie's shoulder. "Looks like your running mate is getting ready to go. Are you planning to stay much longer?"

Catching Victor's eye, Maggie waved farewell. She watched them don their coats as they exited the room. Turning back, she smiled at Helen. "I see no reason to stay any longer. Are you ready to go?"

"Sure am. Do you have a coat?"

"No. I kept it in the car." It was an odd quirk she picked up years ago. If she was parked close enough, she preferred to shed her winter wear so she didn't have to worry about forgetting anything later. During years past, she'd lost enough scarves and gloves to fill a lost and found bin. She still mourned the loss of one of her favorite L.L. Bean ski gloves.

They walked through the hotel and out the exit door, the winter wind pushing at Maggie's thin blouse. She shivered. "I'm across the street. Where are you?"

"Same." They hustled toward the small parking lot. "Get in for a minute."

Helen unlocked her Volvo, and Maggie slid into the front passenger seat. Once Helen closed her door, the whistling wind became muted, creating a calm oasis. She turned toward Helen, who sat with her hands on her lap as she stared through the windshield.

Taking the opportunity to study Helen, she admitted to herself that she found the woman attractive. It wasn't merely her physical features that drew her in. It was her fiery personality and big heart. Every day she directed her energy toward helping adolescents in high-risk communities. She used her law degree not to earn a high salary but to give future generations a real chance at living successful lives, regardless of their backgrounds, their economic standings, or their family makeup.

The streetlight lit up Helen's profile, her cheekbones in sharp relief. Maggie reached out to rest a hand on her shoulder. "What's up?"

Helen grasped her hand and turned, reaching out to capture Maggie's other hand. She regarded Maggie with an inscrutable look, one that made her nervous. "Maggie, you know I value our friendship, right?"

Swallowing hard, Maggie nodded. She felt a prickling on her scalp, and she twitched, wanting to move but afraid to interrupt Helen. She watched Helen's tongue peek out to wet her lips. Helen looked down at their clasped hands, clearing her throat several times. When she looked up, something shifted in her eyes, a sense of determination emphasized by the way she rolled back her shoulders.

"I have a confession to make, and I'm afraid you won't want to remain my friend. It's that fear which has stopped me so many times from saying something, but it's gotten to the point that I can't keep this from you. It's too hard. Whatever your reaction is, at least I'll know and can move forward." She squeezed Maggie's hands. "No matter what, I want you to know that I don't want to lose you."

Astonished by the naked fear she saw swimming in Helen's eyes, Maggie shook her head. "What are you talking about? You're not going to lose me. If I've made you feel like I don't care about you, I'm sorry."

"No, Maggie. No. It's nothing like that. It's…so you remember that day at the beach when I told you I'm gay?"

A small smile inched its way across Maggie's face. "You mean the day you admitted that you're in love with me?" She kept her voice light, seeking to make Helen laugh. She frowned when Helen's gaze shifted again. She squeezed Helen's hands to gain her attention. "You know I was just kidding, right?"

"Well, that's the thing." Helen looked up, took a deep, steadying breath, and leaned toward Maggie, her eyes boring into hers. Beseeching her to meet her halfway.

Maggie's body felt like it was on fire, excitement and fear warring for control. When Helen was close enough for Maggie to feel her hot breath on her lips, her eyes drifted closed. A cascade of sensation bombarded her at the first touch of soft lips. The taste of mint and coffee. The smell of vanilla and musk. The sound of uneven breathing. The feel of fingers curled around hers. She didn't try to hold back a whimper, her thoughts jumbled. The kiss was slow, so slow Maggie struggled not to deepen the kiss. She tilted her head, opening her lips the tiniest bit, inhaling through her nose.

Helen moved a hand to cup her jaw, her thumb rubbing against Maggie's flushed cheek. Maggie felt as if she were going to jump out of her skin. She'd never experienced a kiss like this. Helen shifted closer, and Maggie pulled her forward by the neck, no longer willing to be passive. Although she hadn't anticipated sharing a kiss with Helen, she sure as hell was going to make it count.

Helen's moan made her feel things, things she wanted to explore. Things she hadn't felt before. Not ever. Remaining cognizant of Helen's hairdo, Maggie refrained from sifting through her luxurious tresses. *Next time*, she promised herself. If there was a next time. God, she hoped so. Kissing Helen was addictive.

When Helen began to pull back, Maggie barely held back her protest. She kept her eyes closed, leaning her forehead against Helen's for a moment while she tried to catch her breath. With difficulty, Maggie opened her eyes and leaned back. "Holy shit."

Although her words were whispered, Helen's laugh was welcome. "So, now you know. I realize this is a lot and you probably need to think about things, but now you have all the facts." Helen shrugged, her shy demeanor at odds with her usual forceful personality.

"Well, counselor, you present a strong case." Maggie cracked a smile. "And let me say, before I take it under advisement, that you're an awesome kisser." She was glad to see Helen's resulting smirk and the jaunty tilt of her head.

Trapping her lower lip between her lips, Maggie stared at Helen. "You are hella brave. But, as you know, no guts, no glory." She leaned and delivered a short, intense kiss, swiping her tongue across the seam of Helen's lips. When she gasped, Maggie took the opportunity to brush against her tongue before pulling back. She smirked when Helen chased after her, eyes remaining closed a moment longer before her hazy gaze greeted her. "Rest assured we will be exploring this again. Get some sleep. I'll call you tomorrow."

Helen's stunned look nearly stopped Maggie from leaving, but she wanted to think about the ramifications of exploring this change in their relationship. No matter what happened, she was determined to keep Helen in her life. "Good night, Helen."

Maggie left the warmth of Helen's feelings and strutted to her car, knowing she was being watched. She felt attractive and powerful and coveted. It felt damn good.

Chapter Eighteen

ALICE ENTERED THE HOTEL conference room where Maggie and her team were reviewing policy points for the next day's debate at a near run, making a straight line toward Maggie, who half-rose in concern.

"Turn on the TV. Fox." One of the volunteers retrieved the remote control to do as directed, and as the political pundits filled the screen, Maggie felt dread pool in her belly. For Alice to come in like a bat out of hell, it must be bad. One of Alice's best qualities was how calm she was, regardless of the amount of work thrown at her or how often plans had to be reworked.

"For those of you just joining us, a damaging exposé was released today, merely a day before the final Democratic presidential debate of the year, giving us an intimate view of Senator Ambrose's first marriage and subsequent divorce to Timothy Pearson III, son of the well-known corporate attorney whose clients include Coca-Cola, General Electric, and Gillette. Her ex-husband sat down with Sandra Boustin this morning to discuss their marriage, its breakdown, and why she should not become our next president."

The shot switched from the news anchors to a different studio, where the reporter sat with Timmy. He was dressed in khakis and a button-down shirt, his cowlick sticking up and stubble covering his weak jaw and double chin. The years had not been kind to him.

"Thank you for being here with us today. Can you tell us why you feel it's necessary to come forward with information about Senator Ambrose when your relationship with her ended more than twenty-five years ago?"

Clearing his throat, he bounced his foot on his knee, hands grasping the ends of the seat's armrests. "Yeah. I know it might not seem relevant after so long, but the American people have a right to know who they're considering electing as our next president. It's all well and good when she talks about giving everyone a level playing field and equality for all, but we need a leader who believes in family values, who believes in God. Someone who's a role model for our children. I knew her when she was just starting out. She was a hard worker. I'll give her that. She was ambitious, and she was willing to do what she needed to get ahead."

"Are you saying that's no longer true?"

"No. Well, I wouldn't know. It doesn't matter either way. What matters is the way she goes about it. You see, I married her with the sincere belief that she loved me. I gave my heart to her, and I pledged myself to her in front of God, our families, and our friends. I grew up Catholic, so I took those vows seriously. What I found out much later was that she married me to capitalize on my family's connections. She used me to further her career aspirations, not because she loved me. She came from a horrible childhood, and she was willing to do anything to leave that behind, including misleading me. What's worse is she made a mockery of my religious beliefs. And after all that, it came out that she's a lesbian." He shook his head and shrugged. "Do we really want to elect a woman who makes false promises, turns away from God, and uses people for her own ends? I mean, God fearing people know the unnaturalness of being a lesbian is enough of a reason not to elect her. She's not a proper role model for our children, not that she'd know since she isn't even a mother."

"So, you're saying she never loved you? That she married you so she could advance her career through your family's connections?"

"Yes. I even have a copy of an email she sent to her best friend talking about whether she should marry me. She said she had to weigh the pros and cons, including her being a part of my family, the connections that afforded her, and the influence on her career trajectory."

"Do you have a copy with you?" The interviewer looked like a dog about to receive the juiciest bone ever, her mouth slightly ajar and saliva gleaming on her lips and tongue.

"I'm not going to release it at this time. Look, I realize people are going to think I'm being petty, that I'm digging up old dirt because I'm bitter. That's not the case. Thinking back on our relationship, I realize she needed help, and I didn't see it. I didn't want to see it. No one wants to acknowledge that the person they love is sick. And I felt guilty once I found out why she acted the way she did."

"You say she was sick?"

"She still is. You see, she has a chemical imbalance in her brain that makes her gay. It's comparable to being bipolar. If I'd known I would have helped her, gotten her the medical treatment she needed. Now she's been living like this for decades, and she wants to be our president? No. I couldn't live with myself if I didn't say something. People need to know. Our great nation deserves to know what type of person she really is. Dishonorable, manipulative, immoral, and sick."

"Well, we thank you for stepping forward to warn the American people. With the next Democratic debate at hand, I'm sure your information will serve as a great launching pad for questions regarding Senator Ambrose's capacity to lead our nation. Thank you for being here today."

"Thank you for having me."

As the program continued with the news anchors discussing Timmy's revelations and speculating on how it might affect the election, Maggie sat with one hand on her stomach, body trembling. The anger she felt was white hot and all-consuming. She took deep, slow breaths, counting silently to five with each inhale and exhale. Her eyes became unfocused, the voices around her becoming a constant buzzing. The assertions were outrageous, but she feared Timmy's mendacious words could influence enough voters to impact her numbers. A hand on her shoulder startled her. She looked up into Helen's concerned gaze. "When did you get here?"

"I was close by. I came as soon as I heard." She squatted in front of Maggie's chair, grasping her hands in a firm grip. "We're going to get through this. You have a great team, and they will show the nation all the reasons why no one should take that man-child seriously. I'm sure it won't take long for people to realize that emasculated, sorry excuse for a man is resentful and embarrassed by the information about him found in your memoir. He's striking out to try and embarrass you. But his actions won't work. In fact, it will backfire, because whereas before people may have viewed him as a man who wasn't a good spouse, now he'll be viewed as an inadequate, weak, bitter man. Someone who was never going to be an equal to you."

Sniffing back her fears, her anger, her mortification, Maggie nodded, squeezing Helen's hands. "Thank you."

She took a deep breath, centering herself before looking at the rest of her team. Most had their eyes glued to a computer screen, tablet, cell phone, or the television. Raising her voice to signal everyone to listen, Maggie focused on what needed to happen. "Okay, people. Although unexpected, we need to address the accusations levied by my ex-husband. I want suggestions, action plans, and counterattacks in one hour."

She rose, pulling Helen up with her. "I need some time until then." She held Helen's hand tightly, her politician's face firmly in place as they made their way back to their hotel room.

Once the door clicked close, Maggie sank onto the bed, head bowed. Her mind raced, thinking of Timmy, of her failed marriage, of what she lost through that divorce, of the endings and beginnings. She wouldn't trade any of those experiences, knowing each heartbreak, each challenge, each weakness and trial and failure made her who she was today. Those experiences had pushed her to be honest with herself. Pushed her to take stock in her aspirations, what she was willing to do to obtain them, and what lines she would no longer cross. One of those lessons was how her unhappiness was not acceptable, even when the trade-off was being a part of a supportive family, a powerful dynasty, and a fun circle of friends.

She remembered the email she sent to Lizzie. It was a few weeks before the wedding, soon after Timmy showed up drunk, interrupting her intense studying session for the bar exam. She was upset and frustrated. She wondered whether he would always act according to his own desires, pushing aside her needs. She questioned whether they were getting married too soon, that maybe she was mistaking her feelings for the benefits being attached to him could provide.

"Talk to me." Helen wrapped her in a tight embrace, head resting on top of Maggie's hair. With a sigh, Maggie reveled in the sense of security which stole through her. Even during the first hug they'd shared, she'd felt safe in her arms. Tucking her nose into the crook of Helen's neck, she breathed in her familiar soothing scent. Helen's presence ameliorated all the challenges thrown at her. Her love gave Maggie strength. She squeezed Helen around the waist before pulling back enough to meet her eyes.

"I'm embarrassed. I'm angry." Maggie shook her head. "I thought I'd left that life long ago. It boggles my mind that he did this. And it hurts to think he hates me so much that he would dredge up an email from before we got married, that he would imply I have a brain chemical imbalance, that I was a scheming, heartless bitch using him to get ahead in my career." Tears stung her eyes, and she swiped at them, exhaling forcefully. "And the worst is that I feel he's justified in thinking I used him. I didn't realize I was doing that, not until after the divorce, but I was. He didn't deserve the way I treated him. But I need to get past all those feelings so I can go back into that conference room and figure out how to discredit him well enough that no one will think twice about his accusations."

"This is a mean world to try to live in, but you have a top-notch team to help you. You're not alone. Never alone. And we will find out who pulled the puppet strings on that poor, spineless man who had the chance to spend his life with you and failed to keep you. I'm sure he regrets that. No one recovers fully when confronted with the success of the one who got away. You're powerful and intelligent and funny and beautiful and strong. You're a phoenix, flying high above all the vitriol he spews, all the useless fist-waving, all the rationalizations he spreads for his shortcomings. Anyone with half a brain can see who he is and why you left him. Now." Helen rose, hand extended. "How about we take a nice shower and go downstairs? I know you don't want to go outside, so I'll let the team know to order food for all of us."

Staring at the hand, at her wife, Maggie smiled. "Sounds like a plan."

She took Helen's hand, letting her pull her up into waiting arms. Kissing her on the lips, Maggie hugged her before stepping toward the bathroom, shoulders straightening as resolve flowed through her. She refused to let this sink her campaign. The Pearson dynasty was about to take a major hit. And she was holding the bat.

The headlines were as expected, if not quite as vicious as Maggie had feared: *Voting for the Absence of Family Values, A Modern-Day Marriage of Convenience Gone Wrong, The Inner Dealings of a Conniving Career Politician*, and her favorite, *Is Senator Ambrose in her Right Mind?*

She scoffed, pushing the newspapers away and leaning back in her chair. She looked around the table at her top-tier staffers. Yesterday they'd outlined a plan of attack to discredit Timmy's message, planning to utilize left leaning commentators and liberal groups. They discussed whether she should sit down for a one-on-one interview to discuss the email, the marriage, and the fallout from the divorce. In the end, they decided to get her out and about, business as usual, with an emphasis on stump speeches and photo ops. Since today was the final debate of the year, they expected parts of the interview to be used to attack her credibility. Her group worked feverishly to word possible answers and poll what would be best received, Maggie approving or shooting down what they gave her.

"Let's go over where we are." Maggie waved toward Alice, knowing she would run the meeting.

"You have photo ops at one of the large farms and a factory this morning, and you're meeting with the union this afternoon. We've released statements on all the social media platforms and for the most part, the responses are positive. Bob met with our state field directors via video this morning to give them their marching orders. Eileen's been watching the polling numbers while Zack's keeping track of people's reactions to the exposé."

"Right. Polling's showing a dip in conservative areas, no surprise there. But, from what I can see, you aren't being affected that much. I mean, no one who's endorsed us has pulled their support, and you've been married to Helen long enough that the lesbian angle isn't a surprise. The fact that the email was written so long ago helps, and he didn't do himself any favors by going on television looking the way he did." Eileen Brown, a perspicacious graduate of MIT who had a wicked sense of humor and a sharp mind, looked up from her paperwork, her mouth curled with contempt. "And frankly, anyone who equates gayness with a brain chemical imbalance should get their own sanity checked."

The chuckles around the table brought a smile to Maggie's lips.

"We had an influx of volunteers in the more progressive, LGBTQ-friendly areas." Bob smiled. "From what we can see, the exposé was a bust on their end."

"Good. I'm going to act as if it's business as usual, but I want final drafts of answers for possible attacks I might face at tonight's debate forwarded to me by noon, along with updates on polling and any op-eds mentioning it. Thank you, team." Maggie nodded her head, waiting as everyone except Alice and Darla left. "Anything else I need to know?"

Darla passed her some documents. "Here are the drafts of the op-eds regarding Pearson's interview. It discusses that time in your life, refers to parts of your memoir, and emphasizes how like most young professionals, you made mistakes."

"We decided not to include how female politicians' lives are held up to unprecedented scrutiny and higher standards while being required to remain calm and focused on the issues at all times. Instead, we tapped LGBTQ groups who agreed to write on those topics as part of a series about females in various industries, including tech companies, actors, scientists, and political leaders."

With a nod, Maggie rose from her chair and smoothed down her suit jacket. It was time to get to work.

Throughout the day Maggie kept a smile on her face, even when hecklers called her unfit to lead, even when protesters held up signs telling the world she didn't promote family values, and even when far right supporters called her a witch. It took all of her self-discipline not to stop and cackle, to proclaim herself an acolyte of Laurie Cabot. She pushed away any reckless thoughts and concentrated on ignoring the negative publicity. She was determined not to lose her cool.

On their way to the debate, Alice and Zack peppered her with questions, allowing her to practice by using the agreed upon language for her responses. She wore a navy skirt-suit to project herself as trustworthy, responsible, and qualified, a simple gold chain and her gold watch as accessories. Her hair and makeup were styled to seem as natural as possible while detracting attention from the effects of constant traveling and not enough sleep. She looked the part of a competent leader, and she was ready to prove it.

In comparison to the first Democratic debate, this one wasn't as crowded by candidates. The Democrats who failed to qualify had suspended their campaigns, and from now until Super Tuesday,

Maggie knew the trickling effect would continue, politicians cutting their losses as their polling numbers decreased. Out of the fifteen Democratic hopefuls who had jockeyed for position months ago, only seven remained.

As during the previous debates, Maggie walked across the stage with a bright smile and jaunty wave. She was stationed center stage between Vice President Thompson and Senator Ashford. Pushing everything from her mind but the ensuing questions, Maggie presented a calm demeanor, even when the eventual potshots about the exposé came up.

Congressman Whitman threw the first stone. It was more like a pebble, the criticism on morality too subtle to hurt. "Unlike Senator Ambrose, I have worked hard to make our nation better. I started as a mayor in Pittsburgh, learning about the complex issues facing large cities. I climbed up the ladder, working with the community, partnering with other community leaders. And I stand before you today, ready to keep on fighting to maintain the integrity and morality our nation's politicians must embody to make America great."

Maggie barely held back her incredulity as Congressman Whitman spoke. She knew for a fact that he was connected to organized crime, having seen the investigation documents through the report submitted to HSGA. She knew he would be dragged before the grand jury any day now.

"Senator Ambrose, do you have any response to Congressman Whitman's comments?"

"Yes. Thank you. I applaud Congressman Whitman's efforts to help his hometown and later his state, and I agree that our country has the responsibility of electing politicians who reflect the attributes of an honorable, ethical leader. What I must take issue with is the assertion that I don't qualify."

Maggie stared at the video monitor, speaking with a calm, even tone. "As a young, twenty-something urban professional, I faced many life changing decisions after a childhood bereft of positive role models. I made mistakes, and it took time for me to recognize them. Longer to rectify them. I didn't know what it felt like to be supported by a family, by adults, by anyone who wanted what was best for me. All I knew was how to work hard. All I knew was how to do what I was told from people who I believed had my best interests at heart. All I knew was how to float along, accepting the currents which pushed me in one direction instead of another and to keep my head above the water.

"When my marriage failed, when I lost my first election, when I lost my closest friends and the people who I believed were my family, it felt like I was drowning. But it's been more than twenty-five years. I'm no longer that naïve, passive young lady. I have grown, I have evolved, and I have learned to stand up not only for myself but for those who cannot. The underserved, the underrepresented, those who suffer discrimination due to the color of their skin, due to the accents heard when they speak, due to their socioeconomic positions, due to whom they love. And I will not stop fighting for equality, for safer communities, or for bodily autonomy. We are stronger as a community. My vow is to help everyone—those who have the support of loved ones, and those who need someone to give them that stability."

No further references were made to the exposé, and Maggie was able to reiterate the main planks for her platform. She knew, even before the numbers came in, that she had won the night. She met with her core team after the debate, high on adrenaline and a sense of triumph.

"The numbers are coming in. Support from likely Democratic voters spiked seventeen point two percent after the debate, up six point two percent from before the debate. And your favorability rating jumped nine point one points. Also, according to Google Trends, searches for bodily autonomy spiked more than three thousand percent during the debate, and you were the top trending topic across the US." Eileen looked positively giddy, her face flushed and eyes dancing. She pushed her laptop back and turned it so everyone could read the numbers scrolling in.

Walter took over, passing out the documents he held. "We have a set of campaign ads from marketing for you to review, as well as your itinerary for the next two weeks with appearances, rallies, and photo-ops, and a meeting with the New York police union. Word has it they're leaning toward endorsing you, which will be a big middle finger to Governor Frankel. Once that happens, other large unions will fall into line, like Chicago, Los Angeles, and Philadelphia. The Boston police union's endorsement paved the way."

"All right. We have an early flight tomorrow and once we get back to DC, we'll need to capitalize on tonight's win." Maggie stood. "Get some sleep." She reached out a hand toward Walter for the memory stick with the ads on them, knowing it would take time before she could settle down enough to sleep. "I'll review them tonight."

As Maggie made her way back to her hotel room, security following her, she hoped Helen was still awake. Not that she would begrudge her the ability to catch some sleep. With the campaign kicking into high gear, they would only be able to head back home for a few days. It wasn't ideal, but they would be together for Christmas and New Year's Eve, although they would be attending a black-tie ball in DC to ring in the new year. Still, she looked forward to down time, a few days to regroup before the grueling travel leading up to the first caucuses and the stream of Super Tuesday primaries began.

Stepping into the dark room, she shucked her too-high designer pumps and pulled off her suit jacket. She tread across the carpet carefully, unwilling to make noise if Helen was asleep. She peeked in the bedroom suite and smiled. Helen was curled on her side, breathing in a slow, steady rhythm. Grabbing sweatpants and a T-shirt, Maggie entered the bathroom to change. She removed her makeup and brushed her teeth before closing the bedroom door and settling on the sofa in the main area with her laptop to watch the ads. The six spots promoted her in different ways. Deciding on her top two picks, she sent a text to Walter, Darla, and Alice, knowing any final decisions could be made on the flight home.

The events of the day were catching up to Maggie, her body feeling heavier by the moment. Hoisting herself off the sofa, Maggie stretched her arms above her head before wandering into the bedroom. Thankful for the incredible team helping her navigate the pitfalls inherent with a national campaign and for a partner who kept her sane, Maggie got into bed with a sigh.

Helen wriggled until her backside pressed against Maggie's stomach, cradled by her hips. Helen's hand reached back to find Maggie's hand and pulled it tight around her torso, pressing it between her breasts. Maggie kissed behind her ear. "I love you. Good night," she whispered. Her body settled into Helen's warmth, letting it lull her to sleep.

Chapter Nineteen

AFTER WINNING THE STATE representative election, Maggie found her time eaten up by work, family, and the holidays. Knowing her days as a city solicitor were numbered, she set about getting her cases as organized as possible for her successor. Unlike Victor, she had no one lined up to take her position. Since Lynn employed two assistant city solicitors, she was confident her seat would be filled without a problem. Each day she worked diligently to settle as many cases as she could or prepare the files for litigation if she could not. At the end of each day she dragged herself home, wondering when she might see Helen.

They talked a few times a week about work and the ensuing holidays and the weather. Never about their relationship or the mind-blowing kisses they shared after her election win. Maggie preferred to discuss such matters in person, but it was becoming increasingly clear that their timing couldn't be worse. She consoled herself by indulging in memories of how those kisses made her feel, the warmth, the affection, the promise.

Helen mentioned she would be spending Thanksgiving with her mother and sisters in Boston and Christmas with her father in Florida. When she mentioned she would be returning home on New Year's Eve, Maggie's heart leapt at the thought of ringing in the new year with her.

"Do you have plans for New Year's Eve?" Helen asked. Maggie stared at the muted television as a commercial selling car insurance played out. She was invited to a few gatherings, but she was willing to skip them if that meant she could spend time with Helen. "I was hoping we could spend time together."

"I'd like that. We can order in and watch the ball drop, or if you want to go out, we can attend one of the gatherings I was invited to or go to any you were." Maggie felt as if she were getting too old to wander around Boston on New Year's Eve, but she'd do it for Helen.

"I'd prefer a quiet night in with you if you don't mind. The holidays tend to wear me out. How about Chinese food? We can order from Fantasy Island or Kowloon, and I'll pick it up on my way over."

"Yum. You know I love both."

"That I do." Helen's voice became softer. "I miss seeing you."

"Me, too. Our timing sucks. You know, I could hop in my car and come over right now." Maggie looked around her living room. The only light came from the television. Shadows filled the corners of the room, and although she knew she was the only one present, her eyes strained to confirm it.

"It's too late. I'm getting up at six, and if you come over, I won't get nearly enough sleep to function. I'm sorry." Sorrow dripped off each word. Helen's sigh sounded like the waves pounding sand, its impotent fist splitting apart.

"I know. It's okay." A thought came to her. "I didn't know you have siblings. Tell me?" She kicked her feet out in front of her, resting them on the coffee table. Although she was tired, she wanted to connect with Helen, if only for a few minutes.

"I have two sisters, both older. I was a surprise, and to my parents' eternal disappointment, I didn't fulfill their hope of having a son. Angela is five years older than me, and Lisa is seven years older. Angela lives a few streets away from mom, is married, and has kids. She works as a librarian for the Suffolk County Law Library. Lisa lives in North Reading and is the head manager at Teresa's Prime on Route 62."

"Oh, my God. I love that place. They have the most delicious surf n turf."

"Yes. I like their food, too, although I haven't eaten there in a few years. I think my sisters resented me when we were kids. They often got saddled with watching me after school. The only time we were close was while I attended college. They seemed to warm up to me, but all bets were off once I came out to my family at Thanksgiving dinner about ten years ago. I was missing my girlfriend and made the mistake of mentioning it while asking Lisa to pass the turkey."

Maggie gasped. "That's horrible. So, they stopped talking to you?"

"No. They pretty much ignored the whole thing, and I decided I didn't want to work on relationships with people who were unwilling to accept everything about me. I mean, love is supposed to be unconditional. It's like being with someone and thinking you'll be able to change the less desirable parts. People don't change unless they want to, and really, I don't think a person has a right to judge someone else. We all have our flaws. But being gay isn't a flaw. It's as permanent as the type of blood flowing through my veins."

"I get it. That's part of the reason why I got divorced. I realized a bit too late that I got married because others wanted me to. I let people tell me how to look, what to do, whom to love. I let them strip me of my identity, and by the end of that marriage, I didn't even know who I was anymore. But guess what? I've pulled myself out of that dead end and I'm learning who I am, what I want to do in my life, and who I want to spend time with."

"You do seem more confident nowadays."

"That might have to do with a beautiful lady expressing an interest in me."

"Beauty fades."

"Only when it's outer, physical beauty. When someone is beautiful inside and out, it shines brighter than the sun."

"Smooth talker. I should get going."

Maggie checked her watch, surprised to see how late it had gotten. "Okay, but before you go, can I ask one more question?"

"You just did."

"Smart ass. Another question, then." She ignored the chuckle. "Why are you sharing Thanksgiving with your mom and sisters if you aren't speaking to them?"

"I'm still speaking to my mom. She's always supported me. It's my sisters who haven't made any effort to overcome their bigotry. Mom asked me to come over, so I will. Are you going to your mom's house?"

"No. We'll eat out instead. She doesn't like to cook. It works out better since I'll be able to go to the Thanksgiving Day high school football game. It's fun to see my former classmates and teachers. Anyway, I've kept you up late enough. Get some sleep, beautiful."

"I will. Talk to you soon." Maggie waited until she heard the phone disconnect before lowering hers.

She dragged herself off the couch, switching off the television before entering the bathroom and staring in the mirror. Although she felt as if she was a different person from even a week before, she looked the same. She guessed that, like true beauty, changes in a person weren't always noticeable. She knew no one would see the changes unless she made them see. That meant acting in decisive ways. It meant showing courage. Courageous action. She'd have to think about what that might mean for her. She turned off the light. But not tonight.

***

By the time New Year's Eve came, Maggie was a jumble of nerves. She hadn't seen Helen since the election, and she feared Helen's feelings might have changed. It didn't matter that they normally only saw one another every few months. That was before the kisses. She wondered whether they meant more to her than to Helen. Maybe to her it was no big deal. It was sexy and exciting, but perhaps it was a transient interest, fading thanks to time and circumstance.

She looked at her outfit, wondering whether she should change. She wore tight, black Levi's jeans and a tucked in gold, button-down silk shirt. Her doorbell rang, and she hit the buzzer to let Helen enter the apartment building. It was too late to change now. She looked around the apartment, making sure it was clean. Not that she'd be able to do anything in the ten seconds before Helen walked in. She shook her head and opened the door, watching Helen walk toward her. She was a sight for sore eyes.

"Hello, stranger." Helen's words hinted that she'd missed Maggie, too. At least, that's how she chose to interpret them. She closed the door as Helen set the bag of food on the kitchen table and turned toward her. Helen shed her coat, revealing a white V-neck angora sweater and painted-on blue jeans.

Maggie's tongue darted out to wet her lips before she bit down on her lower lip. She shifted her eyes to the food as Helen turned around, a blush working its way up her neck. She wondered whether Helen would mind if she opened a window.

Before Maggie could decide how to greet her, Helen was in her arms, pulling her close. Maggie melted into the embrace, breathing in her distinctive scent. "I'm so glad you're here." Helen's presence felt like the sun shining on her soul. Maggie felt warm and seen and a bit lightheaded.

"I wouldn't want to ring in the new year with anyone else." Helen broke the hug and stepped back. Her gaze traveled across Maggie's body as if she were running her fingers over every inch. "You look gorgeous. Let's eat. I'm starved."

Maggie watched Helen turn back to the food and shook herself. She was ravenous, too. Dialing back her libido, she took the hint and busied herself with getting plates and utensils. They set up in the living room, Dick Clark's New Year's Eve show on the television, not that they paid it much attention. Maggie didn't know exactly what she had expected, but Helen acted the same way she always had. With one large exception. She kept touching her.

Helen's hand grazed Maggie's while handing her a carton of rice. Her knee brushed Maggie's as she leaned to place food on her plate. Her foot tapped Maggie's calf as she crossed one leg over the other. Each contact left scorch marks, burning reminders of the small touches.

And then the pointed stares began. As Maggie talked, Helen stared at her lips. When Maggie wasn't speaking, Helen's gaze roved her outfit. When Maggie leaned forward to grab more food from the coffee table, she felt Helen's eyes on her back, her waist, her ass. By the time she finished her meal, Maggie's body felt like a live wire trembling with energy, needing an outlet.

Placing her plate on the coffee table, Maggie leaned back on the couch, her heart beating in her throat. She swallowed several times, not sure what to do. She didn't know what Helen wanted, and she was afraid to ask. A hand on her chin stopped her careening thoughts. She allowed Helen to turn her face so their eyes connected.

Helen's pupils were so large Maggie could hardly see any brown left in the eyes. Her face was flushed, her voice unsteady. "I promised myself I'd go at your pace and not pressure you into doing anything you weren't ready for, but I underestimated what those hungry eyes and provocative lips would do to me. Tell me to stop." She moved close enough for Maggie to find it hard to concentrate on the words.

Her breath caught when Helen's parted lips hovered before her. Maggie's lips brushed hers as she whispered her response. "I don't want you to stop. I want you to kiss me. I need your taste on my tongue."

Helen's moan was obscene, and Maggie realized the double entendre a moment before Helen's lips claimed hers.

She tasted exquisite, full of need and desire. Gone were the careful, slow shift of the lips she'd experienced the previous time they had kissed. These kisses were forceful and demanding. They took center stage as the rest of the world dropped away. Fingers carded through her hair, fisting at the back of her head to keep her in place. The passion stirred the embers of her desire, creating a blaze of voraciousness Maggie had never felt before. Her mouth opened under Helen's onslaught, hands pulling her closer as their tongues touched.

Maggie's body shivered, need coursing through her. Helen's tongue entered her mouth, exploring and provoking. The way her tongue slid against hers brought forth the sensation of tangled bodies, spent and sated. These kisses were positively filthy, and Maggie couldn't get enough. She heard her own guttural groan and could hardly believe that it was her voice, her sighs, her need heating up the air between them, pleading for Helen to get closer, to take more, to keep making her feel as if she were going to combust with this desire. The urgency made her feel reckless, but she had no desire to stop or even slow down.

As they continued to kiss, Helen unbuttoned Maggie's shirt with one hand, the other rubbing the back of her neck. As she felt a draft on her chest, Maggie gasped. Helen's hand rested on her breastbone, as if to steady her.

Maggie realized she wasn't doing anything more than returning Helen's kisses. Her hands remained at her sides when what she wanted to do was slip her hands under the clothes that separated her from Helen's tantalizing skin. She didn't want to be passive, allowing Helen to guide this encounter. She needed to touch this woman, explore her with her hands and lips. She reached out, wrapping an arm around Helen's waist. She wanted her closer. Much closer. When she pulled back, Maggie whimpered. Opening her eyes, she watched as Helen pulled off her sweater, revealing a dainty pink bra. Her breasts were small, topped by erect nipples straining against the lacy design.

"Will you touch me?" The pleading in Helen's voice captured Maggie.

Her fingers trembled as Maggie reached out to trace the underwire of her bra. She watched Helen's face, her wet lips opening and eyes glossing over. Maggie leaned in to deliver a soft kiss on the sharp rise of her collarbone, stalling long enough to feel Helen shift against her. Smiling against her skin, Maggie cupped her breast, squeezing gently. She moved her hand in a circular motion, feeling the hardened nub against the center of her palm. She forgot about her open blouse until hot hands surrounded her waist and lips covered her bra-clad breast. The feeling was incredible. She knew she was making noises. Knew her other hand was holding Helen's head steady, encouraging her to stay close. Knew she wanted to climb inside Helen's being and allow her passion to burn away the rest of the world.

When Maggie realized Helen had no intention of stopping her oral explorations, her desire to explore Helen's breasts pushed her into action. She moved both thumbs, brushing against her nipples several times before reaching behind her to remove the bra. Once the straps hung on Helen's elbows, Maggie returned to her breasts, twisting the nipples slightly with her fingers before squeezing them. Helen's reaction was instantaneous.

Hands wrapped around her torso to unfasten Maggie's bra as long legs crawled on her lap. Helen settled on top of her, lips seeking hers. The bruising kiss was complemented by blunt fingernails scratching down her back. Maggie arched, head falling back as Helen broke the kiss and ducked down to latch on to her breast. Heat blazed from her nipple to her core, the sucking motion drawing out her need and intensifying her desire tenfold.

"Oh, God. Yes." She grabbed at Helen's ass, pulling her closer and squeezing. She felt heat emanating from Helen's core, so close to her own. She canted her hips, sucking in a breath as the seam of her jeans rubbed against her wet panties.

Helen bucked on top of her, and without thought, Maggie moved her hand to press between Helen's widened legs. Helen's mouth switched to Maggie's other breast, fingers tweaking the abandoned one mercilessly. She moved against Maggie's hand, her breathing becoming ragged as her movements sped up. Maggie kept one hand on Helen's ass, encouraging her rhythmic motion.

Helen turned her head, resting it over Maggie's heart, her body shaking and arms wrapping around her. Her body slowed down until she rested against Maggie like a ragdoll. She moved her legs so that they were splayed out across Maggie's lap and the couch as Maggie rested one arm across Helen's lap and used her other hand to rub slow circles on her back. She waited for a signal that Helen was okay, that she didn't regret what they did, that she found Maggie desirable. She kissed Helen's bowed head, smiling when an echo of the kiss was delivered on her chest.

Although her body was throbbing in time with her racing heart, Maggie didn't mind. She treasured this moment. Helen always seemed in control. To be the one to make her lose her restraint was a gift. Helen trusted her enough to be vulnerable, and Maggie would do her best to be worthy. She heard Helen take a deep breath and exhale, the humid air wafting on her skin, eliciting a low moan. A hand rose to cup her jaw, and she realized she had closed her eyes and placed her head on top of Helen's thick head of hair while holding her close. Need thrummed beneath her skin, but she pushed it down as best she could, waiting for Helen to indicate what she wanted.

"Maggie?" The question in her voice was enough for her to peer into dark eyes, her lips curling up. She was surprised by the note of uncertainty she heard in them.

"What's the matter?"

"I'm afraid I may have taken things too far. I didn't intend to do anything more than kiss you, but it seems I got carried away."

Stiffening up at her words, Maggie took a shuddering breath. "Do your regret what we did?"

"No." Helen's quick response soothed her, tamped down on her fears. "No. You feel amazing. I'm more concerned with scaring you off. I mean, I don't want you to think I have any expectations for what we'll do when we're together. I don't want you to feel like this is the only reason I'm here."

"I know that. I don't think that you only want me for my body." Maggie wiggled her eyebrows. "Not that I could blame you."

Helen's slap on her shoulder and accompanying giggle made Maggie smirk. It faded when in the next moment, Helen's hand slid to her breast, teasing the nipple into hardness. "But what a fine body it is."

She watched with fascination as Helen leaned in to lave her breast with her tongue, each twitch and swipe reverberating throughout her body. Helen guided her to lie supine on the couch, her hands gentle and lips light.

"Tell me if you don't like something or want me to stop. I promise you won't hurt my feelings."

Not able to imagine any scenario where she'd want Helen to stop touching her, Maggie nodded, a throaty moan ripped from her in the next moment when Helen unzippered her jeans. She lifted her hips to allow herself to be stripped, her self-consciousness fading in the face of Helen's ardent gaze.

"Ever since you said you wanted to taste me, I haven't been able to get the thought out of my head."

"I meant—"

"I know you were talking about kissing, but the thought won't let me go." Helen ran her hands over the outside of Maggie's thighs, leaving a trail of goosebumps. "I want to taste you." She looked up with a pleading look. "Will you allow it? Please? Let me make you feel good."

Not quite sure what that meant, Maggie nodded anyway. Timmy had gone down on her once, and it felt revolting enough that she had written it off as a sexual act she didn't need. Yet the thought of Helen kissing her on her nether lips, of licking and nibbling and stroking her to completion—she wasn't sure she would survive. Before she could second guess her permission, she felt strong hands pulling her legs around thin shoulders and a long, languid lick from her entrance to her clit. Her body jolted, and Helen placed her forearm across her hips to keep her steady.

If anyone were to ask Maggie to describe the next few minutes, she wouldn't be able to capture the ecstasy she felt. Helen's ministrations brought her to the edge of the universe, to the black abyss of desire, within minutes. When Helen pushed her over the precipice with a firm tongue thrashing and a long suck, her body went into a freefall. It was the most exquisite torture she'd ever experienced, and her choked off scream was all she could manage before her body locked up and tears streamed down her cheeks. Helen softened her tongue strokes, one hand reaching up to hold Maggie's. She resorted to long strokes again as Maggie's body sagged, her energy gone.

A tongue twirling at her entrance surprised her enough to make her squeak, the feeling of Helen's tongue entering her slightly calling forth passion Maggie thought she had expended. Helen cupped her ass, pulling her forward as she entered Maggie a bit more each time. The way she wriggled her tongue inside her felt undeniably vulgar. It pushed her higher, her body gearing up for a deeper, more profound unraveling. When it came, Maggie rode wave after wave of her orgasm, legs spreading wider and body moving to capture that wicked tongue. She whined and she whimpered, she moaned and she groaned, sure she would die but needing it. Needing Helen to make her feel so unbelievably good.

One arm covering her eyes, Maggie tried to regain her faculties. "I think you broke me."

Helen's carefree laugh brought a tired smile to her lips. Fingers wrapped around her arm and moved it to her side. She blinked open her eyes and gazed into sparkling, gold-rimmed ones. "Hi."

"Hi." Helen delivered a kiss on her cheek. "Stay here. I'm going to grab water for us."

Maggie pushed herself into a sitting position, feeling her muscles protest. She studied Helen as she came back in the room with two glasses of water. She was nude from the waist up, and Maggie took pleasure in scrutinizing her form. Helen handed her a glass before sitting next to her. Her gaze raked across Maggie, reminding her she wasn't wearing any clothes.

"I've dreamed of being with you for so long, it's hard to believe I'm here." Helen's voice was soft, as if she were confiding a secret. "I thought I had fallen into the old trap of liking the straight girl. I thought it would fade over time." She shook her head. "But how could it when everything you do makes me fall harder?"

"I think it's clear I'm not exactly straight." Maggie shrugged. "I've found myself attracted to men and women." She interlaced their fingers, letting their hands rest on her knee. She sipped the water, rejoicing as the cool liquid flowed down her parched throat. She must have been more vocal than she remembered. Her throat was a bit sore. She felt the temperature nipping at her cooled down body and reluctantly rose to redress. She sat down next to Helen and kissed her slowly, tasting mint. "When did you brush your teeth?"

Helen's chin dipped down. "When I got the water. Sometimes, people don't like to taste themselves on their partner's breath. I didn't want you to become uncomfortable with kissing me." She gazed through her lashes at Maggie. "After all, there's still the matter of the New Year's kiss when the ball drops."

"You think your breath would hold me back from kissing you?" Maggie tucked stray hair behind Helen's ear and leaned in. "Not a chance." She nibbled on her earlobe, gratified to hear her breath hitch. "But thank you for being so considerate." She noticed they still had some time before midnight and decided to freshen up. "I'm going to freshen up, and then maybe we can have champagne? Or wine?"

"Champagne sounds perfect. I feel in the mood to celebrate." Helen's wide smile was infectious. Maggie kissed her once more before rising. She had to agree with her. Tonight was worth celebrating.

***

Yelping as she was pushed into the bathroom, Maggie opened her mouth to object and found Helen's hand covering it.

"Shh. I don't want anyone to see us both in here."

"Then why are we both in here?" They were at Angela's house in Chestnut Hill. Maggie was surprised Helen had invited her to it, and even more surprised Helen decided to attend. Turned out Angela was a supporter of Victor, and by association, her. Once she found out Maggie was a friend of Helen's, she had insisted Helen bring her.

Angela's friendly demeanor was contrasted by her brusque behavior toward Helen. Maggie found herself in the role of attempting to charm Angela into releasing her big sister superior attitude, one that she had no doubt perfected through years of patronizing Helen.

Maggie only wished she could make it clear that she was Helen's love interest. She could understand Helen's request they act as purely friends, though. Maggie was willing to do whatever she could to help Helen navigate her relationship with her family. Even though they knew Helen was gay, they made her feel uncomfortable enough that she didn't want to bring attention to her preference.

"You don't even realize how sexy you are, do you?" Helen locked the door and advanced on Maggie, who leaned against the sink. She pulled Helen closer by the hips, smiling into the kiss she received. "I love watching you work a room, even if they aren't your constituents."

"It never hurts to be friendly. Who knows what will happen in the future? Victor may run for the Senate, and I'll run for his spot. Angela and her friends would become part of my district."

"Six months into your new job and you're already thinking of moving up." Helen's hands smoothed Maggie's shoulders before sliding down her chest and resting on her breasts. She hummed, thumbs rubbing on Maggie's nipples as she leaned in to latch on to Maggie's earlobe with her teeth.

"Stop teasing me, you vixen." When Helen kept touching her breasts and nipping her ear, Maggie retaliated by rucking up Helen's skirt and moving a hand up her leg until she could slip her fingers past her panty line and dip them into Helen's wetness. She turned her head to capture Helen's lips, tasting her desire. She slid two fingers into Helen, swallowing her groan.

Knowing they didn't have long, Maggie set a fast pace, angling her wrist to penetrate as deeply as she could. She punctuated each stroke with her tongue sliding against Helen's. She felt Helen's body tightening, grasping at her fingers, and she pulled Helen's leg around her waist so she could reach even deeper with each thrust, hooking her fingers each time she withdrew them. Helen's body became flushed, heat rolling off of her. With the brushing of her thumb against Helen's erect clit, Maggie pushed her into a strong orgasm.

Helen pulled away from the kiss, tucking her face into the crook of Maggie's neck as she rode out the rest of her climax with slower, more pronounced rolls of her hips. Her sensual moves made Maggie's mouth water. She wished they could do more than this, but she knew she'd have to wait until they returned to one of their homes.

As if hearing her thoughts, Helen kissed her neck and eased away, pulling down her skirt and checking her appearance. Maggie washed her hands and made sure she looked presentable. She was ready to leave when someone knocked on the door. Eyebrows rising, she looked to Helen for direction.

"Be right out," Helen called before whispering to Maggie to get in the shower.

"What?"

"Get in the shower and pull the curtain around it. No one will know you're here. After whoever that is leaves, you can exit. It will look weird if we both leave the bathroom together."

"No, it won't. Women enter the bathroom together all the time. Usually to gossip or touch up their makeup."

"Just do it. I'll make it up to you." Helen pushed her toward the shower, and with a sigh Maggie did as she was told. She stood as still as possible, trying not to breathe loudly, trying not to jostle the shower curtain, trying not to be discovered. A woman and her child entered the bathroom, and Maggie prayed they would be quick.

"Mommy, can I have a cupcake?"

"Yes. But first you need to go potty." Maggie heard the shifting of clothes before the telltale sound of liquid hitting the toilet bowl indicated the little girl was doing as directed. She heard the toilet flush and prayed they would leave soon.

"Wash your hands, honey."

"I can't reach."

"I'll help you. Oh, boy, you're getting so big." Maggie heard the water turn on. "Okay, rub your hands together with soap. Now put your hands under the water. All right."

The water was turned off, and Maggie thought she might actually get away with standing in a tub with only a thin shower curtain separating her from what she was sure would be an inexcusable violation of privacy.

"Let mommy go real quick and then we'll go find the cupcakes."

More clothes rustled, and Maggie bit back her frustration. It took the woman forever and a day to finish up before washing her hands and exiting the bathroom. Maggie hopped out of her hiding space, and once outside, saw Helen's worried face and shook her head.

"I'm so sorry. I had no idea that would happen." Helen's whispered words pulled a small smile out of Maggie. How could she be upset when she wasn't even caught?

"Don't tell me you wasted that orgasm-high by worrying about me." She watched Helen's face morph from worried to confused to confounded to amused. "Ah, that's better. And yes, I do expect you to make it up to me later."

"You can count on it." She schooled her lascivious expression as Angela bustled across the room to them.

"Maggie, I wanted to introduce you to my friend, Kim, and her daughter, Ariel."

"It's a pleasure to meet you both. Oh, that looks tasty." Ariel had chocolate frosting smeared on her face and the remains of a cupcake in her hand. She would bet Helen's IOU for a night of debauchery that these were the two in the bathroom just a few minutes earlier.

"It is." Ariel grinned, revealing a missing front tooth.

"I heard you work with Victor. He's doing a lot of community outreach, which I really appreciate." Kim used a napkin to clean Ariel's face, her attention switching back to Maggie a moment later.

"Yes. Victor's vision on how to strengthen our communities is one of the many reasons I admire him. He believes in public service and advocating for equal rights. And he's working hard to institute legislation which will protect the environment and provide a better place for the future."

Maggie and Victor had worked out similar platforms the previous year, and they often discussed how to combine their efforts to fulfill the promises they made while campaigning.

"Well, I appreciate it. It was a pleasure to meet you."

"Likewise. And it was a pleasure to meet you, Ariel. I think I'll have to try one of those cupcakes now." She flashed a smile and turned toward the dining room where the food was spread out on platters.

"Want to get out of here?" Helen's eyes were alight with mischief, although to a casual observer, she would seem to be conversing about nothing of importance. Maggie had become better attuned to her micro-expressions, though, and she noticed Helen's attempt to bite back her smile.

"You know I do." Maggie smiled across the room at Angela before sneaking a look at Helen. "I need you to make me forget about how it feels to hide in a shower while listening to people pee." Helen's bark of laughter was music to her ears.

"I'll do my best to make you forget everything, including your name."

Maggie sure as hell hoped Helen made good on that promise.

Chapter Twenty

AS HER TEAM FILED into the conference room, Maggie fought back a yawn. She grabbed her coffee mug and drank from it. At least, she tried. Turned out it was empty. She frowned, staring at the empty cup. Someone chuckled and she looked up into Alice's smiling eyes.

"You look like someone killed your puppy." Alice looked at one of the volunteers. "Can you get Maggie a hot cup of coffee? Milk and two sugars."

Maggie pushed her mug toward the young man, nodding her thanks as he scampered off. "Okay. Let's get to it. What's happening with the media?"

Walter's head popped up from behind his laptop, a smile on his face. "Good morning, Senator. We have positive op-eds in the *Times*, both LA and New York, about our education initiative. Of course, we expect to receive push back from the religious lobbying groups about dismissing their school voucher program idea, but we believe if we continue to advocate increased funding for STEM programs, we'll capture the Silicon Valley demographic."

"We just signed off on the *Washington Post* interview, which will be published tomorrow. We got a boost from the article posted in *USA Today*, so we're using that momentum with our biggest donors to secure more funding." Michelle grinned. "And we have that fundraising dinner tonight at Gabby's."

Alice looked at her notes. "Eileen, what are the poll numbers looking like?"

"The favorability rating rose to seven point two percent after last week's debate and has remained steady. Support remains high for Thompson, Ashford, and Frankel, but we expect the other candidates to drop out before Super Tuesday." Eileen sifted through her notes before continuing. "We took a small hit with our stance on more stringent regulations for gun owners. We knew GOA and NRA opposition would come out strong, but our position of making homes safer instead of taking away the guns entirely is holding well."

"How about our environment plank?" Maggie asked.

"Pretty much the same. The big corporations are objecting, but our approval rating is steady at forty-one percent."

"All our travel arrangements for the sweep through the southern states are confirmed. From Iowa we'll fly up to New Hampshire, then we're off to Las Vegas, and then to South Carolina. We come back for a few days before gearing up for Super Tuesday. At that point you might want to take pictures of your loved ones since we'll be on the road for most of March. Which reminds me. Senator, can you give me the dates Helen's able to join us on the road?"

Maggie nodded at Bob and jotted down a note for herself. "I'll get you something today. Some of the later dates are still up in the air, but I can get you answers through the next two weeks."

"Great. Thanks. Rachel, Walter, and I are working with the campaign captains in the districts we'll be visiting to arrange meet-and-greets, rallies, and walking tours. I've sent an updated itinerary to you, but as you know, things will change."

"Thanks to all of you. Get plenty of sleep this week. Even if you're not traveling with me, I'll be relying on you to work your magic from here to keep me updated and visible. Zack and Alice, I'd like to go over the itinerary with you."

As she waited for the rest of the team to file out of the room, Maggie pulled up the document on her tablet. Although the long days were hard, Maggie was excited with how well the campaign was going. By this time next month, the field would have narrowed down significantly, allowing her to concentrate more on her platform and less on counteracting the mudslinging that was prevalent in the election.

"Alice, I need you to dig up whatever you can on the top three frontrunners. Don't dig for dirty laundry that has no bearing on their ability to lead. Focus on the platform, voting records, flip-flopping, that sort of thing. We have to be careful, particularly with Thompson."

"I've been tracking that already and comparing them to their stump speeches and debate answers. I'll draw up some graphics to highlight where we can hit the hardest."

"Good. Thanks. Zack, I need the final draft for tonight's speech by one." Once he nodded, she indicated the itinerary. "Okay, let's go through the schedule. I know I have that radio interview in twenty, so let's make it quick." As they reviewed the document, Maggie took notes, asking questions when needed. "Has HRC endorsed us, yet?"

"No, but they're hosting the watch party for you in Iowa. I think they're close," Zack said.

"That's good. Let's make sure I get to meet with their top staffers before the event so I can get a bead on their concerns." They reviewed the rest of the itinerary in much the same way. At every stop her schedule was packed.

"We confirmed the watch party in Massachusetts at your sister-in-law's restaurant. She's been pretty cooperative." Alice smirked.

"I bet. Okay. Looks like we're in good shape. Thanks." She rose, wanting a few minutes to herself before the interview.

As she made her way to her office, her cell vibrated. Seeing it was Helen, she picked up. "Hello, babe. What are you doing?"

"Oh, you know. Watching a soap opera while eating chocolate and debating whether to take a shower today."

Picturing that tableau, Maggie guffawed. "Good one." She sat at her desk and leaned back in her chair. "I have a radio interview in seven minutes. Did you email me the list of places you can go with me this month?"

"Yes. That's what I wanted to talk to you about. Not the February dates, but the March ones. Are you sure it's a good idea to have the watch party at Teresa's Prime? You do realize our families will be there, right?"

"I do. Don't worry. I'm sure everyone will play nice. And if someone gets out of line, I have a group of people trained to handle it. Besides, didn't you say they were having trouble staying open? This will boost their clientele." Maggie tapped a pen on her desk, eyeing the interview questions advanced to her by the radio station. "I've got to go. I love you."

"Love you, too. Knock them dead."

"I will." Maggie disconnected the call, pushing aside the misgivings she had for the Massachusetts watch party. It was always a gamble when the family was involved, but she had to believe the positive publicity would outweigh the dangers of the wrong person saying the wrong thing at the wrong time.

"It will be fine," she reassured herself. If she told herself that enough times, she might even believe it.

By the time Super Tuesday arrived, Maggie was exhausted. She needed sleep. She needed silence. She needed Helen. Thankfully, at least one of her needs was going to be fulfilled. She would see Helen soon. The watch party at Lisa's restaurant was in a few hours.

Early polls indicated she would win the state and several of the battleground states. Tonight's results would make or break the campaign.

She reviewed the latest polling numbers, thrilled to see that her numbers were increasing. All the rallies, stump speeches, watch parties, and fundraisers had begun to blend, but at least she was gaining endorsements across the country. The rally in Iowa boosted her visibility, and the HRC finally endorsed her. She didn't expect as much support in New Hampshire, but her team had worked their asses off canvassing the state and gathering support from service industry workers. Nevada was a lost cause, the casinos firmly siding with Ashford, the election's living Ken doll who voted against any legislation that would reduce corporate tax breaks or regulate chemical dumping. Still, she managed to nab eleven of the delegates, so all was not lost. The number of delegates was climbing, and three more candidates suspended their campaigns when they placed poorly in the primaries. That meant only she, Vice President Thompson, Senator Ashford, and Governor Frankel were still in the race.

She had received the Boston Teacher's Union, *Boston Globe*, and Boston Police Union's endorsements, and several smaller organizations had fallen in line. She felt confident she would receive pledges from most of the Massachusetts' delegates.

Maggie was looking forward to mingling with friends, colleagues, and even family that night. Her mom was attending, and she had hinted at a surprise for her. Maggie prayed she wouldn't do anything embarrassing. She loved her, but her mom didn't always think through her actions. Helen seemed afraid of her own family's antics. It was interesting to Maggie, how afraid they were that those who were the closest to them would do something inappropriate. She had heard from former colleagues who were planning to attend, and she looked forward to catching up with them.

Although this was a public event, she had added extra security for the event and supplied them with a blacklist. She didn't want hecklers invading what should be a fun night.

As soon as their plane touched down, Maggie called Helen. "Hey, babe. We just landed. Where are you?"

"I'm with your team at the restaurant. Are you going to the hotel or did you squeeze in another event?" Helen's smile could be heard through her words.

"No, no, we're going to the hotel. I need a shower and a nap. When are you heading back?" Noticing people disembarking, Maggie grabbed her bag and filed out, smiling at the flight attendants and nodding at the captain as she passed him.

"We're nearly done, so I'll leave in a few minutes. Want me to bring you lunch?"

"You're a saint. Yes, please."

"Okay. See you soon."

Maggie walked through Logan Airport with a spring in her step, waving at people who called out to her. She got in the car, leaning into the leather seat with a sigh. Her eyes flew open when she heard Alice chortle. "What has you so happy?"

"Breaking news. Senator Ashford's connections with certain lobbyists cast doubt on his assertions that he will push for more initiatives to reduce the environmental impact of large corporations." Alice looked up. "This will sink his plank on requiring manufacturers to go green and lessen their carbon footprints. It's exactly what we needed. Let me contact Zack so he can start weaving this into your speeches."

"Have him include it in tonight's speech, too. Nothing too scathing, but enough to let everyone know we're keeping track of not only his words but his actions."

"On it."

Maggie nodded, knowing her team would not only rework the speech but also jump on polling numbers to see how this might hurt his campaign. Nowadays, every chink in the armor provided the opportunity to land the fatal blow.

By the time they got to the hotel, Maggie was ready to take an hour to unwind. They trooped into the hotel lobby, and as soon as she was given her keycard, she made her way to the hotel room. She took off her clothes and climbed under the covers, setting her alarm for ninety minutes. That would give her enough time to shower and review the latest revisions for her speech before she needed to leave for the party.

Using the technique she'd read about on how to clear her mind and make her body relax enough for sleep to claim her, Maggie focused on each part of her body from her head to her toes, imagining each part becoming heavy. Each time her mind tried to wander away from relaxing, she pulled her thoughts back. She would have time enough later to think about all her responsibilities once she woke up.

The well-known beeping of her cell phone alarm pulled her from the murkiness of her dreams, pushing back the transient tendrils of people pulling at her coattails and the media jockeying for position around her. She sighed as she felt Helen's arm around her waist. She reached out to silence the alarm, turning on her back.

When Helen blinked open her eyes, Maggie leaned in to kiss her. "Hello, love. I'm surprised I didn't hear you come in."

"You were dead to the world, poor thing. You've been working too hard."

"Don't worry. I'm taking care of myself. And when I forget to eat or sleep, I get mother-henned by my staff."

"Making up more words. Good one." Helen got up and turned on the light, coming back to Maggie's side of the bed and extending a hand. "Come on. I brought you a small salad to tide you over. Eat and then we can get ready. If we get there early enough, Lisa said she'd make sure you get your favorite dish."

"The surf n turf? Now you're talking my language." Maggie hopped up, grabbing Helen in a tight hug. "You taking a shower with me?"

"Not this time. I'll take one while you eat."

"Got it." Maggie didn't take her refusal as any type of slight. She knew Helen sometimes preferred to shower alone, using those few minutes to gather her thoughts. She figured Helen was trying to center herself before they interacted with family members. By the time Helen had finished her shower, Maggie had eaten the salad and felt more alert. Her turn in the shower didn't take long. During the months of traveling she'd learned how to be efficient with taking showers, applying makeup, and reviewing information. Managing time was an artform.

***

The restaurant was bustling with volunteers, staffers, and restaurant employees when they arrived. Maggie was glad to see no press or guests present. That meant she had time to eat. Lisa came to greet them, hugging them both before leading them to the kitchen. She'd set up a small table so they could eat in peace. Maggie was touched by her thoughtfulness.

"Mom's going to be here in about an hour. Angela is bringing her."

Helen nodded, accepting the glass of wine Lisa handed her. "Thank you. How about a toast?" She waited until Maggie and Lisa raised their glasses. "To family. We may not have a choice about what family we are born into, but we do get to choose how much effort we put into strengthening those bonds." She looked at Lisa. "I'm glad you're my sister, and not just because I love your restaurant." Her eyes switched to Maggie. "And I chose you as my family many years ago. It's the best decision I ever made."

"To family." Maggie said.

"To family." Lisa repeated. They all took a sip of the dry white wine. "Your dinners should be out any minute. Go ahead and relax while you can. It's gonna be a full house tonight."

Maggie watched Lisa leave the kitchen and jerked her head toward the direction she went. "You've come a long way with her since the first time I met her."

"I would hope so. It helps that she likes you so much. You charmed your way into my family by flashing that signature, winsome smile, the same one that captivated me. After they met you, my being with a woman wasn't that bad after all." reached out to hold Maggie's hand, a tender smile on her face.

"Here we are." Lisa returned with their dishes. "Enjoy."

"Thank you. Everything looks delicious." Maggie cut a piece of the filet mignon and popped it in her mouth. She didn't eat much red meat, but she loved a good steak. She looked at Helen. "How is it?"

Helen was eating the baked eggplant in red sauce. "Very good." She looked up. "I have to fly back to DC on Thursday night. I checked with Alice, and she said I'm not needed until next week."

"You're always needed." Maggie took a bite of the stuffed shrimp. "I appreciate all the traveling you've been doing for me. I know it's hard and it takes away from your work."

"Stop, honey. We've discussed this. I knew what would be expected of me when I supported your run for the presidency. It's okay. I don't want you to worry about my work. You have enough on your plate."

"I know, but your work is important. I want to make sure this isn't too much for you. If it is, we can look at the schedule and do some rearranging."

"That's not necessary. The traveling will slow down soon enough. Now, no more worrying. This is your night. You'll be surrounded by supporters when you sweep the primaries tonight. What you're achieving is monumental."

"She's right." Alice appeared beside their table. "You're making history today. You've got about fifteen more minutes before they start letting people in, so enjoy your dinner."

"Thank you." Maggie meant it. She was fortunate to have Alice on her team. She felt the energy ramping up and concentrated on settling her mind. Helen left her to her thoughts, knowing Maggie needed the silence to prepare.

After finishing her meal, Maggie brushed her teeth and reapplied her lipstick, checking to make sure she looked presentable. She wore a navy blue pantsuit with a robin's egg blue silk blouse underneath the jacket and a string of white pearls, which matched her pearl earrings. Staring at her reflection in the mirror, she put forth her best smile, the one that made the crow's feet at her eyes visible and her gray eyes warm up. Her hair product was working admirably to keep her spiky hair looking stylish. She was ready.

She checked her gold watch. It was eight thirty, late enough for some of the election results to start reporting. *Time to shine.* Exiting the restroom, Maggie didn't get five steps before supporters swarmed around her. She did her best to exchange a few words with each person and thank them for their support. Her face lit up when she saw Terri Lovitz and her husband. She didn't get to spend much time with them, though, since the crowd kept swelling, election results blaring from the overhead televisions.

When she joined her team, she noticed that the restaurant was filled. "Anyone see my mom?" Maggie couldn't see her anywhere.

Helen appeared, placing a hand on Maggie's shoulder. "She's here. We brought her to the kitchen so you could talk in private for a few minutes. Come with me." Helen took her hand and they weaved their way through the crowd. As soon as they entered the kitchen, Maggie heaved a sigh of relief. It was much quieter. "Over here."

When she saw her mom, it became clear why they were in the kitchen. Sitting next to her was Mike. He jumped up as soon as he saw her. "Surprise, sis." He held out his arms, and she stepped into them for a hug.

"Holy shit. When did you get out? Why didn't I know this?" Maggie was happy for her brother even as she felt guilt nibbling at her for not keeping better track of what was happening with him.

"Nah, no worries. It was all up in the air. I didn't find out until last week, and I asked mom to not say anything in case it fell through. You don't mind that I'm here, do you? I can leave through the back…" He indicated behind him with his thumb, a look of uncertainty on his rugged features.

"Don't be ridiculous. I want you here. This is a wonderful surprise." Maggie hugged him again before stepping back. "And you…" She shook her finger at her mom. "I can't believe you kept this a secret." She shook her head, laughing as she delivered a kiss on her mom's cheek. "Okay then. Let's get back out there. Try not to talk to the press. If they start pestering you, tell them you'll be glad to talk to them later. Or pretend you can't hear what they're asking."

"There ya go. I like that." Mike said with a grin.

Maggie sauntered out of the kitchen with her family following her. Zack intercepted them near the stage at the back of the restaurant.

"Now's a good time to say a few words. Thank them for being here and supporting you. Numbers are coming in, but no states have called it, yet. It will be about another hour. Massachusetts polls closed an hour ago. Most of the elections closed voting between seven and eight o'clock, but that means we won't get results for the western states like Texas and Colorado until late."

"Got it. Who's introducing me?" Maggie looked around the restaurant, a small smile on her lips. She was surprised to see so many former classmates, including Lizzie, Kevin, and another woman who was the spitting image of Lizzie only younger. *That must be Gemma*, she decided.

Victor's daughters were also present. She missed him. He had been such a gentle soul. When he'd died a few years ago, it had hit Maggie hard.

"Congresswoman Cromsby." Zack waved to Sarah, and she made her way to them.

"Sarah, it's so great to see you." Maggie hugged her. She looked over her shoulder at Cheri. "Hi, Cheri. How are you?"

"Good. Glad I'm just a spectator here." Instead of entering politics, Cheri chose to become a high school history teacher in the public schools. Maggie admired her choice, knowing she was molding tomorrow's leaders. Cheri gave her a hug before stepping back. "Mom sends her regards and said to tell you she voted for you."

"Oh, please let her know I was asking about her." Maggie turned to Sarah. "I hear you're introducing me. Thank you for making the trip from DC."

"Are you kidding? I'm honored. You're going to be our next president, and I can honestly say that you deserve it."

"All right. Let's get this party started." Zack led Sarah to the stage, making sure the microphone was turned on. He stepped back to allow Sarah to take his spot at the podium.

"Hello, Massachusetts." Sarah's raised voice and her chipper attitude stirred up the crowd. Their cheers reverberated off the walls. "Thank you for being here tonight to support the best presidential candidate who, coincidentally, hails from our state, the land of the brave. Nowadays, you really do have to be fearless to run for public office, and Maggie Ambrose has overcome not only the typical challenges any politician faces in an election, but also the added obstacle of being a female politician. She's an inspiration to us all. Please welcome Senator Maggie Ambrose to the stage." Sarah led the thunderous applause, her bright smile reminiscent of her father's.

Maggie grabbed Sarah's hands in hers and thanked her for the introduction. She stood in front of the microphone, ready to deliver her rousing speech, but first she wanted to tell a story about Sarah. "I met Congresswoman Cromsby for the first time when I won my very first election as a state representative back in nineteen ninety-seven. I had joined forces with the man who beat me in the same election two years before, her father. Victor Cromsby was a great man, a great politician, and a great trailblazer. He taught me how to learn from my mistakes, to cooperate with others—even when that meant pushing aside my bruised pride—and how to craft policy. And

Congresswoman Cromsby has furthered those ideals, as I knew she would way back in nineteen ninety-seven. How did I know? Not five minutes after meeting me, she asked me for a job as an intern." Maggie laughed along with the crowd. "She knew what she wanted even then. Keep up the good work." She shot a smile at Sarah, amused to see how flushed she was.

"Now, tonight we are making history. We have worked hard to get to this point. Canvassing the neighborhoods, joining with national grassroots groups, getting the signs out there, calling friends and neighbors—many of you opened your doors and invited people in for intimate discussions. I learned about what was important, what was worth fighting for, and how I can best serve you. It all comes down to making sure no one has to fight to survive. Everyone should have an equal chance to live a happy, fulfilling life. We've promoted a platform we believe can help the common American. And if I'm elected to be your next president, I will do everything in my power to implement legislation which will be meaningful and progressive. We are a complex nation with complex problems, but that's not a valid reason for leaving any American behind. It's time everyone is given the opportunity to live full, happy lives. So, let's get to work, America."

As soon as she finished uttering her tag line, the place erupted. She waved at everyone as she left the stage, stopping at the side where Helen waited for her, Christine and Evan standing next to her. She saw Helen's mother and pasted a smile on her face. "Thank you for coming." She kissed her on the cheek. "How are you?"

"Oh, I'm fine, honey. Nice speech."

Angela arrived with a glass of water, which she handed to her mother. "That was a great speech, Maggie."

"Thanks, Angela. And thanks for coming."

"Wouldn't miss it." Angela's eyes widened. "Is that your brother?"

Turning her head, Maggie caught sight of Mike talking to a few guys near the bar. "Yes. My mom's here somewhere, too."

"That's nice." Angela's voice held a note of uncertainty, and Maggie grinned. Helen handed her a glass of white wine, not bothering to enter the conversation.

Alice came over, tablet in hand. She tipped it toward Maggie so she could see. "Zack's going to start making announcements as the numbers come in. You're doing great."

The night flew by, the announcements getting progressively better. She ended up winning eleven primaries, including Massachusetts. It was a glorious night, and not even hearing the press shouting questions about Mike could dampen her mood.

"Are you pushing for the decriminalization of marijuana convictions to help your brother? Are you hoping to get his record expunged? Is it true he received special treatment while incarcerated?" One reporter shouted out.

"I've always advocated for rehabilitation and mandatory reintegration employment programs rather than the current policy of punishing a person for breaking the law and throwing them back on the street after they've completed their time without any support to help them gain their footing. Likewise, those who commit non-violent crimes, such as possession of marijuana, should not carry mandatory minimum sentencing. Mike has served his time and deserves to be given the opportunity to rejoin society and live his life. If you'd like to discuss this aspect of my platform, please contact my team to schedule a time to discuss it further."

Although she was high on adrenaline and the sweet taste of success, she knew by the time they returned to the hotel that she would need to get some sleep. They entered the room, Maggie reading the newest articles on the election results as she kicked off her shoes.

"Let me draw you a bath. It may help you relax a bit. And I must insist you put that aside until the morning." Helen raised her eyebrows. "And don't look at me that way. You know what I'm saying is for your own good."

With a sigh, Maggie plugged her phone into the charger. "You're right."

"Of course, I am. That's why you love me."

"One of the many reasons why," Maggie murmured. "One of the many."

Chapter Twenty-one

THE HUMIDITY WAS THICK enough to make Maggie feel like she was walking through a sauna instead of strolling down Ocean Street with Helen. They tried to take a walk around the neighborhood at least a few times a week to stretch their legs and to deter them from sitting in front of the computer to do more work after dinner. Maggie cherished the quiet walks, needing them to reconnect after long workdays.

"I love that smell."

Maggie wrinkled her nose, her upper lip lifting as she identified the aroma. "You do?" She didn't try to disguise her disgust. She shook her head.

"Well, yeah. I mean, I don't know why, but I love the smell of skunks. Maybe because it reminds me of when me and my dad used to go camping during my childhood."

Maggie stopped, pulling on their clasped hands to keep Helen from walking any farther. "That smell is not from skunks."

"Are you sure? It smells like it."

"I'm sure. It's marijuana."

"No." Helen shook her head. "That can't be true."

"And yet it is. The smell's coming from that backyard." She pointed at a house they had passed, about fifteen feet away. "My bet is that they're toking right now. Want to investigate?"

"No, thanks." Helen pulled on her hand.

"Are you sure?" Maggie teased.

"You just ruined my most cherished childhood memory. I don't need you to hit the final nail in the coffin."

"I'm sorry, babe." Maggie swung their hands between them and started walking. "But you still have your memories. Who's to say someone was smoking weed while you camped? Maybe it was a skunk."

Maggie peered at the Queen Anne Victorian houses, the ones she'd grown up with. The Diamond District boasted mammoth houses built in the late eighteen hundreds and early nineteen hundreds. Many had wraparound porches and multiple fireplaces. Some owners had restored their homes to their former glamour, while others had allowed the old houses to fall into states of disrepair. It seemed to be an apt reflection of Lynn—parts were well taken care of while other areas were falling apart, the onslaught of time and disregard apparent. Many of these houses boasted hardwood floors, crown moldings, built-in cabinets, high ceilings, and ocean views. Their clapboard siding, shutters, and gables harkened to a time long gone, and some of the houses even had a widow's walk on the roof. Maggie imagined the views overlooking the bay must be phenomenal.

For a while, she felt like these houses. She learned to look the part of an up-and-coming professional, how to dress and converse, her desire to fit in with the Pearson's and their social standing paramount. Yet even as she mingled with the elite, she felt broken inside. She feared they would see the decay of her soul, the defectiveness of her spirit, and the tenuity of her façade. She learned to repackage herself but as time passed, the stressors of living a life she didn't enjoy cracked the veneer. A slight pull on her hand caught her attention. She realized Helen had asked her a question.

"What are the petty actions I've taken against others? Wait. Do you think I was being petty by telling you what that smell was?"

"No, silly. I was thinking it could have been quite embarrassing if the wrong person clued me in. So, answer my question."

"Hmmm." Maggie quirked an eyebrow. "How can you ask me that? I'm not petty."

"Oh, come on. We're all petty at some point. We're all selfish and immature and vindictive at times. It's all well and good to rise above those feelings and take the high road, but we aren't always able to talk ourselves out of lashing out, particularly when someone has hurt us. So, spill it, lady."

Maggie shook her head. "I have no idea. I can't remember anything off the top of my head."

"How about with Timmy? Did you do anything to him, like during the divorce? You must have felt pretty angry and hurt with the way he acted, not to mention those who took sides."

"Wow. You're not pulling any punches. Okay, okay." Maggie pulled her across the street to walk toward Lynn Shore Drive. "You know I had to move out, and he got the house." She watched Helen nod before they crossed the street to the beach. She found an empty bench and sat down. "I was bitter about that. In my more level-headed moments, I could admit to myself that I didn't want to live there anymore, but the fact that he got to keep it was hard to accept." She looked at Helen, biting her lip.

"Uh-oh. What did you do?"

"I would drive past the house late at night and hit the car alarm fob. It was loud."

"You didn't." Helen's cackle invited Maggie to join in. "Oh, God. You did it more than once?"

"A few times a week for months." She shook her head. "So immature, I know, but surprisingly satisfying." She plucked at the bottom of her shorts, thinking back on those days.

Helen covered her hand and squeezed it. "Okay. No dwelling on the yucky feelings. What else did you do?"

"Nothing. Wasn't that enough? I mean, it's totally out of character for me. I felt bad about it. Enough to leave the car fob in his mailbox one day. But I thought about doing tons of other stuff." She chortled. "Like digging up the tulip bulbs or locking him out of his high school alumni email account."

"Well, I'll have to remember to keep on your good side." Helen sputtered, her eyes sparkling with merriment.

"Yeah. Every time I thought about vindictive ways of hurting him, I reminded myself of how much I had already hurt him." She squeezed Helen's hand. "Keeping on my good side's easy. Plus, we didn't get divorced."

"Well, we'd have to be married for that to become a possibility."

Maggie froze for a moment, replaying the words, and turned in her seat to fully face Helen. "Do you want to get married?"

Helen gaped at her, her mouth dropping open and eyes widening. "Are you asking me to marry you? Here? Like this?"

"Well, yeah. I guess. Or I'm asking you to think about it." Maggie shrugged. "We've been together for nearly four years. It wasn't a true consideration before, but Vermont has civil unions now..."

"Okay."

"Okay?" Maggie studied Helen's face. Her face was animated, eyes bright. She practically vibrated on the green bench. She was serious.

"Oh, my God." She pulled Helen in for a hug. "You're crazy. You should have held out for a more romantic proposal. And a ring." She turned her head to share a kiss and pulled away when her lips met teeth. She scowled. "Smile with your heart and not your lips so I can kiss you." She swallowed Helen's laughter.

***

Maggie stood by the side of the stage at the Boston Marriott, waiting to be introduced by her longtime friend and colleague. Victor trotted up the steps as if he were much younger than his seventy years. Just eight years ago, he'd convinced her to run for the US Representative spot while he took a shot at the available US Senator seat. She shook her head.

Victor had dropped in without notice in two thousand three, much like he had in nineteen ninety-seven, and while treating her to lunch at the 21st Amendment, her favorite watering hole near the Boston statehouse, he had lobbed the idea of her running for his US Representative seat. He offered to run the campaign with her on one ticket, although he had enough support to not need her help.

Her career had morphed several times during the past decade—from litigator to city solicitor to state representative to US Representative. They had both won the two thousand three elections, reinforcing the nickname they were given in nineteen ninety-seven, the dynamic duo. On the Hill it was commonplace to see them together, discussing policy. It didn't matter that they worked in different houses or clashed on what policies they felt were most important to push through. Their relationship was built on respect and trust, which encouraged senior leaders to adopt the same attitude toward Maggie. And now she was running for the junior US Senator's position with Victor as her running mate once again.

For the two thousand twelve election, they did something rare for the US Senate race. They built a party platform with Victor running for reelection and Maggie running for the other Senate seat. They crushed everyone in their way, and tonight the polls would confirm what they already knew. They were going to win. She was going to be the junior senator. All due to Victor's efforts to pull her along as he ascended to higher elected offices.

Victor only had one opponent, an inexperienced corporate suit. It only took one debate to highlight how unprepared Victor's challenger was to represent his constituents on the Hill. Maggie had more competition, but Victor's declaration that they were a team and had worked together successfully for more than a decade soon caught voters' attention. He named her a rising star, and people listened.

Sarah introduced her father to the people waiting to hear the results and celebrate with them. "My father has worked tirelessly for Massachusetts, first as a city solicitor, then as a state representative, US Representative, and for the past several years, as your US Senator. We have received word that the other candidate has conceded the race after seventy-seven percent of the polling sites reported that my father, Senator Victor Cromsby, has received an astounding ninety-seven percent of the votes. Let's welcome him to the stage." The room erupted in applause as he crossed the stage and hugged Sarah.

"Hello, Boston." Victor's voice carried across the crowded venue, and people turned to listen. "Isn't she great?" He smiled at Sarah before turning back to the crowd. "As you know, Sarah has started down the same road I traveled. She started out as an attorney, fighting the good fight to protect children caught in the crossfire of abusive homes. After gaining experience with navigating the law, she became a state representative, and I'm confident she is doing her best to help her constituents."

An aide ran to him and whispered in his ear. Victor nodded, his thoughtful expression turning into a delighted smile. He looked around until he spotted Maggie and winked.

"I want to thank you for your support and for trusting me all these years to advocate on your behalf. I've always had an open door policy, and that will continue. I believe in our nation. I believe in our communities. I believe when we work together, we can create a society that supports its people.

"Now, let me talk to you for a moment about a politician I believe in, Maggie Ambrose. Congresswoman Ambrose has traveled the same path I have, and I've been fortunate enough to be along on that journey with her. I've worked with her for years, and I can state one immutable fact. She is the real deal. She cares. She works hard. And she embodies the attributes we need in a leader."

Maggie felt her eyes welling up as Victor spoke. Helen discretely rubbed her back as they stood close together. She knew she had to get herself under control. Women in politics learned that showing emotions was dangerous. It might be construed as showing her humanity or revealing her fragility.

"I asked her to run for Senate with me, much as I asked her to run for the state representative and the US Representative seats in the past. Each time I asked her to roll the dice with me, I did so for one reason. She has no hidden agenda. I know who I'm getting when I vote for her. I know what you're getting when you vote for her. And I want to work with someone who is on the Hill to represent your needs. Now, you might have seen Adam scurrying up here a moment ago. He was giving me the latest numbers for Congresswoman Ambrose. As you know, polls closed an hour ago, and thanks to modern technology, we now know who the winner is. So please help me welcome up to the stage Senator Ambrose."

The noise was deafening as Maggie made her way to Victor. He pulled her into a hug before raising her hand in his. Their supporters cheered and hooted as waves of exaltation flowed across her. Her face warmed, but she ignored her sudden bout of shyness, pushing it away. She had fought hard to win this election, and she was damn sure she was going to enjoy this moment.

Victor squeezed her hand before stepping to the side, yielding the stage to her. Maggie nodded her head. "Thank you, Senator Cromsby." She turned toward the crowd, smiling brightly. "Wow. What a night. I want to thank you for your faith in me. For being here. For showing your support. For getting on the phones and passing out the flyers and displaying the signs and talking about me. It was due to your efforts that I'm before you now, ready to work for you. And I'll have my guardian angel, Victor Cromsby, lighting the way for me, as he always has. We are going to kick butt and take names, my friends. We are going to cut through the games and work for the betterment of this nation. The dynamic duo works for you, and I can't wait to get started."

***

A knock on her office door interrupted Maggie's concentration. She closed the folder and looked up. A man she didn't recognized flashed a smile. He wore a light gray suit with an off-white Oxford shirt and blue tie. "Hello. I hope I'm not interrupting. I'm Senator Ted Stapleton."

Standing, Maggie smiled. "Please come in, Senator. It's a pleasure to meet you." She sat down once he took one of the chairs in front of the desk.

"I heard you're a rising star and wanted to reach out to you. Victor's been talking about you for years." He chuckled. "Thinks of you as a daughter. I know he'll be guiding you as you get up to speed, but I wanted to offer my help, too."

"Thank you. That's kind. I do have a steep learning curve ahead of me. It's amazing how different it feels being on this side of the house." Maggie waved. "And I don't mean the offices."

Ted smiled, nodding his agreement. "As the junior senator, you won't have many choices as far as which committees to serve on or which bills to introduce. Many times, new senators rush to prove themselves. My advice is to sit back and observe the process. Get to know who the other senators are and where their interests lie. The rest will fall into place."

"Thank you, Senator. I appreciate your advice."

"Call me Ted." He rose, holding out his hand. Maggie shook it, a slight smile on her face. "I'll be seeing you around." She watched him walk out the door, whistling a tune she didn't recognize.

It turned out she saw him again much sooner than she anticipated. She was wandering the Smithsonian National Air and Space Museum with Helen a week later, staring at the tin cans which masqueraded as spacecraft, when she heard her name called. She turned to see Senator Stapleton and a teenaged boy.

"Senator, what a pleasure. May I introduce my wife, Helen."

"A pleasure, and please call me Ted. This is my son, Scottie. Looks like we both had the same idea."

"Hi, Scottie." Maggie watched as the tips of his ears turned bright red. He was at that age where he was all arms and legs. His ears seemed large on his head, and he didn't seem comfortable being the center of attention. He looked like a Picasso painting with odd shapes pieced together. "Are you interested in being an astronaut or a pilot?"

"Maybe." He shrugged, shoving his hands in his pockets.

"Oh, come on, son. You can do better than that."

Scottie looked up. "Sorry. I want to build things. Dad said I might like to build engines or spaceships." He glanced at the spaceship in front of them. "It's pretty cool. I mean, the calculations have to be exact or it could blow up. I know that's happened before. I read about it in class."

"It's pretty dangerous. Astronauts are brave to get in those ships, if you ask me. Yet someday, maybe once you're an adult, we may be able to travel the stars, like Star Trek."

"Or Star Wars." Scottie's enthusiasm was short-lived as his eyes flickered to his father's disapproving stare. "Yeah. Well, maybe someday."

"I won't keep you ladies any longer. Enjoy your day."

"Thank you, Ted. See you on the Hill." Maggie waited until they wandered away to look at Helen. "And that is Ted Stapleton, the senator who stopped by my office last week to offer some unsolicited advice."

"Interesting. I can't wait to see how this story unfolds."

"What do you mean?" Maggie held up her camera to take a picture of the Star Trek Enterprise model spaceship.

"Don't you ever feel like there's history that hasn't happened yet when you're in someone's presence? Like a premonition of someone who will impact your life?"

She studied Helen's pensive expression and nodded. "Yes. I felt that way about you. About Victor. So, you feel that way about Ted?"

"Yeah. Or maybe it's his son. Only time will tell." She linked her arm through Maggie's. "Come on, Senator. This girl's hungry."

"That's criminal. We'd better get you fed."

***

Maggie tried to hire Alice after reading an op-ed in *The Boston Globe* she wrote about women in politics. In it, Alice discussed the fine line female politicians were forced to walk and the unrealistic expectations foisted on them. Political caricatures often represented them as mean, angry, crazy, or elitist. They were viewed in various unattractive ways, including as lightweights if they were too meek, opportunistic if they used their connections, or dissembling if they didn't disclose every detail of their lives. When forceful, the woman was found to be aggressive. Female politicians who dared to display anger were categorized as having a disagreeable disposition and a temperament unsuited for politics. Worse was the undertone that women should be thankful to the men who helped them get into office. Fifty-eight percent of people polled supported the idea of men but not women running for president because they felt most of the women who ran for the office weren't likable.

After laying out the damning statistics on how many women were elected to office and how voters viewed them, Alice discussed how to unravel more than two centuries of bias and assumption to perform the slow, painstaking work of dismantling the patriarchal attitudes. She pointed out how society still struggled with seeing a woman at work instead of at home, and how women have not found a balance between work *and* home. Much of the article could be applied on a broader scale.

Maggie appreciated Alice's examination of the common biases and prevalent hypocrisy women faced. Complaints about how women were abandoning their children and destroying family values were underscored with evidence of women being held to a practically unattainable standard while under unprecedented scrutiny. Everything from the way they walked and talked, raised a family, dressed for events, reacted to false accusations or blatant discrimination—all these factors played into the complex world of female politicians.

Her final paragraph cited how seventy-five percent of Congress was made up of white men. Although the statistic was slightly lower than five years ago, it wasn't good enough. Not by a long shot. Her call to arms was inspiring. Maggie contacted her office that day and scheduled a phone meeting.

Once Maggie connected with Alice, she learned that the Massachusetts assistant district attorney had grown up in Dorchester, returning to her stomping grounds after passing the bar exam. Maggie offered her a job in her Massachusetts office and was turned down. Instead of feeling insulted, it solidified her belief that Alice would be a great addition to her team. She used the rest of their meeting time to discuss what challenges Alice faced in her particular role.

"Nothing you wouldn't guess. Lack of funds. Too many cases to prosecute and too little time. At the end of the day, it's a business. That bothers me because we're affecting people's lives, their freedom, their futures. We're prosecuting even when we don't have a strong case. We're passing on cases when we foresee it will take too much time and money to prosecute. We're picking and choosing based on politics, on optics, and on motivations we're often not privy to."

"That sounds pretty bleak." Maggie was at the point in her career where she might be able to push for criminal reform. "Tell you what. Email me a list of the top five areas you feel need to be improved, along with your reasons why. I'll do some research and we can talk again. If that's acceptable to you." She heard the cautiousness in Alice's voice when she agreed, and Maggie chuckled. "I promise I have no other motive than to help."

"It's just unusual. I mean, why are you doing this?"

"That's an easy question to answer. Some of our laws are woefully outdated and unwieldy. I have the power to affect change, and I intend to use it. Besides, I might as well get as much done as I can before people realize I don't have children and decide I'm a bad example for family values." Finally eliciting a small laugh from the serious woman, Maggie smirked. It was a start.

Although they didn't discuss it until much later in their association, Maggie knew Alice faced additional challenges as a professional black woman, prosecuting people from her own neighborhood. Maggie kept in touch with Alice, and every so often she offered her a job. One day Alice confided how she was prosecuting a black man who she'd known since she was a girl.

"He accused me of turning my back on my community and selling out to the white man."

Maggie was furious. She heard the hurt in Alice's voice. It was too easy for people to throw stones. She deserved better. As if Alice didn't have to rise above discriminatory behavior every day while attempting to enforce the laws.

As had become the custom at the end of each conversation, she offered Alice a job. "You know, you can leave the DA's office and work for me at the statehouse. No relocation is necessary. I need someone with integrity to run it."

Instead of Alice's usual "thanks, but no" response, Alice remained silent on the line.

"Still there?" Maggie asked.

"Yes, I'm here. You know what? I think it's time for me to take you up on that offer."

Maggie nearly fell out of her chair. It only took three years of monthly job offers to get Alice to accept. Only. She was ecstatic.

"Great. When can you start? No, wait. Better you think about that before answering. Tell you what. I'll have HR send you the job proposal, and you can correct the start date if needed. I'm hanging up now before you change your mind. Bye." She heard Alice's laughter before she disconnected the call.

Once Alice became a part of her team, Maggie would work on getting her to relocate to DC. She knew it wouldn't happen right away, but she didn't mind. Maybe by the time she was up for reelection in three years, she'd find a way to lure Alice to the Hill. Alice's agreement to work for her was all the proof Maggie needed to reinforce her belief that when she kept working toward her goals, even when the challenges before her were daunting, she was bound to reach them. Like the ocean's relentless tide smoothing a rough rock to a polished stone surface, so Maggie edged ever closer toward her objectives, always believing she would reach them.

Chapter Twenty-two

THE DAYS LEADING UP to the Democratic convention were a blur for Maggie. Governor Frankel dropped out of the race when he failed to carry his state in the New York primary. That left Vice President Thompson and Senator Ashford in the race—the old establishment or the not-so-hard on the eyes, pretty boy. Maggie kept asserting her progressive platform, poking holes at her opponents' proposed policies and circumlocutory speeches.

Arriving at the DC office, Maggie was surprised to find several people grouped in front of the television. She wandered closer to find out what was happening. The crawler on the bottom part of the screen proclaimed Senator Ashford had suspended his campaign.

"Senator Ashford suspended his presidential bid after running out of money to finance his campaign. This comes as a big surprise since he was supported by several large corporations and big money businesses, including Caesar's Palace, ExxonMobil, and Cigna." The political pundit read the names of several other businesses, but Maggie had heard enough.

"There's something fishy about this." Maggie didn't realize she'd voiced her thoughts until she looked around to see her team staring at her.

"I agree. He had plenty of money." Alice stepped toward the desk and retrieved a steaming cup of coffee, handing it off to Maggie. "Good morning, Senator."

"Thanks." She took a sip and hummed. "I'm not used to wandering into my own office without anyone noticing me."

"Take it as a gift. Your days of anonymity are dwindling fast." Alice clapped for attention. "All right. Let's get it together. Although Senator Ashford is no longer in the race, we are. Meeting in ten."

Maggie sat at her desk, booting up her laptop. She was tempted to read up on Ashford, but she knew her team would fill her in. Better to use her time to review her speech for the ACLU event she was attending that night. She made a few notes in the margins, not looking up until her team was present and spread out on the other side of the room. She carried her notes and laptop to the empty seat at the head of the table. Alice swept in, detouring to the desk to grab Maggie's coffee before taking a seat.

"Thank you." Maggie took a large swig of the rapidly cooling coffee before clearing her throat.

"Ashford dropping out is a mixed blessing." Zack looked down at a document. "Some of his supporters will shift to us if only to avoid supporting the present administration. On the other hand, some of his largest money contributors will switch to Vice President Thompson since they'll want to keep the tax breaks they enjoy now. It's probably a good idea to do some digging on the real reason why Ashford dropped out, or at the least why he's claiming his funds dried up."

"I'll take a look at his donor list and see what I can find," Alice volunteered. "I have a feeling those lobbyist connections had something to do with it."

Maggie nodded and moved on. "Let's review his list of endorsements and contributors and divvy them up. I want each one contacted to feel out what it would take to gain their support. With the race down to two, we need to renew our attack on the weak points of Vice President Thompson's platform and do our best to differentiate ourselves. How are we polling?"

Eileen piped up to answer Maggie's question. "Our plan to better regulate face and biometric recognition technologies is polling well. People don't like the idea of having their privacy invaded at the whim of the government, and after last week's fuckup at the airport, people are concerned about the reoccurring inaccuracies popping up. We're also polling well for the Workplace Bullying Initiative and the Education for Every American proposal."

"And the bad news?" Maggie didn't expect anything unusual. Conservative Democrats didn't like her humanitarian stance on immigration and asylum seekers. NRA continued to protest her plans to better regulate gun licensing. And the oil companies hated her, although her op-ed piece on how the Keystone XL Pipeline was killing the environment gained her support from the National Audubon Society and the Sierra Club.

"We're struggling with the healthcare initiative. Big pharma took out some big ads in the *New York Post*, *Boston Herald*, and the *Nashville News*. We're already working on it. CNN tipped us off that a guest commentary against big pharma is going live tonight."

Maggie nodded at Eileen and switched her focus to Darla. "Where are we with endorsements?"

"It looks like the National Farmers Union is leaning toward endorsing us. Also, Young Leaders of America and NAACP. Tomorrow we head to West Virginia where you'll have a walking tour with local business owners and a photo-op at a bakery."

"Right. Let's see whether—" A knock on the open door interrupted Maggie. She looked up to see one of her executive assistants.

"Sorry to interrupt. President Sugarman is asking for a meeting at the White House."

"When?" Maggie didn't think she had any appointments this morning.

"Now." Maggie's eyebrows shot up. She looked at Alice. "Do you know anything about this?"

"No, but the timing can't be a coincidence. If I were to hazard a guess, it must be about who he's going to endorse." She shrugged. "I don't see how he could endorse you unless Vice President Thompson bows out."

"Great. Come with me so you can brief me on this week's itinerary."

By the time Maggie stepped into the Oval Office, she was fighting to keep calm. She was surprised to see Vice President Thompson already seated there, a small smile on his face when he greeted her.

"Sorry to summon you without notice." President Sugarman shook her hand and guided her to the seating area where Jimmy rose to shake her hand.

"Hi, Maggie. Seems different to see you without a podium in front of you." Jimmy waited for her to sit down before he retook his seat.

"I'm sure you're wondering what's going on here. With Senator Ashford suspending his campaign, and the two of you left to duke it out for the Democratic nomination, I'll need to endorse one of you soon." The president turned to Maggie. "I told you when you first informed me of your intention to run that I'd back Jimmy unless he dropped out. Although I haven't taken that step, he's backed by most of my supporters."

Maggie nodded, trying to appear unflappable and more importantly as if she had all the time in the world to be told things she already knew.

"When I began my campaign, I did so with the sincere belief I could continue the initiatives President Sugarman put into place throughout his administration and introduce some more progressive ideas to fall in line with our younger demographics. I know our platforms coincide with some of these objectives." Jimmy rubbed the back of his neck. "Here's the thing. Gina's sick."

Maggie's hand flew to her chest. Jimmy's wife was a vivacious woman who had her hand in countless organizations, including GLAAD. "I'm so sorry, Jimmy. If there's anything I can do…"

"She has a long road ahead of her, one which I refuse to let her travel alone. I'm going to suspend my campaign and endorse you. All I ask is that we have a sit down after you get elected so we can discuss some of the planks I supported, to see if you might be willing to push some of them through." Jimmy held up a hand to stop her from saying anything, although she was shocked enough that her mind blanked. "I'm not asking for any promises now. I trust your integrity, Maggie."

"Of course, we'll meet. My God. I'm happy to do that." Maggie leaned back in her seat, blinking several times. She'd just been handed the keys to the kingdom. She glanced at President Sugarman, wondering why this meeting was taking place in his office.

"After he releases the announcement, I plan to endorse you and put the full weight of the White House behind you. You're going to make a fine president." President Sugarman stood and stuck out his hand, a wide smile on his face. He looked like a proud papa. Maggie rose and shook his hand.

"Thank you. Both of you." She looked at Jimmy. "I'm sorry you have to drop out, but I admire your willingness to place family first. Please give my best to Gina."

"I will." He nodded. In that moment he looked much older, worry lines creasing his forehead and pulling at his eyes.

She saw President Sugarman step back, a sure sign the meeting was over. She took her cue and left without looking back. It was time to sprint to the finish line.

Walking through the front door once she arrived home that night, she felt as if she'd drunk ten cups of coffee. Energy sizzled through her body, and all she wanted to do was celebrate with her wife. Entering the kitchen, she saw Helen cooking at the stove. The smell of garlic tickled her nose. She leaned in and kissed her neck. "Smells good. What are you cooking?" She peeked in the pan and saw vegetables and chicken covered with brown sauce.

"Chicken stir fry. It'll be ready in a few minutes if you want to freshen up."

"Okay." Maggie wandered away, kicking off her shoes and making her way to the bedroom to find something to wear. She took off her business suit and donned sweatpants and an oversized Suffolk Law School T-shirt. After finding her slippers, she scampered down the stairs, ready to eat.

"Good timing, hon." Helen dished out their meal as Maggie opened some red wine. "How was your day?"

"The best." She noticed the time and stood, taking her plate and wine with her. "Come in here with your food," she called over her shoulder. She sat down in the living room and flicked on the television, changing it to CNN.

"Why are we in here?" Helen sat next to her, curling one leg under her.

"Big announcement. Ah, here it comes." Maggie watched as Jimmy announced his decision to suspend his campaign.

Arms pulled her in for a tight hug, Helen's voice high with excitement. "Holy shit. You got it. Is the president endorsing you? He must be. This is incredible." Helen delivered kisses all over her face and Maggie laughed, joy infusing her.

"I know. I had to sit on this all day." She told Helen about the morning meeting, her happiness counterbalanced by the reason Jimmy dropped out of the race. "Now we can concentrate on getting in the White House without worrying about our own party slowing us down. All the former Democratic candidates are publicly endorsing me and pitching in to strengthen our attacks on the Republican platform. They're even getting me to the table with some of my largest critics to see how we can work together. I don't expect all the animosity to disappear, but I'm excited to have more opportunities to at least start the conversations we need to have to change policy."

"I'm so proud of you." Helen wrapped her in another hug, this time delivering a toe-curling kiss. Maggie protested when she pulled away. "None of that. Eat up. You need your strength."

Pouting, Maggie did as she was told. She was hungry, and the stir fry tasted delicious. She swallowed the dregs of her wine, letting go of the glass when Helen's hand wrapped around it. She watched Helen place it on the coffee table before turning to her with a predatory expression. Maggie's pulse jumped.

Helen tangled a hand in Maggie's hair, kissing up her neck and nibbling on her ear before capturing her lips with an intense kiss. Maggie whimpered, her body heating up. Helen's answering moan pushed her arousal higher, their kisses becoming rougher and movements more desperate. They clutched at one another, bodies molding together as Helen gently pushed her down on the couch and covered her with her body.

Maggie's body was on fire. Helen knew every inch of her, knew where to touch, and what she liked. Maggie didn't try to hold back her breathy sighs, responding to Helen's raspy voice filled with need. Helen twined the fingers of her free hand with Maggie's as they moved together. She felt need coiling in her belly, spiraling outward in tingling waves of desire. Helen sucked on her pulse point, biting down hard enough to push Maggie into a glorious release. Her body jerked, knee pushing against the apex of Helen's thighs. With a breathy gasp, Helen climaxed, her body gyrating as Maggie held her close. They lay together for several minutes, ignoring the droning television. A sense of peace cloaked Maggie, a feeling she only had when in Helen's arms.

"I love you." Helen's whispered words filled every part of Maggie's spirit.

She dropped a kiss on Helen's hair. "I love you, too." She tried to sit up, but Helen held her down.

"Not yet." Her whining tone was adorable.

"No? I was hoping we could continue this in bed. But if you have other plans…" She laughed when Helen hopped up and grabbed her hand to help her rise.

"My only plan is to continue this in our bedroom." Helen delivered a short kiss before pulling her toward the stairs.

"You always have the best plans."

***

The time between her meeting with President Sugarman in May and the November election was a blur of endless primaries and planned appearances. She traveled to as many states as possible to romance big money donors, meet with her supporters, and deliver rousing stump speeches. The schedule was punishing.

As promised, Vice President Thompson and President Sugarman endorsed her, and within the week endorsements from her former contenders came in. She became the sharp point of the Democratic arrow, and as the shaft was pulled back, as she was aimed toward the bullseye, Maggie concentrated on making it to their goal. Her goal.

During the summer months ramping up to the Democratic National Convention, Maggie worked through a list of possible running mates. Her team did a great job of sifting through the political pool to narrow down the choices. In the ideal world, she would have chosen a female running mate. In fact, Jackie Anderson was her top choice. She liked the idea of adding her on the ticket after the New York governor failed to carry the state in the election. It fed into her puckish sense of humor. Her team was quick to educate her on the impossibility of winning with a female running mate. Instead, she met with the top six picks, and by the time they announced her pick, Senator Julian Rodriguez, Maggie knew they would make a powerful team.

The Democratic convention was an experience she knew she would never forget. Hours and hours of orations by important people within the Democratic Party. Established politicians. Up-and-comers. Present and future leaders. When she was introduced as the Democratic candidate, the crowd's response was electrifying. The sea of people swayed while shouting her name, their emotions swelling to a crescendo of support. She was buoyed by the ebb and flow of their harmonious clamor, and she allowed their acceptance to flow over her. It was an interesting paradox. She felt grounded in its rightness and yet lifted on a wave of solidarity, pushing her toward the election.

By the time she arrived at the presidential election watch party, held at the Boston World Trade Center, Maggie was nervous. She did her best to distract herself by mingling with the crowd while she waited for the poll results.

"Here. Drink this." Helen handed her a glass of white wine. "Don't worry. I'm keeping track."

"Thanks, love." Maggie took a sip, her eyes scanning the room. "Where's the family?"

"They're at a table near the front. Mom wanted to be in a place where they could take good pictures when you gave your acceptance speech." Helen chuckled. "See, you still have her wrapped around your finger."

"Are your sisters with her?" Maggie's eyebrows rose when she spotted Mike and her mom talking to Christine and Evan. Helen followed her stare and snorted.

"Yes, my sisters are with my mom, and yes, I find it hilarious that Christine and Evan love talking to your brother and mother. I've never met a more mismatched group, and yet it works. All of them seem happy to chat when they're at gatherings together."

"It is interesting." Alice appeared at her elbow, a smile on her face. "That smile suggests good news. Hit me with it."

"It doesn't look like we're going to have to wait much longer for the Republicans to concede. You secured some of the battleground states. Since we weren't relying on Pennsylvania or Florida, they're pushing us along. And get this. Ohio came out for you." Alice pointed toward the television on the wall streaming numbers. "We're waiting for the western states, of course. I'll check back in with you when I get more numbers."

"Thanks." Maggie turned to Helen, excitement rippling under her skin. She reached out to squeeze Helen's arm. "Did you hear that? This is incredible."

"Yes, it is. You are. And soon you will be our president." Helen leaned in. "I can't wait to see you behind that desk, ready to change the world. You and Julian are going to make history tonight."

Maggie smiled. Julian Rodriguez was a three term senator out of Texas. He carried the Latino vote, although that wasn't why Maggie agreed to have him become her running mate. When she sat down with him, he impressed her with his vision of what America could become if they worked together. He wanted equality. He wanted people to have the opportunity to do whatever made their hearts sing. He wanted safe, supportive communities across the US. He wanted to put into place many of the same planks she was promoting. "Speaking of Julian, any idea where he might be?"

"Yes." Helen jerked her head toward the left side of the room. "He was talking to Sarah."

Taking one more sip from her glass, she handed it to Helen. "Back to circulating around the room. It won't be long now."

"No, it won't." Helen's smile softened. "Go do your thing. I'll catch up to you in a bit."

By the time she received the concession phone call from the Republican nominee, Richie Collins, Maggie already knew she'd won. The California numbers clinched it for her.

She heard Senator Sarah Cromsby introducing her to the roar of the crowd, and after delivering a peck on Helen's smiling lips, Maggie strode across the stage, arm raised in a wave and a smile firmly etched across her face. Her heart was racing, and although she tried, she couldn't focus on anyone. She reached Sarah and gave her a hug before turning to the crowd.

"We did it!" She raised her hands high above her head in the classic pose of celebration, allowing her supporters to cheer, to celebrate her win, their win. "Today is the beginning of a new tomorrow. Thanks to you, to your hard work and unflagging belief that we could do this, Julian and I are ready to put into place the initiatives we've discussed throughout this campaign." She called Julian to the stage, shaking his hand and turning toward the crowd.

"Meet your new vice president, Julian Rodriguez." She raised their clasped hands above their heads as another cheer filled the room. She let go, and Julian stepped back. Maggie smiled at the cameras, knowing her acceptance speech was being broadcast nationally. She felt Helen step up beside her and a sense of calm flowed through her.

"I received a call a few minutes ago from Senator Collins. He congratulated us on our campaign, and I congratulated him. I congratulated him because through this campaign I learned about some of the areas that need attention. That need to be strengthened. Strengthened not only by our belief in a more inclusive nation, but by definitive action to translate those beliefs into reality." People's voices rose as one with approval, and Maggie waited, allowing their euphoria to bolster her. Camera flashes were constant, and she did her best to keep a small smile on her face and a relaxed stance.

"The voters have spoken. They want to be represented by people who are like them. People who know the challenges ordinary

Americans face. People who understand what discrimination feels like. What it feels like to work hard every single day to provide for oneself, never mind for a family. Voters want leaders who have their constituents' best interests in mind, and who aren't so far removed that they've forgotten what it feels like to struggle."

She paused, her gaze sweeping the crowd before resting to her right, where Helen stood. She looked at her wife, whose bright eyes and matching smile served as a beacon of hope. She looked back at the crowd, past the media, searching for familiar faces. She saw her brother, Mike, who beamed at her and gave her a thumb's up. She saw her mother's smile. Saw Helen's mom and two sisters. And she saw friends and colleagues and peers, people she'd met throughout her life's journey. Lizzie, Kevin, and Gemma. Emma, Nancy, Stella, Paulie, and Brett. Anita Cromsby and her daughters, Cheri, and Sarah. Christine and Evan. June and other Lynn school educators. Scottie, David, and several of their friends she'd met at Scottie's apartment. Attorneys she knew. Democratic politicians who'd pledged their support. Her entire team, including Alice, Darla, and Zack. So many familiar faces, reflecting her bad choices and her triumphs, her failures and her successes—they all led her to this moment. An ineffable joy at being able to experience this moment swept through her, and she gripped the podium to ground herself before she continued.

"The Statue of Liberty represents friendship, liberty, and enlightenment. She guides us all to a better tomorrow, lighting the way with her torch. With your help, we intend to continue down that path to make our nation a better place to live."

Taking a settling breath, she lifted her chin and stared into the cameras before she uttered her slogan. She wasn't surprised when the crowd joined in, and they spoke the words together.

"So, let's get to work, America."

Epilogue

THE OCEAN'S WAVES WHISPERED to Maggie while cradling her in gentle arms. Her tired mind enjoyed the break from having to respond to its voice. She listened to the seagulls talking and the buoys clanging and the people splashing. She breathed in a deep lungful of ocean air, content to float on the current without any need to worry. She'd fought hard to reach a point in her life where she could enjoy such halcyon days. Although she would only be able to remain at the beach for a short while longer, she was glad they were able to clear the summer afternoon for an impromptu visit to the North Shore.

A wave pushed her up before speeding toward the shore. Maggie sputtered a bit as some of the water slapped across her face. She shot up, bobbing on the water while blinking several times. Scanning the area, she was happy to see Helen sitting under an umbrella reading a book. Helen looked up and waved her arm back and forth in wide arcs until Maggie waved back.

"Everything okay, Madam President?" One of her Secret Service agents asked. When Maggie requested a good swimmer to accompany her to the beach, Nora Brooks had volunteered. Like Maggie, she grew up by the beach and was a strong swimmer.

"Yes. I think it's time to get going, though." Maggie swam toward the shore, allowing the tide to push her until she could get her feet under her. She headed toward Helen, who rose and held out a towel for Maggie. "Thank you, love."

"You're welcome. Are you ready to leave?"

Maggie considered the question. She thought of her life, of the path she had traveled to become a second term president. She thought of her wife, of the partnership they built to share their lives together. She thought of her personal growth, of the courage she found to reclaim her life instead of living it for others. She nodded, looking around King's Beach once more before turning her attention back to Helen.

She wasn't that little kid floating along, doing her best to fit in, to survive and do as she was told. She wasn't the girl who worked hard to fulfill other people's needs at the cost of her own. She was a strong, determined leader. She had learned how to swim against the tide, and she knew she would not allow anything to pull her away from her path—certainly not the undertow.

About Jazzy Mitchell

Jazzy Mitchell is the proud publisher of Launch Point Press and on the founding Board of Directors for OPUS Literary Alliance. She believed in supporting writers with telling stories, as she tells her own, one word at a time. Knowing how powerful words are, she enjoys connecting them in different ways. Her writing has evolved through poetry, short stories, fanfiction under the name Jazwriter, and novels. Each project has taught her how to integrate what she's observed. She's warned loved ones anything they say or do may show up in her next novel.

During the past thirty years, Jazzy has reinvented herself several times. She taught English for a decade to inner-city, underprivileged middle school and high school students, giving back to her hometown and the school system which helped her. She encouraged countless students to express themselves through their writing by exploring their artistic sides. Law school drove the creativity out of her, but as time passed, her artistic instincts reasserted themselves. Through the years, she has taught adults about ethics and the law and, through the Lightarian Institute, energy work.

Jazzy's the author of four other contemporary lesbian romance novels: *Lost Treasures*—which received an Honorable Mention for the 2016 Rainbow Awards, *Musings of a Madwoman*, *You Matter*, and *Leveling Up*. Jazzy lives in Portland, Oregon, with her loving wife, three energetic children, and sassy dog.

Connect with Jazzy

Facebook – JazzyMitchellauthor

Email –publisherl@launchpointpress.com

Website – www.launchpointpress.com

From the Author

    Lynn, my hometown, is a city on the North Shore in Massachusetts, less than four miles away from Boston. It contains a broad spectrum of socioeconomic and cultural diversity. While growing up, Lynn was a paradox to me with its beautiful coastline and depressed downtown. The dichotomy between safe and dangerous areas, affluent and underprivileged communities, well-kept and decrepit properties hints at the larger personality of one of the oldest colonial settlements in the Commonwealth. The land is drenched with history, and one need only wander down old cow trails cutting through the city or hike across the wonders of Lynn Woods reservation, the largest municipal park in New England, to learn how layered Lynn's personality is. My stomping grounds act as the backdrop for much of the book, imbued with the characteristics of the ocean it hugs. A natural femme fatale.

    This book has demanded my attention for years. For a long time, I didn't feel up to the task of revealing the essence of my hometown. Perhaps I needed more time to discover its voice. Likewise, my characters took time to grow. Maggie was known to me by another name until halfway through the manuscript. It hadn't sounded right, and when I finally listened, really listened, I heard her tell me who she was, what she believes in, and how she's persevered. Her challenges may seem familiar to you. Her mistakes and poor choices may cause you to like her less. Yet, don't we all travel down the wrong road at some point? Maggie experiences trauma, neglect, and abuse, and those scars take much longer for her to face, to process, and to overcome. Her struggle not merely to survive, but to thrive, drives her to make some questionable choices. It's that humanity, those mistakes, which color her character and mark her as a fascinating person. Unlike most people who can face their mistakes in private, Maggie must confront her past deeds and admit her mistakes before an entire nation. This is her journey.

    No book comes into being without help. I'm blessed to have the support of many talented writers, supportive friends, and my family. My wife, Peggy, has jokingly said she was going to create a support group for writers' significant others. Seems she's missed me during the months while I toiled away at writing the book, cursing my limited vocabulary and inept attempts to write something worth reading. She and her sister, Karen, even helped me settle on Maggie's name after hearing me whine about the original name choice one too many times. Thanks for supporting me, babe. I know the tortured artist cliché becomes old pretty fast, but you've weathered my moods brilliantly. Love you. Ditto for the kiddos, Drake and Katie. They knew when I was tapping away at the laptop to leave me alone. I know it was hard at times. Juanita is all grown up and doesn't have to deal with any of the growing pains I suffer while writing, but she's always showing up at my author readings and book fairs. I appreciate that more than she'll ever realize. Family support is important to me. My mother and father both buy and read my books. It's both wonderful and awful. (I mean, come on, my parents are reading sex scenes I wrote.)

I want to thank my local writing group, the Portland Lesbian Writers Group (PoLeWG). A couple of years ago, I was introduced to Lori L. Lake, and she invited me to attend a meeting. Since that first introduction I've become friends with several wonderful women. Lori shares her wisdom and resources without hesitation, and I've utilized many of her lessons. More important to me is the friendship we have developed. This lady is a class act. I'm richer for knowing her.

KC Luck, Amy Stinnett, Kay Grey, Hannah Dubrow, Linda Vogt, Patricia Hansen, Shawn Marie Bryan, Reba Birmingham, Dolores Maggiore, Sandra de Helen, and Jane Cuthbertson—these are some of the awesome writers I'm fortunate enough to know. As sister polliwogs, they share their love of the written word and support me in various ways. It's a great group. If you're in the Northwest, you should look us up to see whether you might want to join our merry band.

Louisa Kelley, another polliwog, was kind enough to read the manuscript and give me feedback which prompted me to reconfigure the timeline and write out the final (and most important) election results. I'll admit I was afraid it would sound like the other scenes with election results, and okay, maybe I was becoming a teeny tiny bit lazy. You can thank Louisa for giving me some tough love. I do.

Another polliwog member who provided helpful comments on the manuscript is Luca Hart. I appreciated her eagle eyes and willingness to take the time to smooth out the rough edges of the manuscript.

Another group I belong to is LGBTQ Romance Authors Northwest. I was part of an author retreat with several writers from this organization in the winter of 2020, not long before the pandemic shut everything down, and it was a gift in many ways. I was able to spend time with some wonderful, talented writers, who unreservedly offered their friendship and support. Thank you, CJane Elliott, Rick R. Reed, Charley Descoteaux, Dianne Hartsock, and Ben Brock. I'm humbled by your talent, generosity, and willingness to welcome me into the fold.

C.A. Farlow has read my stories since I first began writing fanfiction. For more than ten years, she's helped me work on my writing skills, always offering support, guidance, and kind words. She was the one who introduced me to Desert Palm Press, and our friendship continues to strengthen over time. I owe you a beer, my friend. Thank you for always being willing to clear your schedule to read my scribblings.

David A. Clarke is another awesome friend I met through writing fanfiction stories. Our friendship has become one which I treasure. My family has welcomed him and his family into our hearts, and we will always look forward to the next occasion we can spend time together. David, thank you for being a great friend. Hugs!

And last, but certainly not least, I must thank Desert Palm Press. Through this publishing house I've learned what it takes to make a manuscript publishable. Sometimes the learning curve was steep, but we all persevered. I'm grateful for the lessons I've learned. I'm in awe of the talent this publishing house attracts. Thank you, Lee, for giving me a chance, for helping me become better, and for investing your time and money on my stories. Thank you, Natty Burns, for editing this story. I asked for you specifically, knowing you would be the perfect person to whip this manuscript into shape. I always try to listen to my gut, and your guidance reinforced my belief that you were the best woman for the job. Michelle Brodeur, thank you once again for creating a beautiful cover. You always find the perfect way to reflect the story's essence. I love knowing the photographs I took years ago of King's Beach now decorate the cover of this book.

www.ingramcontent.com/pod-product-compliance
Lightning Source LLC
Chambersburg PA
CBHW070647100726
47907CB00007B/2134